ISBN-13: 978-1-7337467-1-7

love among the shamrocks collection

the next generation

Book Three

Chasing After

Moonbeams

M. KATHERINE CLARK

Other works by M. Katherine Clark

The Greene and Shields Files
      Blood is Thicker Than Water
      Once Upon a Midnight Dreary
      Old Sins Cast Long Shadows
      Tales from the Heart, Novelettes

Love Among the Shamrocks Collection
      Under the Irish Sky
      Across the Irish Sea
      On the River Shannon
      The Land Across the Sea, an Emmet O'Quinn Short

Love Among the Shamrocks Collection the Next Generation
      In Dublin Fair City
      Song of Heart's Desire
      Chasing After Moonbeams
      You Don't Own Me – Coming Soon

The Wolf's Bane Saga
      Wolf's Bane
      Lonely Moon
      Midnight Sky
      Star Crossed
      Moon Rise
      Moon Song, a Companion Guide

Dragon Fire
      Heart of Fire
      Will of Fire
      Born of Fire – Coming Soon

Soundless Silence, *a Sherlock Holmes Novel*
The Rest is Silence, *an Edmond Holmes Novel*
Silent Whispers, *a Scottish Ghost Story*
Silent Night, *a Scottish Ghost Story Christmas* – Coming Soon

Dedicated to all those who made this book possible!

I couldn't have done it without you!

Thank you!

Chapter One

Meditation had always been a large part of Naomi Moon's life. It grounded her, centered her. Many people probably thought it was silly. She would rise with the sun and meditate out in her small Zen Garden. But ever since she was a young girl, her mother taught her to be one with nature and herself. With her mother gone, it was a way for Naomi to be close to her.

The only music around her was the soft warm breeze of Florida's Emerald Coast and the crash of the Gulf of Mexico's waves on the shore. Though she knew it was only a matter of time before the hustle and bustle of the tourists roared the city to life, she cherished those moments just before the inevitable.

"Honey! I'm off to – Oh! Sorry," the sound of her father's voice calling from inside their bungalow made her smile. Then, his attempt at a whisper, followed by the thumps and bangs as he tried to *be quiet* in the kitchen, made her chuckle.

Taking a deep breath, she came out of her meditation, bowed low, her forehead to the floor, and whispered.

"Until next time, Mama."

Then, standing, she again filled her lungs with the salty, humid air. Her eyes opened to see her mother's name etched in the stone. "I love you."

Turning to take the three steps up from outside into the kitchen, she saw her father sitting at the island, chewing a toasted bagel. He looked up and smiled.

"Sorry to interrupt, honey," he said.

"You didn't, dad," she answered kissing him on the cheek and moving to the pantry. Pulling out the box of cereal, she continued. "I was almost finished anyway."

"I know but being married to your mother for nearly thirty years, I know not to interrupt. I had her wrath more than once," he chuckled fondly.

"Loving wrath," Naomi winked.

"True," he replied and tossed back the remaining orange juice in his glass. "I'm glad you continue her tradition, honey. It keeps her alive in our hearts."

"It feels weird not to meditate. It's my time with her," Naomi said putting a slice of bread in the toaster.

"I know, love," he replied, then sighed. "It's hard to believe she's been gone ten years."

"It is hard," she agreed pouring the milk.

"You remind me so much of her, Ni," he smiled. "So beautiful and kind and stubborn."

She laughed. "Can't forget the stubborn."

"Never," he beamed. "She would be so proud of you."

"I do miss her."

"I know. We both do."

They were quiet for a long moment until they both finished their breakfast.

"Well," her father began. "I'm going to check in at the Sanderson's, make sure everything is going well."

"Have they paid for the extra lumber yet?"

"Not yet," he said.

"Dad..."

"I know. I'll talk to them."

"Be sure to. We need that money."

"I know, Ni. Where will you be today?"

"I'm going to check on the reno at the Emerald Coast Condominium. Then, I have the planning meeting with Olivia over lunch," Naomi explained.

"Oh, that's right. I forgot that's today?" He said as he shrugged into his paint overalls.

"Yep. The eighteen-year high school reunion planning is in full swing."

"Why is this reunion so important?" He asked grabbing his baseball cap.

"I have absolutely no clue," she replied. "Liv said something about it being the same amount of years since we graduated as we were when we graduated. Eighteen-year-olds. God, were we ever that young?"

"You're one to talk, honey," he teased. "Thirty-six isn't bad at all. Just wait until you hit sixty-six. Then talk to me about eighteen."

He grabbed his keys off the peg by the door and headed out. "It's just odd, you know? You never hear about the odd numbered reunions, just the big ones. Oh, well, have fun. Let me know how the condo's going. Oh! Can you pick up a couple things at Publix tonight? We need a few things for around the house. The list is on the fridge."

"Sure thing, and I'll swing by Lucky Sam's and get us dinner."

"Delicious, thanks, love," he leaned over and kissed her cheek.

"Bye, dad, be safe."

He trotted down the steps and toward his old nineteen seventies rust colored pickup truck. Naomi waved at him after he finally got it started and pulled out of the driveway.

"Good morning, Mrs. Kirkpatrick," she called to her neighbor as she headed to the mailbox.

"Good morning, dear," the old woman said. "How's things?"

"Things are wonderful as always. And you? Is your granddaughter coming down this summer again?"

"Oh yes, she and her young man will be here in a month or so," Mrs. Kirkpatrick said. "How about you, dear? Any young man in your life?"

"Oh, no," Naomi shook her head. "No *young* man need apply. I'll never date a man younger than me again." Not that she really had. The youngest was only a few months younger. But could have been in dog years with how different they were.

Mrs. Kirkpatrick laughed. "Well, don't put it past them. You know women in their thirties are marrying younger men. They have enough stamina to keep up," she winked.

Naomi chuckled. "I have to get ready for work. I hope you have an amazing day, Mrs. Kirkpatrick. Weatherman says it'll be perfect to be by the pool today."

"Oh, don't worry, dear. You need to be home by three, though."

"Oh? Why?" Naomi asked wracking her brain for the reason. "That may not be possible, I have a meeting at three."

Mrs. Kirkpatrick went on as if Naomi hadn't spoken. "Maximillian will be here. He's cleaning my pool today."

"Oh, of course," Naomi muttered low while forcing a smile.

"Did you know he just broke up with his girlfriend?"

"Imagine that," again, Naomi muttered through a gritted teeth smile.

"You know how handsome he is. And he always likes seeing you."

"Well, I will do my best," Naomi lied. Then, with a wave and a *see you soon*, she shut the door and leaned against it.

Blowing out a breath, she huffed. It wasn't as if she didn't like men, it was more everything that went along with them. She couldn't handle another lying cheater in her love life. Her ex-husband really did a number on her. She couldn't blame her neighbor and it was very sweet of her to think about her, but Mrs. Kirkpatrick only knew she had a divorce and moved back home. No one except her dad knew the truth of Emilio's infidelity.

"Enough," she said aloud. Pushing off the door, she headed to her bathroom for a quick shower. Then, changing into her jeans, branded tank top, and boots, she locked up the house and headed to her truck.

Chapter Two

Oisín O'Quinn stared into the clicking camera with as sultry a look as he could muster while sand dug into crevices of his body he didn't know existed. The ocean shoot was every models' dream, at least, that was what his manager assured him as they flew from New York City to Panama City Beach, Florida nearly three weeks ago.

And if he was being honest with himself, it was exciting. The sun shining down on his bare back, the water crashing over his legs, the heat of the warmed sand under his chest, the screaming fans. Aye, Oisín was in heaven.

"That's great, Osh," his agent, Tony called from under the umbrella chairs, a Bloody Mary at his elbow. "Looks fantastic."

"I would like a few of you coming up out of the water," the photographer, who had the ability to make his life hell, said. Oisín smiled at him and turned over, checking that his swim trunks hadn't ridden up too much before he stood.

Grateful he had conditioned his skin to bear the Florida sun, Oisín still winced as he felt the beginnings of sunburn on his right shoulder. The glorious Irish blood pumping through his veins made him proud to be Irish and yet caused far too much maintenance when in the sun.

A few more shots and the photographer called a break.

Sloshing out of the surf, Oisín gratefully took the offered towel and wiped his face and chest, then used it as a shield to cover his shoulders.

"I love you, Oisín!" one in the crowd of screaming fans yelled.

"I want to have your babies!" another cried.

"Marry me!"

Oisín chuckled. Fan girls were one of his favorite parts of the job. One-night stands were all any of them were looking for, a boast to their friends back home, and he was perfectly fine with that. It wasn't as if he was going to settle down anytime soon. He had just turned thirty and his modeling career was in full swing.

Five years ago, he was helping his mates move a man from his Dublin flat to a retirement home after he had fallen once too many times. As owner of the *Rough and Buff* moving company, Oisín oversaw the project with a keen eye. The company was made up of university friends and the only stipulation was they had to be all attractive and willing to wear nothing but a kilt and boots. It was quite the hit with the ladies. But the move five years ago, Oisín remembered vividly. The man was a flamboyant seventy-two-year-old and he kept staring at him. Not that Oisín cared about being looked at, he was used to it and prided himself on his physique. But the man's gaze was not one of interest or even lust, it was curiosity. After the lads had loaded up the truck, Oisín was going through the checklist with the man and after everything was cleared the man turned to him.

"I could make you a star, lad," he said.

"A star?" Oisín had questioned.

"Aye, have you ever considered modeling?"

The question had taken him aback.

"I still have contacts in the industry. You could be the next Mark Vanderloo."

"I don't know who that is."

"Look him up. Then call me," he offered his card. "We're talking New York, LA, Paris, Milan, everywhere a young man like you would love. Think on it."

And Oisín had thought on it. Searching the internet for information well into the small hours of the morning and that next day, he called the man. The rest happened so fast, Oisín could hardly remember, but as he sauntered over to the women screaming his name, his feet sinking into the warm white sand, he knew he would never give up that life. He loved it.

After signing breasts and taking selfies, he made it to his agent who was typing on his phone.

"More sunscreen," Tony snapped his fingers without looking up. Oisín relaxed into the chair under the umbrella. "I have you booked in at seven tomorrow, and we will need to take a helicopter to get to the island. So, I have a five am wakeup call going to your room in the morning."

Oisín nodded, no party that night. "When's my free day?" he asked as one of the crew rubbed sunscreen on his back and shoulders.

"You get a few weeks off as discussed for vacation but until next week, you're booked. We booked a beach house for when we're done here, so you'll have your pool party."

"The fact you can read my mind is scary."

"Trust me, I know. Fortunately, it's not all the time."

Oisín chuckled then moaned as the woman began massaging his shoulders.

"I'm going to grab a few things from the store tonight then. I'm tired of take away and delivery," Oisín said.

"I've never met anyone who has ever said that."

"I know, but I do miss a homecooked meal and since we can't go out..." he pried.

"Not yet," his manager replied. "You know the rules, no beer, no sugar, no bread until the shoot is over. I'd hate to have to photoshop out a little bloat."

Oisín looked down at the eight protruding muscles on his stomach.

"Does it look like a little bloat is possible?"

"Beer and bread? Anything is possible. But I trust you. Go with your bodyguard after we finish here."

"I'm going for a run and a swim first. Then I'll go," he revealed. "Coming with me, By?"

The stoic man beside him merely nodded once. The bodyguard was an impressive man, standing nearly seven feet tall and larger than Oisín. Byron was a beast with milk chocolate skin and closely sheared black hair. But Oisín enjoyed his company. Both of them were displaced for a job and he was quiet but interesting.

There were times Oisín sat with him and asked for advice. Byron was ten years older and had lived a life before becoming his bodyguard four and a half years ago.

"When you're ready, Oisín," the photographer called.

Taking a deep drink from his bottled water, he thanked the young woman and headed back out into the sun and salt water.

Chapter Three

"Ah! Oh my god, oh my god, oh my god!" Olivia always greeted everyone as if it had been years since she had seen them even if it had only been a week or so.

Naomi braced for one of Liv's crushing hugs and was not disappointed even if the air in her lungs seized and her ear drums vibrated with her squeals.

"I've gotten us a bottle and cannot *wait* to show you my sketchbook! This reunion is going to be auh-maze-zing!"

"Can't wait." Naomi forced. "So excited."

"I knew you would be!" she took Naomi by the hand and led her over to the four top table where a bottle of chilled white wine waited, two glasses were already poured. All of Olivia's notes, sketches, and ideas were sprawled out.

"I was so worried you weren't coming. You know, after the," Liv looked around, leaned in, and dramatically whispered. "The divorce. I worried you wouldn't want to plan. But don't worry, I will tell everyone the talk of ex-husbands, divorce, and marriage is banned from the party. I'll make sure no one brings it up."

"It's been two years, Liv. It's okay."

"Sweetie," she huffed and her bottle blonde curls bounced. "It's devastating! You're thirty-six, not a spring chicken! And you need to think about that biological clock. It's ticking away and you've wasted two years!"

Naomi ignored the flare of pain that always lit in her chest at the thought of children. "Liv, as much as I always enjoy our conversations," she said tightly. "I have a long afternoon planned. Could we begin talking about the reunion? I just simply cannot wait for you to show me what you have planned."

Olivia giggled. "You know who else said that? Dave Prince! I ran into him the other day at the car repair shop. My little Scooter dinged the Porsche last week."

Who in their right mind allows their seventeen year old son drive a Porsche is beyond me, Naomi thought.

"But anyway, Dave and I met in the waiting room, and he recognized me right off the bat, no idea why."

Probably because he slept with ninety-nine percent of the girls in high school and you slept with ninety-nine percent of the guys, Naomi thought.

"But I told him all about our plans and he couldn't wait to be there. He even asked us both to save him a dance."

"Oohoho, no," Naomi replied. "Dave Prince had wandering hands in high school. No way I'm dancing with him."

"Oh but you *have* to! He just got a divorce too. He said he wasn't going to go unless we both promise him a dance."

"Then I guess we're one done on the RSVPs because it isn't happening."

Olivia stared at her for a long moment, mouth gaping open, then a sly grin appeared on her lips.

"You *like* him!" she squealed. "Oh, this is perfect! You like him and are scared to show it. Oh! That makes me so happy! This year's theme is going to be fairytale and it's perfect! You two can run as reunion king and queen!"

"One, no I don't like him, never have. Two, this isn't prom. There are no kings and queens."

"There will be," she clapped her hands excitedly. "Oh my goodness! So happy!" She did a little shimmy dance in her seat.

Naomi knew better than to argue. She took the wine and drank a large gulp. She'd need it to get through the next hour.

Oisín jogged alongside Byron on the dry sand. The sun was bright at midday but the gentle breeze from the water cooled him considerably. Still wearing his swim trunks, he had pulled on a shirt, sunglasses, and hat to shield his identity but from the looks of beachgoers, it did little good.

Pulling up to a stop as they reached the pier, Byron looked over at him.

"Ready for a swim?" he asked.

Oisín put his hands on him hips and took several deep breaths. He hated cardio but it was needed to keep his physique.

"Tell me something, By," Oisín began. His bodyguard did not answer, only nodded. "What were your thoughts when you turned thirty?"

The man rose dark, thick eyebrows. "Where's this coming from, Oisín?" Byron's southern accent made his name sound more like the large body of water rather than his traditional Irish pronunciation.

"I don't know," he replied. "I guess you only turn thirty once and it's pretty impressive. But I have all these thoughts in my head."

"Like what?" he asked.

"Well, like now any woman younger than twenty-five looks like a child. It was almost an overnight thing. I also need to be more of an adult. And that makes me worry." He chuckled.

"You can't eat and drink whatever you want now, eh?" Byron laughed.

"Something like that. Guilty," he winked from behind his sunglasses.

"Listen, you're a great man," Byron began. "I've seen what you've done with your money. You have set your parents up for life and all your siblings and nieces and nephews. They will never have to worry thanks to you. I know many people in the industry who are selfish and use their millions only on themselves. You are in fantastic shape and could have any woman you bat an eye at."

"True, but there's no challenge in that," he complained.

"You know my daddy used to tell me, if there's no challenge in getting her, there will be a challenge in keeping her."

Oisín thought for a long moment. "Have you ever wanted to settle down?"

"I did. A long time ago. Before war, there was a girl. But... she's married now."

"And not since?"

Byron shook his head. "No one really understands the job. And I've seen what long estrangements do to relationships. More than one guy in my platoon got a *Dear John* letter. It's not for me."

"Yeah," Oisín nodded, his eyes on the horizon.

"What brought this on?"

"Nothing really, just... I got a call after we were done with the shoot. My brother Lachlan and his wife Corinne just announced they're pregnant again for the third time and even my other cousin Liam is getting married. Trevor and Cassie are about to have their first. I'm surrounded by births, marriages, and even some death, but I just feel like I'm in a bubble. I'm sure I'll be all right. I'm just a little homesick."

"You know the cure for homesickness?" Byron asked. Oisín shook his head. "A homecooked meal. Come on. We can put that kitchenette in the condo to good use. Jump in the shower, we'll head to the store."

"I like it."

"And just because you can't have beer, doesn't mean one whiskey or a glass of red wine is out of the question. You just have to know how to stop." Byron winked and Oisín laughed.

"Rebellion. I love it. No one does rebellion better than us Irish."

"Except the south."

Oisín slapped him on his shoulder and grinned. "I still have a lot to learn about American history, my friend, but I'm sure you're right. Come on."

Walking back to their condo, they trudged up the dry white sand, toward the boardwalk. Rinsing their feet in the small showers provided, they headed up to their two-bedroom condo to shower properly and change.

Chapter Four

Naomi subtly checked her phone. It was just after four and Olivia had ordered another bottle of wine an hour ago. Having only had a couple sips of the too-sweet wine, Naomi was not at all surprised Liv was still drinking. But after sending a text to her dad when she paused to use the restroom, Naomi cancelled her visit to the other property she wanted to see at three. There was just no stopping Olivia when she got going.

Finally, the wine was finished and before Olivia could order another, Naomi jumped in.

"Liv, I'm so sorry to cut this... uh... short, but Dad asked me to pick up a few things today and then dinner, so I'm going to need to run across the way. Will you be all right?"

"Oh honey, of course! Oh my, is it already four? I had no idea. Time flies when you're having fun. I need to pick up some chicken for tonight's dinner, I'll go with you. Uh, *gar-con,*" she called snapping her fingers and mispronouncing the French word. "I'm going to need you to drop everything and run my ticket." She ordered handing her credit card to the waiter.

The waiter forced a smile and took her card. Naomi knew what he must be feeling. Olivia was very demanding and usually the waitstaff of any restaurant ran the other way when she arrived.

"Mm," she grabbed her glass and drained it. "I tell you this is like candy to me, a few more sips and I'll be dancing on my head. Well, I am so glad to have your help planning this with me, Mimi. It's got to be perfect." She reached over and covered Naomi's hand with hers. "It'll be just like high school. Except now we can legally drink!"

"Oh god I hope not," Naomi muttered.

"What was that?" Liv questioned.

"Oh god I hope so," Naomi forced. "And it will be perfect, you know why? Because you're planning it."

"Awe, you are just so sweet," she patted her hand and grinned. "Kinda like that wine, huh?"

The waiter came back with her card and receipt.

"Well, did you see that? Not even a thank you," Liv stated when the waiter left.

"We have been here for over three hours and only ordered wine. He probably wants to flip the table."

"Well, excuse me. See if his highn-*ass* likes the tip he gets from me."

Naomi watched in horror as Liv put a two-cent tip on a sixty dollar tab. Having worked in the restaurant industry, Naomi knew what customers like Olivia Harrison were like.

As Liv signed her name with a flourish and gathered her things, Naomi opened her wallet under the table and pulled out the last of the cash she had. Though it wasn't as much as she wanted to give, business hadn't been good and she and her dad had to scrape by, she held it surreptitiously. She'd be damned if she let Liv insult the waiter like that.

"Now. Coming, honey?" Olivia asked as she stood and smoothed out her sundress.

"I'll be right there, got to use the little girls' room. I'll meet you outside," Naomi said.

"Twice in an hour? You might want to get that bladder checked, hon. You are at that age," she winked and teased brightly.

"It's the water," Naomi gestured to her empty glass.

"Well, momma always said drinking water is better than drinking wine, but if you drink wine, be sure you can walk the line." Her annoyingly vociferous laugh followed her out the door.

Naomi dropped her face in her hands. There was a reason she only saw Olivia on rare – *very* rare – occasions.

"Should I clear up?" the waiter's voice came from beside her. Looking up, she saw the strain around his lips and eyes as he saw the two-cent tip with the snarky note written near the tip line; *maybe if you smiled more and treated your customers better you'd get more than my two cents.*

"I am so sorry," Naomi said. "You've been run off your feet and she didn't help."

"It's okay. I'm sorry if I made your day less enjoyable."

"No, not at all," Naomi stood and faced the waiter. "Can I ask, how old are you?"

"Nineteen," he said.

"You're working to save up for college, I bet."

He nodded but looked away. "I just need to get a good job. My parents can't afford to send me, so I'm working."

"That's admirable and nothing to be ashamed of. My parents couldn't afford to send me to college either. But I worked my way just like you. You'll get there. Do you have any construction skills?"

"I helped my dad build a shed out back a couple years ago."

"My dad and I own a construction company. We don't have much work but give us a call," she handed him her card. "We might have something soon."

"Really?" His eyes lit up.

"Really," she smiled. "And I know it's not much but take this. Thank you for all your hard work and I hope your day gets better. Don't let the Olivia's of the world get you down. The best way to survive is not to care about that sort of person. You be you. That's all anyone has the right to ask of you."

She pressed the twenty-dollar bill into his hand. His eyes grew wide.

"I wish I had more, but this is all I can do for you. What's your name?"

"Bobby."

"Well, Bobby, I'll see you next time. Be sure to give us a call with some availability."

"Yes, yes, ma'am. Thank you."

"And keep that smile, Bobby. It'll all be worth it in the end."

With that, Naomi got her handbag and headed out the door to meet Liv on the sidewalk.

Oisín and Byron walked up and down the aisles at the local Publix, two baskets on their arms, already laden with the essentials; foil, paper towels, seasoning, and whiskey. They made their way to the fresh meat and deli area. First stopping to get some vegetables, Oisín picked out some bell peppers and a cucumber. Byron grabbed a handful of brussels sprouts. Oisín looked at him curiously.

"Don't tell me you've never had them," Byron said. "They're like miniature cabbages... isn't that big where you're from?"

Oisín chuckled. "Nasty stereotype, By. But I've had them. They're just not my favorite. My gran used to boil them."

Byron made a face. "Mine did too, but my momma bakes them with some olive oil, salt, and lemon juice. Trust me. You'll love 'em."

"I'm trusting you on this, By."

"Good. I'll go to the butcher and get us some steaks. You want some shrimp?"

"That'd be great and if they have some mussels or oysters?"

"I'll check. You get a few more things and I'll meet you at the checkout. No sugar though."

"No worries," Oisín waved him off. Truth be told, he hadn't had a single pastry or donut in ten years. The only sugar was a piece of cake on his birthday and maybe a snuck cookie around Christmas. As he headed toward the deli, he stopped when he saw the imported cheese selection. That was his kryptonite. A little cheese platter, some fruit, drizzle it all with some lavender honey on a warmed French baguette, his mouth watered.

Looking to see what options they had, his eyes lightened on a magazine stand beside the counter, his face on the cover.

From O'Quinn to Oh God!

Inside playboy Oisín O'Quinn's Steamy Bedroom from Someone Who Has Been There!

Oisín had to chuckle. There were women who came forward claiming to have been intimate with him all the time. Everyone wanted their five minutes of fame and most of the time, he couldn't even remember their names. The picture of the cute brunette did jog something in the back of his mind, but nothing else. Shaking his head, he turned back to the cheese selection.

A few Dubliners, a Brie, and a smoked Gouda and he was ready to go. Grabbing the imported Irish butter, he smiled. Though most of the time anything imported to America from Ireland tasted like shite, he loved his butter and cheese.

Meeting Byron at the checkout, they said nothing as they waited for their turn.

The magazine on the shelf had his face as big as a full page but with his Panama City Beach baseball cap and aviator sunglasses, he was sure he could slip by without the fuss of being recognized.

He hoped...

Chapter Five

"I'm thinking chicken cordon bleu. What about you?"
Olivia asked. It was the fifth recipe she had mentioned in twenty minutes. Usually not an issue, nor one to get upset or annoyed easily, Naomi was about to lose it. Liv had wasted three hours of her day, a day that was already extremely busy. She held it together, proud of herself and her meditation that morning.

"Ooh, lookie!" Liv grabbed a magazine off the rack and held it for Naomi to see.

"Who's that?" she questioned. The man on the cover was gorgeous. Far too good looking. His light brown hair was cut close on the sides, but the top was longer in a Pompadour style. But his dark mocha chocolate eyes drew her in and sucked the air out of her lungs.

"Who is that?" Olivia asked incredulously. "What do you mean, *who is that?*Have you been living under a rock? This is Oisín O'Quinn! Only the hottest male model in the business. Seriously, Mimi, you need to get out more. He's gorgeous."

"Probably a huge pain in the ass. Most models are self-centered." As soon as she said the words, she knew she was stereotyping and as someone who looked different than a lot of people, holding to her mother's Hawaiian heritage, she knew what it was like to be stereotyped. She even felt a little guilty.

Liv wasn't listening as she opened the magazine and read. "Listen to this! *He's an animal! He had me on my back, on all fours, on the bed, against the wall, and on the carpet all in the first round."*Olivia's voice grew husky and sultry. *"His stamina can only be matched by that of an animal. He's a lion!"*

"You know, lions are very lazy creatures," Naomi said. "And I can't believe they actually printed that. Is nothing sacred anymore? I'm sure he doesn't like having his... abilities aired out."

"Sex sells, babe. Don't tell me you wouldn't hit that if it came up to you," Olivia shoved the magazine with a picture of him, nearly naked, only wearing a pair of cotton tighty-whities, thumb hooked in the waistband and looking into the camera as if he was a true predator and the camera was his prey.

"Sure, I'd hit him," Naomi said nonchalantly. "If he came any closer, I'd give him a good right hook across that all too perfect jaw of his."

"Oh now, don't be jealous."

"I'm not."

"It says here, he has an apartment in New York, London, and LA. Gawd, I'd melt from one glance."

Naomi shook her head. Was Oisín O'Quinn attractive? Yes, very. But in that perfect model way where it's nice to look at but not touch. Like a porcelain toilet seat.

Olivia tucked the magazine in her cart and grabbed another. Pushing it into Naomi's basket, she giggled.

"For later."

"No thanks, I'm good," she said.

"Oh come on," Olivia whined.

Instead of fighting, she sighed and accepted the magazine. Wanting nothing more than to head home, grab a beer with her dad and sit out in their small garden listening to the waves. They couldn't see the water from their house, but the small oasis they had created was her sanctuary.

Every year, every time they renovated a condo, Naomi's dad would draw her to his side and kiss her temple as they looked out at the emerald green water.

"One day, honey," he would say. But that day had yet to happen.

Finally, Naomi had everything in her basket and headed to the checkout. Olivia thumbed through the magazine occasionally moaning at the pictures. Soon, once the groceries were paid for, the magazine costing ten dollars more than she wanted to spend but she wasn't about to let Liv know she couldn't afford the added expense, she said a quick goodbye in the parking lot and powerwalked away from Olivia.

Reaching her rusty pickup truck, the door stuck, of course, but soon she got in and sat in the stifling heat of the car sitting in the Panhandle Floridian sun. With the air conditioner not working, she cranked the windows down. Resting her head back on the headrest, Naomi heaved a sigh. Olivia was a sweet woman, always had a crazy streak but she meant well. Still, it drained Naomi whenever they were together.

Looking over at the three bags of groceries, one of the chocolate colored eyes of the hottest model to don a pair of Versace underwear peeked out of the plastic. Rolling her eyes, she sat up fully, started the car, and, looking back, began pulling out of her parking space.

Out of nowhere, a figure appeared behind her. She gasped and slammed her foot down on the brake, hearing a bang as the figure's hand shot out reflexively to stop the truck. Throwing the gear into park, she unbuckled and raced out of the car toward the figure.

"I'm so sorry, are you okay?"

"Aye, fine," he answered, and she heard the lilt of an Irish accent. Looking up at him, impressed she had to crane her neck to see his face. He was tall and for her five-foot ten-inch height it was refreshing to be dwarfed by him.

Then locking eyes with his, as he fixed his sunglasses, she recognized the chocolate-colored orbs.

"Oh shit," she breathed.

"Oisín!" she heard a man yell and soon, a larger man was pushing him behind him and inserting himself between them. "I told you to wait for me," he scolded him, still glaring at her with menacing eyes.

"It's fine, By. I'm not hurt," the first one... Oisín, Naomi gulped, said. The big guy glanced back at Oisín then her suspiciously. Finally, he moved aside and Oisín stood before her again.

"Really I am very sorry. I looked but I didn't see you."

The corner of his mouth quirked up in a teasing smirk.

"This is where you apologize for not seeing my lights and me trying to back up and thank me for my reflexes, successfully not hitting you." Naomi waited but he still said nothing. "Ooookay," she breathed and stepped back. "I'm sorry I almost hit you, but you need to watch where you're going too. Deal?" she struck out her hand and his grin tipped up on both sides of his mouth.

"You know, I've had women try a lot of things to get my attention, but you're the first to try to run me over."

"What?" she questioned. "I didn't... I wasn't..."

"Of course," his grin widened, and sweet baby Jesus, his dimples popped. He was gorgeous. But she had a serious aversion to him. "But you know, a beautiful woman like you doesn't have to nearly kill me to get my attention."

It took Naomi a second too long to answer. "I didn't nearly kill you. You walked out behind me without looking. If anything, we both are to blame."

The gorgeous smile turned devastating. "You're cute when you're impassioned. I'd like to see more of that. Why don't you come by my condo tonight?"

Naomi stared incredulously at him. "Excuse me?" Was he seriously propositioning her? In the Publix parking lot? *Asshole.*

"That's what you wanted, isn't it? I mean you do sort of owe me, after all."

Naomi couldn't stop her hand. She tried, not really, but she told herself she tried not to, but she did. The sting on her hand, the way his head snapped to the side, and how the huge guy behind him stepped forward only for Oisín to place a hand on the guy's chest to stop him, brought what she had just done crashing down on her.

"Oh god. Look, I'm sorry I almost hit you, but I'm not sorry for slapping you. Just because some women would jump at the chance to... jump you, not all of us sleep around for no reason. You need to learn how to respect women. I'm sure your mother would not be happy with your choices. Find someone else who wants you. Unlike you, I have some self-respect."

With that, she stormed back to her truck, got in, watched as the two men waited for her to pull out and drove away. Her cheeks burned hotter than the sand on a clear summer day. God, she hoped that would be the end of her involvement with Oisín O'Quinn.

Driving felt good. It had been a long time since Naomi had driven just for the sake of driving. The scenic route was always her favorite but soon, the sun began to slip closer to the horizon and her gas tank got closer to empty.

With a regretful sigh, she turned her pickup around and headed home. The thought of sandwiches from Lucky Sam's completely forgotten.

Oisín O'Quinn was exactly as she expected; gorgeous but arrogant. Still, she hated how her body had reacted when he asked her back to his condo. And she wasn't talking about the slap. It had been an awfully long time since a man had called her pretty and shown an interest in her. Why did her traitorous body have to like it from *him?*

Shaking off her emotions, she pulled over on their little street behind her dad's pickup.

"Ugh, dinner," she groaned and leaned forward, her forehead on the steering wheel. "It's okay," she leaned back. "I'll cook something." She cringed remembered the bare cabinets. Getting out of the truck, she grabbed the groceries and headed inside.

"Dad?" She called. "You home? I forgot Lucky Sam's. I'm so sorry. You will not believe the day I had." She set the bags on the kitchen island. "The condo looks great, by the way. The fresh paint really adds to the view. I'm thinking we could up the selling price by ten." She put the things away ignoring how the only food in the house was Ramen and opened the refrigerator door. "Olivia says hi, by the way. Or actually as she would say: *oh my god, tell your dad I said hiiiiiiiiiii,*" Naomi raised her voice to imitate Olivia's mousy tone. "Seriously, I swear that woman lives on energy drinks and wine."

She grabbed the much needed beer and popped the tab on the opener imbedded into the side of the kitchen island. "Oh, and you couldn't even begin to imagine who I bumped into today... literally. I'll give you one guess. He's an arrogant, egotistical, self-centered, asshole who thinks the sun and moon rise and set on his shoulders. You will never believe the audacity of this guy. He actually thought I wanted to go back to his condo with him. I mean can you imagine?" She walked down the short hallway, kicking off her tennis shoes and drinking from the bottle. "Any guesses?" Rounding the corner to the living room, she froze. Her father stood from the chair and gave her a nervous smile but what caught her eye was the man sitting in the other chair, dressed in a blue suit, crisp white shirt, unbuttoned at the collar, and tan dress shoes, holding a whiskey glass between his middle finger and thumb. A smirk on his lips. The same smirk he wore earlier.

"What the hell is he doing here?" she demanded.

Oisín O'Quinn's smile grew. "Dear me, sounds like you've had an interesting day. So have I," he stood.

"Mr. O'Quinn and I were just talking about possibly working on his new place. He just bought that old mansion off Bay Tree Lane," her dad said.

"That rundown plantation? I thought they were going to tear that place down," she replied.

"It was put up on the market for flippers and Mr. O'Quinn purchased it," her father explained.

"I like giving things a second chance," Oisín said. "And I need a good construction crew to help make my vision a reality. I need a place to go when city life doesn't agree with me. And when you..." a smile toyed on his lips. "*Bumped* into me, I saw the logo for Moon Construction and had Byron look you up. I was just discussing the particulars with your father."

"Particulars?" she questioned.

"Mr. O'Quinn wants to hire us to handle the reno," her father said.

"Oh, hell no," she replied.

Chapter Six

Oh little Miss Moonbeam is beyond adorable when she gets passionate, Oisín thought. Having been the only woman to play hard to get with him in his life, he was intrigued.

After she positively buzzed with sexual tension, Oisín wanted nothing more than to see her let her hair down. When she drove away from Publix, he saw the brand on her truck and had Byron look her up. His bodyguard harrumphed but eventually did as he asked. His driver drove him to Moon Construction, a residential area off Nautilus Street between Scenic 98 Front Beach Road and I-98. The little sign for the construction company pointed to the back entrance of a two story sea blue house with a charming mermaid fountain in the flowerbed.

When the man who Oisín discovered was Naomi's father, opened the door, Oisín immediately put on his mega-watt smile and won the older man over with his charm. But the purely European Caucasian man before him, did not look like his daughter. Naomi's Hawaiian heritage was clear in her striking features. The man before him looked... ordinary.

But as soon as he entered the home, on the construction offices side at least, Oisín understood. Photographs of a woman bearing a strong resemblance to Naomi littered the area and Hawaiian artifacts and decorations stood out against the eggshell painted walls. Though he had never been to Hawaii, Oisín appreciated the culture and the tradition of such an ancient people.

When Mr. Moon had offered him something to drink, he had refused a beer blaming his agent's strict diet, though it was a lite, and accepted some of the Japanese whiskey in the drinks' cabinet. They had just begun speaking of his newest acquisition when the door opened and he heard her voice.

She was railing on him, and someone named Olivia, and he couldn't help but smirk. She wanted him, it was obvious, and he was more than willing to oblige. But as soon as she turned the corner, taking a long drink from her beer, her eyes connected with his and shock followed by the cutest rage, entered her eyes.

"What the hell is he doing here?"

His smile grew and he wanted to tease her. Finally, her father explained Oisín's ruse for seeing her again and though it wasn't a lie, he did just purchase the old plantation house on Bay Tree Lane, it was the beach house down the access road he wanted to renovate first.

He had planned to start the reno on his own and ask for some of his old friends from the *Rough and Buff Moving Company* to come over and help, if any of them would talk to him anymore. When he left Ireland for his modeling career, he had left of them without jobs.

The view from the beach house was amazing with his own private beach and he couldn't wait to create an oasis where he could sit back and relax. And though he could do most of it himself, Naomi Moon and her father were an added benefit.

Well, Naomi was. But from what he could tell, they weren't too well off and could do with the money. Their reviews were excellent, but there was always someone who could do it cheaper and quicker.

Naomi's "oh hell no," brought him back to reality. Mr. Moon looked even more nervous as he glanced at him.

"Would you excuse us for a moment, Mr. O'Quinn?" he asked.

"Take your time," Oisín motioned for them to speak and when they left the room, he sat back down and took a long drink of the whiskey, not even attempting to cover his eavesdropping.

Naomi was fuming by the time her father stopped in the kitchen. He turned to look at her.

"What's going on, honey? This is a big job. He's all ready to write a check for whatever we need. This could really put us in the black again. You know Emilio's company is kicking our asses and poaching our guys. We were three down at the Sanderson's today alone. We need this. He's offered any amount we need to get started."

"Yeah, you know who does that? Rich guys with more money than sense."

"Honey, I've never seen you like this. Why don't you like him? I mean it's not like he's not handsome, I would have thought you would smile a little at him."

"I'm not shallow dad," she spat. He held up his hands in supplication.

"I didn't mean it like that, sweetheart. What has you so... upset with him?"

Naomi grumbled. "Is he hot? Yes, of course, he's a model. But he made... we met earlier as you heard, and he made... he said some things to me and it made me what to hit him harder."

"You hit him?"

"I *tapped* him with the truck then slapped him when he propositioned me."

"He propositioned you?" Her dad's face went red.

"It was nothing."

"And you hit him?"

"Yes."

His eyes bounced to the entrance. "Good. But honey he's a model, you can't hit him harder, unfortunately, he could sue us. Though I have a good mind to go back in there and deck him myself. Look, if he makes you uncomfortable, we can refuse."

"No," she said sternly, surprising herself. "No, we can't. You're right. We need this gig. But unlike some women, I'm not blinded by a six pack and an averaged sized..." she looked at her dad and bit her tongue at the word she almost used. "You know what. He's an asshole. We can take this job on one condition. I don't have to be alone with him. Nor do I have to hear him flirt with me. I'm sick of men like that."

"Agreed, honey," her dad nodded once. "I'll take care of it all. He's offered pay plus labor and expenses. If we can cut down on labor costs to just the essentials, you and I can do the bulk of the work."

"Dad, us doing the bulk of that place is insane. We can't do it. Besides you can't do ninety percent of the stuff you used to do before the—"

"Before the heart attack, I know," he cut her off. He never like to remember that day three years ago when he lifted too much lumber. And Naomi definitely didn't want to remember seeing her dad clutch his chest and fall to the ground. "So let's negotiate and get a team together. We can cut down on new crew by pulling some guys from the condo renos. You know I hate the way he treated you, but we could truly benefit from this. You okay with it?"

"I will be." She huffed a sigh. "You're right, it's a big deal." She took a long drag of her beer.

Her dad rested his hands on her arms and kissed her forehead. They walked back out to the living room to see Oisín still seated in the chair, a smirk toying at his lips as he locked eyes with her.

"It's eight actually," he said.

"What?" Naomi questioned.

"It's not six, it's an eight pack," he explained.

Naomi rolled her eyes and drank from her beer.

"And about the *other* thing you mentioned..." he prompted. "It's not average."

"It's smaller?" Naomi spat.

Oisín chuckled but stood, finishing his whiskey. Setting the glass on the small table he gave her a sidelong glance.

"I like you, Naomi."

"Trust me, the feeling is entirely one sided," she stated.

He grinned again and extended his hand to her father. "I believe I overheard some of your terms and if I have caused offense by my proposition earlier, you have my most heartfelt apologies. Both of you." He looked pointedly at Naomi, but she couldn't tell if he was sincere. "However, I do agree to your terms and if Miss Moon doesn't feel comfortable around me, I will limit my visits to the site. I wouldn't ever want to be the cause of any woman feeling uneasy. I have a mother, two sisters, and many cousins, nieces, and aunts. Sometimes I forget my behavior would reflect badly on my family and how I would feel if anyone spoke to my female relations the way I do."

Great, now she felt badly, *how did he do that?*

"That being said," he began again. "I do hope to take you both to dinner to discuss the contract."

"We can drop it off at your condo tomorrow."

"Tomorrow won't work, I'm afraid. They have me on an early chopper out to Fort Morgan for a shoot. It'll take all day. Would dinner be all right? We can meet at my condo and I can have my driver take us anywhere. I've heard there's a wonderful little place down the beach that has the best seafood tower. The Sand Dollar."

"Of course," Naomi scoffed. "Only the most exclusive and expensive will do."

"Is it expensive? I had no idea," he grinned. "Bring the contract." He fished a set of keys out of his pocket and offered it to Mr. Moon. "Let yourselves in. I assume you know where my new property is located. I'm interested in your opinion. There's a beach house just down the boardwalk—"

"Duckboard," Naomi corrected.

"I'm sorry?"

"That's the first apology I believed."

"Naomi," Mr. Moon whispered.

Ignoring her father, she continued. "Wooden paths in residential areas are called duckboards not boardwalks."

"Oh..." Oisín's grin returned. "Well, that just ruined my fantasy of reenacting the famous song about a boardwalk. You're full of disappointment today, aren't you?" he winked. Turning his attention back to her father, he continued. "I'd like to start with the beach house so I can move in while you're working on the main building. Draw up what's needed. I'll sign whatever. Also, could you have an outline of what your vision is? I'm a very," he looked over at Naomi. "Visual learner."

"What style do you prefer, Mr. O'Quinn?" Mr. Moon asked. "We can do a virtual tour of the place and share our ideas but if you could give us a style or color palette. It will help."

"Oh, please, Mr. Moon, call me Oisín."

"Bill," Mr. Moon motioned to himself.

"Well, Bill, I'm pretty laid back. I like secondhand things. Giving them a lift to their true potential but I like fancy too. I'm hoping the mansion will be the fancier southern style you Americans always show in your movies."

"You fancy yourself a real Rhett Butler, don't you, *Ocean?*" her deliberate mispronunciation of his name made him grin.

"Are you offering to be my Scarlett O'Hara, lass?" he pinned her with a stare that rose the hair on her arms, then turned. "The beach house, I'm looking at open, airy, serene, peaceful. I do love me some shiplap and as far as color palettes go, I'd say beachy; blues, greens, browns, off whites, you know, bring the beach and gulf inside. That sort of thing."

"We'll get started," Bill said.

"Excellent. I'm looking forward to working with you. Until Wednesday evening. Say seven o'clock? You know where I'm staying, I'm in room one eleven, building one. I'll let the guard know to expect you and will meet you at the stair just before the walkway. You'll see it. If you have questions, ask the guardsperson. Davis will drive us. I hope you don't mind, but my bodyguard will need to come with us. He'll get us settled at the table and hang out at the bar nearby. He won't interfere."

"Of course not, we understand."

"Do we?" Naomi questioned.

"Thank you for the whiskey, Bill. It's one of my favorites and still allowable on my diet." Oisín offered his hand to her father and winked at her.

"My pleasure," Bill said. "We will meet you at your condo."

"You have my phone number, if anything changes, please let me know."

"I will," Bill promised and walked him to the door through the kitchen. As soon as it was firmly closed behind Oisín, Bill looked over at his daughter.

"What is with you two?"

"What? He's an asshole."

"The sexual tension between you two is through the roof. I felt it and I'm your father."

"No, nuh uh, nope," she finished her beer. No way was she attracted to him. "Not at all!" She called over her shoulder as she walked back to the kitchen.

Chapter Seven

Oisín gazed out at the beautiful landscape before him. The chopper ride to Fort Morgan dropped them near the old Civil War fort. The curator had opened early for them and showed them around. The old fort was incredible. The pentagonal walls still had indentations from old cannon balls and bullet ricochets from the famous battle. The tales of heroism, death, and war intrigued him but as his grandmother used to say, where there's violent deaths there's spirits and he felt it. The old fort was eerie but to someone who grew up in *the old country* as his grandma used to say, his senses were heightened and on more than one occasion felt like he was being watched or saw something out of the corner of his eye. Byron looked to be feeling the same. His usually stoic bodyguard was even more… stoic.

"What are you feeling?" Oisín asked.

Byron looked at him surprised and then shrugged. "A lot of things. Good soldiers died here, and slaves were used to build this place," he revealed. "I'm getting an eerie feeling of both."

"It's definitely quiet and peaceful now."

"Still," Byron looked about as uncomfortable as any man could be.

Oisín was sorry to have to leave such a beautiful spot, especially with all the history, but was happy to walk out those doors to get to the shoot. Even Byron relaxed more once the fort was behind them.

They stood on the beach just a stone's throw from the fort but looking out at the blue-green water, he took a deep breath.

"Alabama," Oisín said softly as his agent strolled up looking down at his phone. "It's just as beautiful as Florida in its own way."

"Yeah, the beach is," Tony replied. "Inland is a little too… country for me."

"Spoken like a true city boy. I grew up in the country," Oisín reminded him.

"The *Irish* country. It's different than American country."

"I don't see why. Everyone I've met is overly friendly and not in the *I wanna get in your pants* kind of way."

"Everyone wants to get in your pants, Oisín. That's one of the things I love about you."

"Awe, Tony, I'm touched," he grinned. "Didn't know you went that way."

"Makes you marketable, O'Quinn," Tony, his agent, said.

"Just a piece of arse to you," he pretended to be hurt.

"A very profitable piece of ass. We're waiting on hearing back from Metric. That's a million plus."

"Any word on that?"

"Not yet. Their request for a couple weeks is normal. Don't worry you're a shoo in."

"Keep me posted."

"Will do. Let's get to work. Andrina will be here soon, and the shoot calls for solo pictures."

Oisín nodded and walked over toward the costume and makeup tent set up near the sand break to help with the wind. Seeing various clothing set out on the rack, he took a second to run his finger down the sleeve of an old, yet modernized World War II military jacket.

"No fingering the clothes." The voice of his hair and makeup artist, Sheila Polk came from the front of the tent.

"Jaysus, Sheil," he sighed. "Scared me to death."

"Just keeping you on your toes, O'Quinn," she answered sashaying up to the makeup chair set in front of his mirror. "Sit." She ordered.

"Yes, ma'am," he replied and hopped into the chair.

Sheila studied his head critically as usual as she contemplated the best hairstyle.

"I'm guessing we're doing a military shoot. Hence the fort and the jacket," Oisín said.

"They're wanting an Errol Flynn type look. Fortunately you already have the main type of haircut back then, short back and sides. We'll start with the mousse."

She grabbed a canister from her belt, shook it, turned it upside down, and pushed the button. The familiar sound of the mousse being released from its pressured container soothed Oisín. Knowing Sheila wouldn't want to talk until she had his hair working with her, which could take anywhere from ten minutes to half and hour, he pulled out his phone and checked his texts.

Two were from his brother, one showing an ultrasound photo of the new baby and another funny meme about animals that only a veterinarian like his brother would understand. Still, he replied with the appropriate reaction to the picture and another to the meme.

Another was from one of his friends in New York telling him about the latest fashion news.

One more from his cousin Trevor, a famous Broadway star, and opera singer. Trev was just cast in the revival of *The Scarlet Pimpernel* Musical playing the titular character and he was off-the-charts excited to be working with the tenor who originated the role and Trevor's idol. Oisín grinned and sent back a congrats and a request for two tickets for opening night in a couple months. Trevor sent back a thumbs up emoji almost immediately.

Then, he clicked over to the unprogrammed number showing up on his feed. He grinned. Naomi must have gotten his number from her father and was texting him. His grin grew with every insult she hurled at him as he typed back.

It was refreshing to have someone immune to his charms for once. But as he turned off his phone, her face flashed in his mind again for the millionth time since he woke up that morning and for once in his life, he was interested in getting to know a woman in more ways than between the sheets.

Naomi Moon intrigued him. She was beautiful, but more than that, her stubbornness, sass, and genuineness made him interested in her more than anyone else.

"That's a smile I've never seen before," Sheila said breaking him from his thoughts. He caught her eyes in the mirror then saw his hair.

"Nice work, Sheil," he said.

"Uh huh," she replied then pointedly look at his phone in his hand.

"Something new."

"A girl?" she questioned, her southern accent caressing the word.

"You know you're it for me, love," he teased.

"Nope," she replied. "There's an old saying... don't shit where you eat."

"And interesting saying," Oisín said. "I believe my ma mentioned that before I left Ireland."

"Smart woman."

"You know I'd light up your world, lass," he grinned.

"I don't date white guys, you know that," she said.

He took in her mocha-colored skin, enhanced by the sleeve tattoos, nose ring, and braided hair.

"It's a pity," he replied. "But if I ever want someone more gorgeous than me on my arm, I know where you work."

"Arrogant bastard," she replied.

"Cheeky wench," he grinned.

"Well, whoever she is, I like the smile she puts on your face," Sheila said.

Oisín caught the look on his face in the mirror and had to blink to make sure he saw himself correctly. Sheila was right, he was smiling a different smile than usual. That worried him.

No matter what, he only wanted to play. A different smile could mean trouble. Naomi was becoming more of a distraction than he bargained for.

Naomi drove behind her father toward Bay Tree Lane. Grumbling and lamenting the fact that even though she took her father's phone the evening before to share Oisín O'Quinn's contact information, she still woke up thinking about him. Even after she sent some scathing texts, she woke up feeling badly about them and texted an apology then grew angry that she had apologized when it was clearly his fault.

As she showered and brushed her teeth that morning, she remembered his smirk. When she got to the kitchen, she gasped as she saw the magazine out in plain sight. It had been tucked away in the fruit basket on the side of the island until she could throw it away. What angered her even more was there was a message written across it in a man's handwriting.

You can't believe everything you read, but in this case, you can. Next time feel free to ask for my signature. See you at dinner. – Oisín O'Quinn

She groaned in frustration. He must have seen it on his way out. Hearing her dad coming down the stairs, she quickly tossed it in the trash, picked up her phone, and sent another text to Mr. O'Quinn.

Naomi: Trust me, I DON'T believe everything I read, especially not the fictitious and spurious blather that comes from an over eager child looking for her five minutes of fame. Let me guess, you paid her to say those things about you. You know she was only twenty-one?

Naomi saw the three bubbles as he typed a response.

Ocean (Asshole) O'Quinn (as she had programed his name into her phone): She was legal and hot.

Naomi scoffed.

Naomi: Seriously?! Is that all you men want? Whatever happened to chivalry? Decorum?

Ocean (Asshole) O'Quinn: I've often wondered that, too. Oh, and by the way, no, I didn't pay her. Nor influence the article. I would have much rather been likened to a tiger or bear instead of a lion but hey, King of the Pride, right?

Naomi: King of the Pride? Often characterized as lazy, good-for-nothing, horny jackasses who are never satisfied with one woman and who think they run the show but honestly would die of starvation without a woman around. I've changed my mind, that part I do believe. You are just like a lion. It gives me a design idea for your bedroom.

Ocean (Asshole) O'Quinn: Thinking of my bedroom, love? I'd be happy to show you around.

Naomi groaned in anger and looked up to see her father.

"What's wrong honey?" he asked.

"Nothing. Let's eat and head out."

Her dad looked at her for a long time before moving toward the fridge to pull out the orange juice. Naomi's phone buzzed on the island again, but she ignored it, put two slices of bread in the toaster, and poured a cup of coffee. She would work with her dad on the houses because it was what she loved to do but she would not allow Oisín O'Quinn's dancing eyes to make her weak. She'd been down that road before and never again would she put herself in the predicament of coming home to see her man in bed with another woman. She would never let that happen. And Oisín O'Quinn would be that type of man.

Chapter Eight

As Naomi and her father pushed open the old door to the mansion, they both coughed and waved their hand through the dust in the air.

"A good day of windows and doors open is called for," her dad said.

"Or just tear it down," Naomi replied.

"And lose all the history? Honey, no."

"Let's just look around and see what needs to be done and then head to the beach house."

"Okay," he shrugged and tried the light switch on the wall beside them. It clicked but nothing happened.

Naomi pulled out the iPad she always carried and opened two apps. The first was the camera and the other was the design checklist her cheating ex-husband developed specifically for her, early in their relationship. She still used it because there was nothing quite like it on the market. Never in her dreams did she think he'd sell it and make millions then try to take down her father's company.

She snapped a photo of the ancient wiring and switch then tapped on the electricity button on the app. What she loved about it was all she had to do was enter the basic schematic of the building, age, square footage, etc., and then what needed to be fixed or updated and began a running tally of expenses based on cross-referencing companies she had inputted and used in the past. As she typed up a quick explanation on the notes portion, her dad went to the window and yanked back the heavy drapes. He coughed as a cloud of dust descended around him. Naomi turned to check on him but stopped when her eyes caught the room. The soaring ceilings held the largest chandelier Naomi had ever seen, uncovered, the crystals tinkled in the soft breeze from the open door. A large round marble table stood beneath the splendor, caked in dust but it didn't take away the hidden beauty. Two staircases ascended to the second story farther back and flanked a slightly smaller than life size imitation statue of Michelangelo's *David* standing on another table in front of a door.

"Oh wow," her dad breathed standing next to her. "This place is incredible."

"They just left everything?" she asked.

"We'll need to check the terms of his purchase, if it doesn't include inside items, we'll need to look for next of kin."

Naomi wasn't listening. She walked further into the foyer and instantly saw the true potential. Houses spoke to her and sometimes if she was lucky, it showed her what it wanted to look like.

Her dad walked up beside her, a smug smirk on his face. "Still think it needs to be torn down?" He chuckled.

She gave him her best side eye and rolled her eyes. "Just surprised Mr. Underwear Model had enough braincells to buy it," she replied.

"Now now," her dad chuckled again. He looked around and shook his head. "So much potential. It's a pity it's so rundown."

Naomi walked over to the window where her father had pulled back the drape to let in the sunshine. It was a door leading to the rounded portico. Snapping a picture of rotted stripping and clicking on the window insulation button on the app, she typed more notes as her father continued.

"The floor looks good. With a good sweep and some polish, it'll be good as new," her dad said crouching low and swiping his hand across the two-tone black and white tiles. Naomi added *air out* and *deep clean* to the list.

"What are we up to now?" her dad asked.

"Electricity, new windows, clean, polish, about twenty thousand," she answered. "If HVAC isn't up to code though…"

Bill Moon nodded and walked to one of the staircases. "Ni, look at this," he called her over and pointed to where the first step had pulled away from the tile.

"Oh shit, foundation?" she questioned.

"Let's hope not," he answered as she bent and snapped a picture.

Bill walked past the stairwell to the hallway and disappeared. Naomi took the moment to look around the foyer again.

"Beautiful," she murmured.

"Ni, come here, look at this!" her dad called. She walked down the darkened hallway to see another room with light from an open window flooding the space. She stepped over the threshold to see what would classify as a living room, if old plantation houses' grand rooms could be reduced to a twenty-first century nomenclature of *living room*. A stone fireplace filled one wall, floor to ceiling windows overlooking the portico were to her right, an archway led to the dining room. That space held another large chandelier, a twelve-seat dining table and a china cabinet on the back wall. Antiques, every single one of them, including the fine bone china in the cabinet. She followed her dad's call to the side and gasped at the music room off the dining room. An old ornate piano stood proudly covered in dust and cobwebs in the middle of the room. Wandering through it, she came out on the other side of the space and stood frozen in the doorway. An empty long rectangular room with black and white tile continuing in its basic but beautiful pattern met her eyes. Looking up, Naomi saw the second level open to look below and again, chandeliers hung from subtly gilded rose crown molding. Archways with red curtains pulled back, led to small rooms on the side. Apparently, for some quiet talking or other pursuits back in the previous century. The music gallery above the built-in mahogany bar looked in need of some repair and Naomi headed up the stairs to check and take photos.

"This place eh?" her dad called up.

"It's amazing, honestly," she said adding some notes and descending again.

"Some windowpanes need replacing," her dad said pulling back one of the drapes. She took a picture and keyed it into the system.

"Might be best to replace all the windows," she said. "I bet they're all over fifty years old."

"As an add on, just in case he wants a smaller number than what we are giving him."

"Good idea."

"Look at this view," her dad said opening one of the set of French doors leading to a stone patio. "A little loving pruning and you could see down to the water."

Naomi added *landscaping* to the list.

"What's the total?" her dad asked.

"For just downstairs and landscaping? We're looking at fifty without window replacements."

"Not bad, honestly for such an old building."

"But that's not including mold and asbestos tests."

"Go ahead and add it in, we're going to need it."

"And lead paint."

"True," he nodded as she typed in her iPad. "We haven't seen the upstairs nor basement or kitchen. I bet the plumbing is ancient. When Oisín and I talked, he was figuring two-fifty."

"Tighty-whities might be right," Naomi replied.

"Tighty-whities? How do you know what sort of underwear he wears?" her dad turned a critically lazy eye on her.

"I don't, but he's a Versace model, dad. Not like they make 'em breathable."

Bill burst out laughing. "So, this has nothing to do with the magazine on the counter at home that has a full page of his – ahem, *tighty-whities?*"

Her cheeks flamed red. For the first time since collage, she blushed in front of her dad.

"It wasn't mine. Olivia forced me to buy it."

"Riiiiiight," he drawled. "That's the story you're going with. Got it."

"Let's just finish up here so we can go to the beach house and spend more of his money. That's the one he really wants done first."

"We get a good enough crew, we may be able to do them simultaneously."

She was grateful her dad changed the subject without much complaint. Though she was sure he'd poke fun later, she was glad to stop talking about Oisín O'Quinn in nothing but a thin pair of white underwear and a sultry look on his face.

"Let's get the number and a timeframe first before we do that," Naomi said. "I agree but I don't want to stretch us too thin."

Her dad nodded in agreement, and they continued their review of room after room. As Naomi thought, the HVAC was about twenty years out of date and not up to code. As far as kitchen appliances went, the refrigerator looked to be out of the fifties and the stove range and ovens were too corroded to work even if they had power. They also found evidence of rodents chewing the power cords.

The bedrooms upstairs were in decent shape and Naomi put down some much-needed paint and supplies along with furniture and light fixtures, seeing the total keep ticking up.

Finally, the basement was the last on their tour. The smell was a mixture of musk and salt air. They needed to check the foundation and see if there was any water damage. Naomi held her breath as her father checked the hot spots with the flashlight on his phone.

"Looks good, bar one. The spot over here will need to be checked. Looks like there was some flooding. Let's check the flood zone permits and make sure they're up to date," he said. "Just to be sure, let's get Martin out here."

Martin Knowles, PCB's best foundation expert and building inspector, ex-military though he never said what branch, and all around nice, good-looking guy. Also happened to be Naomi's ex-boyfriend from High School. She made a note to call him.

As she looked around the space with its exposed brick, duct work, and dark wood beams, an idea kept niggling in the back of her mind. She saw an image of what the basement wanted her to do to it and she smiled. A genuine smile. She could do it. She always liked to do something special for their clients, make a special place for them that really marked their personality. It was her little touch on something they never knew they wanted.

"I like that smile," her dad said. "Is it for Martin?"

She looked back at her dad and laughed. "No, no just my little project taking shape."

"Oh... ah," he grinned and looked around the space. "I look forward to seeing what you create. But let's go and tally everything then head to the beach house." Her dad wiped his hands on his jeans.

Following her father up the stairs, she stopped at the first step then looked back. Her idea coming to her like a movie projection. The plan cementing in her mind. It was a special place, and she knew exactly what to do. For once, when she thought of Oisín O'Quinn in that space, a smile lifted the corner of her lips instead of her usual eye roll. For the first time since she met him, she didn't hate him. That thought should have worried her, but it didn't, and a sort of giddy feeling churned her stomach.

Chapter Nine

Oisín checked his watch once more as he heard the door lock beep and the heavy hurricane style door open. Byron walked in and looked over at him.

"Davis is pulling the car around," he said.

"Any sign of them?"

Byron shook his head. "Maybe text her?"

"Nah," he answered. "You saw the traffic. They're probably stuck there. I'll give them another ten minutes."

Byron nodded and sat on the couch, picking up the remote to the television. Turning it on to a national news network, he listened a little, but Oisín felt his eyes on him.

"Everything all right?" he asked turning from the kitchen where he had grabbed a water bottle.

"Yeah, of course," Byron answered looking at the television.

"Out with it, By," he said.

"What are you really doing with this girl and her father?"

"Don't mince words," Oisín chuckled.

"I'm serious, Osh," he said. "She's not your usual. I'm not sure I like the idea of you being around her too much. She could have hit you with that truck and she did slap you."

The memory of the sting of her hand swiping across his cheek echoed, but he shrugged. "Don't know. They're a good contracting company apparently. I want to get that place up and running. I'm losing money on it as it just sits there."

"And all the flirting, that's just you wanting to get into her pants?"

"Something like that," Oisín replied. "What has you so worried, By?"

Byron sighed. "I don't like how she treated you. I'm not sure I like the idea of her in your most intimate space."

"I haven't gotten her in my intimate space yet." His eyes twinkled.

"You know what I mean. She's going to be designing your home here. Are you sure you want her to know that much about you?"

"It's her job," he shrugged. "I'm not too worried. Honestly, I appreciate your concern and I acknowledge it. But I know what I'm doing."

"All right," he threw his hands up and sighed. "All right, I've said my piece. Just promise me you won't let her hurt you."

"No one can hurt me, By, but I appreciate you looking out for me."

Byron nodded once and then raised a hand to his ear listening on the device tucked into the back of his shirt and embedded in his ear. He looked up at Oisín and nodded.

"Understood, *Aquaman* on the move," he said into his cuff. "They're here."

Oisín nodded. "Still lovin' that codename."

"None of us can pronounce your name correctly so instead of mispronouncing it to *Ocean*, we thought, next best thing. Aquatic Superhero."

"And let's face it, he's a badass superhero."

"Yes he is," Byron grinned. "Let's go before I change your name to *Lover Boy*."

Oisín laughed as he walked out of his condo and down the stairs to the main entrance. Byron always had them on the lower level near an exit just in case they needed to move quickly. Oisín never understood it's convenience and would much rather been in the penthouse suites, but it was nice not to have to wait for an elevator.

Hands suddenly sweaty, Oisín wiped them on the back of his white dress slacks. Glancing at Byron in his usual black slacks and black Oxford shirt, he was glad to see the car waiting. Unable to see Naomi and her father, he kept walking. The white of his pants reflected in the streetlamps as the sun was slowly beginning to set. Wearing one of his favorite midnight blue button-down shirts from his Dolce and Gabbana modeling days, he put a little more swagger in his step as he walked beside his bodyguard and allowed him to open the door to usher him in.

The image that hit him when he entered the backseat of a limo, took his breath away. Naomi sat beside her father wearing a little black dress that hugged curves that should have been illegal. Her dark brown hair was pulled back into a low ponytail and short sections of hair framed her face making her sharp features appear softer. Her dark wheat colored skin looked flawless and natural as he noticed she only wore a small amount of mascara. She looked up at him with those russet-colored eyes and he lost his ability to speak. Correction, he lost his ability to stop himself from speaking.

"Damn, you look hot."

"Excuse me?" her father and she said at the same time.

"What I mean is," he stammered. "You look great in that dress, but I bet you'd look even better out of it."

"I don't appreciate you speaking to my daughter that way, Mr. O'Quinn."

"Shit, sorry, I – ehm," he looked over at Byron who was staring at him with wide eyes.

"All set, Davis, let's go," Byron said quickly.

"I'm sorry," Oisín finally said clearing his throat. "I do apologize. Sometimes I forget myself and Byron has to reel me in. Miss Moon, I apologize. What I should have said is you look very lovely this evening and I am honored to be escorting you and your father to dinner."

"Cut the shit, O'Quinn," she said, and the use of his last name only sent a shiver through him. "I think we both know exactly what you meant. Fortunately, this is a business dinner, and I promised my father I would be nice to you. That being said, you say one more quip about me, I think my father may use some of that military training he's been hiding for so long."

Bill's eyes glanced at Byron who watched them both like a hawk. "I don't think it would work but I'd give it my all."

"I think I'd let you, Mr. Moon," Byron said. Then with a look at Oisín he went on. "You really screwed that up, Osh. He has every right to deck you."

"I know, and if he does, you stay out of it, By."

"Oh I intend to," Byron answered.

Bill grinned at the bodyguard. "I think I like you."

"Semper Fi," Byron said.

"Semper Fortis," Bill answered.

"Ah, a squid," Byron grinned.

"Ten years, Marine," Bill stated.

"Where did you serve?"

"The Pearl," Bill admitted sliding over to sit closer to Byron.

"Damn," Byron whistled.

"Let me guess, Afghanistan?"

"Leatherneck in Helmand."

"I appreciate your service."

"And I yours."

"Since my bodyguard and your father apparently have become BFFs, let me take a moment to please say how sorry I am for my rude behavior," Oisín whispered to Naomi as Bill and Byron kept talking. "You honestly took me off guard and when I'm off guard, I have no control over my tongue."

"I think you have full control over every part of your body, Mr. O'Quinn, but that doesn't mean I am one of those women who want to find out. Your words are just words. Yes, they're annoying as hell, and yes, I wanted to slap you again. But I'm not going to let you, or anyone make me feel uncomfortable in my own skin. Already happened in my life and will never happen again."

"I understand."

"Do you?" she eyed him up and down. "I doubt it."

"Would you believe I was extremely overweight as a child?" He asked. Her brows furrowed. "It's true. All throughout primary and secondary school, I was obese. My parents weren't sure what was wrong with me. I tried working out and dieting but nothing helped. That's when my brother, who was studying to be a veterinarian found this hormone called Leptin. Apparently without it, the body doesn't realize it has body fat and causes immediate hunger. My brother found this out and helped create a dietary plan for me. Come first day of sixth form, I was six foot four and a solid two-forty. I know what it's like to be made fun of. And I never want you to feel like I'm judging you or teasing you."

Naomi simply looked at him for a long moment then nodded once. "Thank you for complimenting how I look tonight. Even if it was poorly done at first."

Oisín smiled and was glad to see forgiveness in her eyes.

"Did you get a chance to see the houses?" he asked.

"We did," she replied. "Do you happen to know the terms of your purchase? Do you own the furniture still in the home?"

"Yes," he answered. "As you Americans say, I own it lock, stock, and barrel." He winked.

"Good, that takes part of what we had in mind out."

"Did you like it?"

"It's a beautiful property," she said. "The views will be amazing once pruning is done."

"That's what I thought too. I have a couple ideas for the upstairs. I would like an office and I would like as many of the bedrooms renovated as possible. All but two can be generic."

"And those two?"

"Mine of course, and I want Byron to have a say in his. He'll have the room across from my room."

"Do you know his style?"

"I don't, but I bet you your da' will after their conversation."

She was quiet for a moment. "When will you be finished in Panama City Beach? Are you going to another shoot soon?"

"No actually," he said. "I'll be done after another shoot at Pier Park, day after tomorrow. Then I'm on vacation. My agent rented a house for me near the pier, I'll get you the address…" then seeing her jaw tick, he hurried on and said, "in case you need to get a hold of me. I promise I'm not trying anything on with you."

A look appeared in her eye that he couldn't discern but she nodded once and pulled out her phone. He had given her the address just as they pulled up to their stop. Byron and Bill stopped speaking of military times and his bodyguard opened the door to step out. Oisín, familiar with the protocol waited. Naomi tried to open the door next to her, but Oisín made a sound.

"I'm sorry," he said. "But I need you to wait."

"What? Why?" She asked.

"Byron's making a sweep, honey," her dad explained. "Oisín lives in a different world than us."

"Thank you for understanding," Oisín said.

"I was on diplomatic detail a few times, I get it," Bill stated.

"It gives me a chance to apologize to you for my behavior."

Bill waved him off. "So long as my daughter has forgiven you, that's all I care about."

"I have," she answered then glanced at him. "For now."

Byron stuck his head back in. "All clear."

"Here we go," Oisín grunted as he slid out of the limo, slipping his sunglasses on even though it was darker than before. They were parked under the overhang of the restaurant and a man dressed in black slacks and a white shirt with a black pinstriped vest was waiting for them. He smiled but not in an overeager way and stepped forward.

"Mr. O'Quinn, may I say what a pleasure it is to have you dining with us tonight," the man said.

"Thank you," Oisín replied.

"We have a table ready for you in a private room with a beautiful view of the beach. Once you get settled, I would be happy to raise the window so you can get the breeze on this beautiful night."

"That would be nice, thank you," he said. Naomi and her father stepped out of the car. "This is Mr. and Miss Moon they are my guests for tonight and of course you know my bodyguard."

"Yes, of course, welcome to The Sand Dollar, Miss Moon, Mr. Moon. I hope you will have a wonderful meal. I am Vincent, the general manager and your contact for anything you need tonight. I have two of my very best servers attending you this evening. If you follow me, I'll take you directly to the table."

Byron spoke low into his cuff as he followed directly behind Oisín. Naomi and her father walked to his left. Vincent led them through the door and down a private hallway to another door. Pressing a card to the reader, the door beeped, and he pushed it open.

"This is the only way in, but there is an exit near to your table. The servers have to scan in and no one is allowed back here. We do cater to many rich and famous and want to make sure we have that extra layer of protection for you to make your stay with us just that much more pleasant."

"It is appreciated, Vincent, thank you," Oisín said.

"Will this do?" he asked turning toward Oisín and standing next to the lone table in the room.

Oisín took in the space. The cherry wood walls reminded him of his local pub back home, but the tasteful decorations and copper stamped ceiling tiles elevated the space to the exclusivity he had been hoping for.

"Yes, this will do very well," he answered, taking off his sunglasses.

"And would you like the window open?" he asked.

Oisín looked at the *window* in question. It was more a floor to ceiling garage door with an elegant railing just beyond like a Juliet Balcony. The sand and surf just a stone's throw from the opening.

"I would," he looked at Naomi and her father. "That all right with both of you?"

"Fine," she answered.

"Excellent." Vincent hurried to a hidden panel and pushed a button. The window lifted until it was directly overhead. Vincent offered a seat to Naomi and she sat to the right of where Oisín was eyeing. Bill sat to the left. Taking the head of the table, he almost felt badly for Byron. But knowing his friend and bodyguard would never sit with him when he was on duty in a strange place, he let it go. "Now, the wine you ordered is on ice, should I bring it to you now, or would you prefer to see our cocktail list?"

"I would actually like a whiskey," Oisín said.

"Of course, do you have a preference on region?"

"An Isla single malt, if you have it," he replied. "Highland, if you don't."

"We have Oban, Ardbeg, and Laphroig."

"Ardbeg, neat, please."

"And for you, Miss? Sir?"

"A Lemon Drop?"

"Lemon Drop martini, absolutely," Vincent bowed slightly to Naomi and looked expectantly at Bill, who looked a little lost.

"Uh, um," Bill started. "Ah, I'm – ah, not sure."

"Certainly, I can give you a few minutes to check the menu if you would like. But I can highly recommend our martinis or a whiskey," Vincent said.

"Do you like Isla malts?" Oisín asked. "I recommend Ardbeg."

"Okay, yeah, I'll have one of those. Ice please," Bill said.

"Wonderful," Vincent replied. "I will have those prepared and I'll bring some water for the table. Still or sparkling?"

"I prefer sparkling, with lime," Oisín said.

"That's perfect," Naomi agreed.

"I'll bring a pitcher for the table and some glasses."

"And you will take care of my shadow back there?" Oisín tossed his head in Byron's direction.

"Yes, oh absolutely," Vincent bowed slightly and headed out the door to put in their drink orders.

Once alone, the three of them opened their menus. Conversation flowed around what sounded good and how beautiful the setting sun looked on the water. When Vincent returned with two others in tow, he passed around the drinks while one of them poured the water. With introductions to the two servers, Vincent bowed again and left them to their orders. The white wine Oisín had preordered arrived after their cocktails were finished and a soaring tower of seafood was placed in the middle of the table. Shrimp, crab legs, oysters, smoked salmon, caviar, and lobster were all laid out in a beautiful silver three tier platter.

The waitress opened the bottle of white, after showing him the label and allowing him to check the temperature. Once the waitress had poured a small amount for him to taste and it was to his satisfaction, he nodded and the waitress poured first Naomi's glass, then her father's, and finished with his.

When they were alone again, apart from Byron leaning against the built-in bar area, munching on a fresh platter of shrimp, Oisín lifted his glass and toasted.

"Slainte, to new friends, a prosperous relationship for the both of us. And to forgiveness and second chances," he winked at Naomi who breathed a laugh and shook her head amused.

"Cheers," both she and her father said and clinked their glasses.

"So, what do you think of the place, Bill?" Oisín asked taking an oyster and prepping it with one of the lemon wedges they provided. "Naomi told me a little of what she thought of it on the drive over. And to answer your question, I own everything in the house, anything the previous owners left behind is mine."

"Oh excellent," Bill said shelling one of the shrimp. "There are some lovely antique pieces that we can really spruce up to shine."

"That's what I was hoping for," Oisín tossed back the oyster savoring the buttery lemon flavor.

"The potential of the mansion is phenomenal," Bill said.

"Did you get to see the beach house?" Oisín reached for another oyster.

"We did," Bill answered. "Naomi has some great design ideas to show you. But we also want to run a few things by you. We have some numbers," he looked over at Naomi who pulled out her iPad from her purse.

"What did you think of the beach house, Naomi?" he asked.

"The view alone is worth everything," she said clicking on her tablet. "There's some foundational issues with it, not surprising being so close to the sand and salt. But we're confident we can figure something out. The only issue is getting in the heavy machinery that we need to lift the house in order to reform the pilings. But it was obviously done before, we can figure it out. Maybe with some clearing and landscaping of the woods surrounding the plantation, we can get the cats and cranes in."

"We have drawn up some immediate things that need to be taken care of and resetting the pilings are a must if you want to keep the house as is," Bill explained.

"I do," Oisín answered. "That is exactly what I want to do."

"Good, because these two properties have so much potential," Naomi said. "After seeing the buildings, I want to work on this project. It deserves the love and attention we can provide."

"I had no doubt," Oisín smirked. "So what did you have in mind?"

One of the servers came back to refill their wine glasses and take their orders for the main course. Once he was gone, Naomi continued.

"To bring both houses up to code, we will need to install a new HVAC system, bring an electrician out for the wiring, have a plumber check the plumbing, and test for mold and asbestos. The plantation house as a whole is in much better shape than the beach house. We have a foundation expert and building inspector on standby. He can check the houses and give us a clearer picture of any structural damage. According to our calculations for just the plantation house, with the right team, we could get it done in eight to ten weeks."

"Wow, that soon? I didn't expect it."

"Like I said so long as Martin doesn't find anything majorly wrong with the structure, it's a piece of cake. The beach house, not so much."

"Okay, what do you have for me on that one? As I mentioned, that's the one I really want done first so I have a place to stay while I'm in town waiting for the main house," Oisín reminded her.

"Yes, but here's the thing," Naomi took a drink of her wine. "To do everything externally for that place would take six weeks alone and that's cutting it a bit short it's more like ten weeks. Just from what we saw. Again, once Martin takes a look, we'll have a clearer picture."

"Understood. So what's the rest of the beach house look like?"

"The deck is wonderful but about eighty percent of the boards are rotted. It would be safer to take the entire thing down and rebuild it," Naomi said.

"That's a lot of lumber," he answered. "And man hours."

"Exactly," she agreed. "So again the pilings, deck, siding, all of that needs to be done before we do anything inside. It's currently not stable enough to work. And if you want to take out any walls or open the space up, it might take longer. Here's my thoughts," she turned the iPad around to show him mock ups of the design. "There's not enough natural light in the living areas and since it's a private beach, we figure knocking out this outer wall from here to here and installing sliding doors. Then, place three floor-to-ceiling windows on either side, opening that space up and bringing in the light and view in a nearly three hundred-sixty degrees. The main structure is circular so if we continue the windows on the upstairs we could possibly build a small balcony off the master bedroom which would be just to the right of the main deck. My thought is, if you like the idea we can consider adding stairs from the master balcony to the main deck. The kitchen as it stands right now is in desperate need of a rehaul. I say we knock down the half wall and open the space up even more. Put a large kitchen island here," she pointed to a spot on the design picture.

"And have an overhang for stools and a place for breakfast. Bring in some recessed tract lighting throughout the main floor and convert the old wood burning fireplace into a gas one. Then, extend the fireplace up to the master directly above. There's three bedrooms on the second floor, as you know. The master, we build the balcony off the front where that small window is and place two more windows here and here," she showed him. "That will let in the light that's needed in that space. Then, for the other two rooms, I have two options. Two guest bedrooms or break down the wall separating them and combine them into one big entertainment space. Build a spiral staircase up to the loft area and add a lookout. Close off the current stairwell from the second floor up to the third and give the downstairs dining room vaulted ceilings move the stairs here. In the loft, we can do bunk beds or futons for guests. The two bathrooms upstairs can then be extended to give you more space.

"With the added space we can create a master oasis with standup shower, bath, and separate, but connected water closet. The guest bathroom we can extend without that wall there and give you double sinks, a large walk-in shower, and commode. On the deck, you will have enough room for a private getaway. I also want to plant some palm trees to give you shade on the deck and since the deck goes all the way around, I figure we can enclose one part of it and make it an all-season room just off the kitchen, so you have a place to read or even use as an office all while overlooking the Emerald Coast. Color scheme would be grey and white with a splash of blue and green and give you that shiplap you love in the living room and master."

Naomi paused and all Oisín could said was, "wow. That's amazing."

"It will really look good and bring new life to the structure."

"And you think all that can be done in ten weeks?"

"No," she shook her head. "That's just the outside, deck, windows and doors cutout, pilings, siding, etcetera. The rest of it will take another six to eight weeks."

"And what is the price tag on the beach house alone?"

"Depending on which option you want for the upstairs—"

"I like the idea of the large entertaining space."

"Good, then we're looking at seventy-five thousand," she said.

"Sold," he answered. "I love the design. It's exactly what I was looking for. Open, airy, beachy. What do you need from me?"

"Well, I'm glad you like the design," Naomi said. "Do you want to do both the beach house and the plantation? You haven't heard the design plan for that."

"Whatever it is, I know it will be great. The beach house was a test of your skill and you passed with flying colors." Oisín took a drink of the wine and smiled. "But I would love to know what your plans are for the ballroom."

The servers came back with their main entrees and Oisín ordered a bottle of champagne to celebrate. He caught Byron's raised eyebrows. Naomi glanced back to see them looking at each other.

"Is there a problem?" she asked.

"No, he's just surprised I'm drinking white wine and champagne. I have another shoot and I'm on a strict diet. Seafood I can get away with, but wine turning to sugar not so much. I'll pay for it tomorrow. He'll get me out for more cardio on the beach which is not my favorite thing."

Naomi laughed softly. "I run the beach every other morning, I understand."

"It's just the loose sand. My trainer says it takes more to run on the loose sand but I hate it."

"I can imagine, that would suck."

Oisín grinned. They had found common ground. "If you ever see me running on the beach, feel free to call to me and tell me something crazy happened with the reno. Anything to get out of it." He winked.

She laughed again. "I will remember that."

He loved the sound of her laugh.

"So what is the total price for both properties, landscaping, repairs, whatnot?" Oisín asked.

"From my *estimate*," she stressed the word. "It's about three hundred thousand."

"And about ten weeks give or take each place?"

"About that yeah," she replied.

"So conceivably by the end of September early October I could have both done."

"If we did it concurrently. If not, then mid to late October," Bill said.

Oisín nodded slowly and took a bite of his filet. "All right. Where do I sign?"

Naomi broke into a grin as Bill relaxed into his seat. She clicked a few times on the iPad and then turned it around for him.

"This is the contract. We usually put ten percent down."

"Make it twenty," he said. At her confused look, he continued. "I want to be your biggest priority."

She rolled her eyes again, but this time he noticed it wasn't out of disgust but more humor.

Oisín accepted the stylus and signed his name on the line. Naomi then turned the tablet around and signed her name, adding the date. The server brought the champagne and popped the cork. Pouring three glasses, she handed them to each of them then returned the bottle to its ice bucket.

Oisín toasted them. "Thank you. I am happy to have *bumped* into you. I hope this is the beginning of a prosperous relationship." They clinked and sipped. "Now, business is out of the way, let's talk. How did you get into construction, Bill?" he asked.

"My father worked in the shipyard most of his life. Here in Florida. He taught me everything I know. When I was in the Navy, I was stationed in Hawaii, Maintenance Division."

"Hawaii, is that where you met Naomi's mother?" Oisín asked.

"Yes, it is. How did you know?" He asked.

"I hold a great respect for Polynesian and Hawaiian culture. I've studied a great deal of it."

"Mmhmm," Naomi replied. "And the actual truth is?"

He stared at her for a long moment. "All right, fine. I watched *Moana* with my nieces, all right?"

"I knew it," she grinned. "Another Disney convert."

"Guilty. Though I have been to the Islands. It's a beautiful state."

"It is that," Bill answered. "I fell in love with Iolani. She lived near the base and would come visit me. When I returned to Florida, I was discharged after my eight years but I never lost touch with her. I flew out the day the ink dried on my discharge papers and proposed to her in the sand where I first saw her that very next day. We were married thirty years when she got sick."

"I'm so sorry for your loss," Oisín said sincerely.

"Thank you," Bill replied. "But she gave me the greatest gift. My daughter. Naomi looks just like her mother."

"I can understand why you were enchanted then," Oisín answered.

Naomi rolled her eyes but chuckled.

"Do you still have the boat repair side of things?"

"I do, but it's not nearly as profitable since the fiberglass and computers took over. I prefer the old-fashioned boats. And there's so many repair yards in this city alone, it's almost impossible." Bill took a drink of his water.

"Are you thinking about getting a boat?" Naomi asked him.

"I grew up on an island. I love boating. I was thinking about it. Would want to store it somewhere though, I don't want to ruin the view with a dock."

"It would be difficult but not impossible to have a dock built near, but I agree, it would sully the view," she said.

"How did you get involved in the business, Naomi?" he asked.

"I've been working with Dad my whole life," she stated.

They were quiet for a long moment. Oisín waited for Naomi to continue but when she didn't, he smiled and drank more of his wine.

"How did you become a model, Oisín?" Bill asked. "It seems like a tough industry to break into."

"Aye, it was tough, still is. I've been fortunate. I caught the eye of a retired agent and he got me connected with the right people. But it's still tough. There are companies who don't want me, think I'm too big, too tall, too… Irish, but I don't pay them any mind and I am who I am. I like myself and my bank account."

"Do you have any family?" Bill asked then waved his hand stopping him from answering. "My apologies. We should keep this professional. You don't have to answer that."

"No, no worries, I don't mind. I love my family. And yes, we're a large family. Irish, you know. Ma, da', an older brother and two older sisters, then there's about twenty-four cousins and numerous aunts and uncles."

"That is a large family," Bill agreed. "I'm an only child and so is Naomi."

"Sometimes I wish I was too," Oisín teased.

Their waiters came around to see how everything was and when they offered to refill their wine, Oisín realized he hadn't touched his food after the initial bite. He took a forkful of the buttery garlic mashed potatoes and closed his eyes. At their silence, he opened his eyes again.

"Sorry, carbs, I've missed them."

"Must be tough having them tell you what to eat or drink," Mr. Moon said cutting into his Mahi-Mahi.

Oisín eyed Naomi out of the corner of his eye as she speared a piece of Monkfish and lifted it to her mouth. How he wished to be able to ogle her without fear her father might pull out a gun and shoot him. Naomi was Bill's little girl and if the man knew what was going through Oisín's mind, he'd definitely want to kill him.

The rest of the evening past in appropriate conversation about his style tastes, wire transfer information, how he was enjoying Florida, and when he finished the best Key Lime Pie he ever had, Oisín signaled for Byron to have the car pulled around. Vincent was appropriately thankful for his patronage, and he was appropriately complimentary. They drove back to his condo, and he thanked Naomi and Bill for a wonderful evening. He watched them pull out of the carpark and drive away. Sighing, he headed up the stairs, Byron right behind him and pulled off his suit jacket as soon as the door was closed. His shoes followed and he ducked into his room hearing Byron do the same. Washing his face, brushing his teeth, and changing into his sweatpants and a white t-shirt, he headed out to the balcony with a water bottle.

He leaned against the balcony railing looking out to the inky blackness before him. Florida was beautiful. There was something majestic about the warm salt air and the expanse of water surrounding them. He loved it there and could not wait until he had a house on the water. Someplace to call his own, a place he could share with someone special.

Naomi's face flashed before his eyes. She was beautiful, perhaps the most beautiful woman he'd ever seen. She was strong, confident, and yet, she cared about her dad. There was nothing sexier to him than a confident woman. He wanted to get to know her better. That thought should have scared him, but as he thought about it, the more he was interested in chasing after Miss Moon.

Chapter Ten

Naomi tossed and turned in bed. It was well past the witching hour and as she looked over, two o'clock shown in red neon lights on her nightstand. Even the soft rain that pelted her windowpane, Oisín's dancing eyes and laughing smile kept playing as if on repeat in her mind. No matter how many times she told herself she didn't like him, couldn't like him, she still caught herself thinking about him.

With a huffed sigh, she admitted it to the darkness. "Okay, so he's hot, really hot and I'm not dead. Of course I'm going to find him attractive, but the hell if I'm ever going to let him know that. Besides, just because I may find the shell attractive, doesn't mean he's a nice guy. He's a jackass and thinks he's god's gift to everyone. There's no way I can like him. That's it. Just no way."

She squeaked when there was a knock at her bedroom door.

"Honey?" Her dad's muffled voice came through the door. "Are you okay?"

"Yeah, dad, I'm good. Can't sleep is all," she called.

"Oh okay, need anything?"

"Nope all good. Thanks." She loved living at home with her dad. He needed her help and it helped neither of them to be lonely but there were times she missed having her own place. Somewhere she could rant on Oisín O'Quinn without worrying about her dad's reactions.

Still, the thought of some warm milk or Tylenol seemed to always help her insomnia. Pulling on her robe over her sleep tank and shorts, she padded down the hall to the stairs. Her dad stood in the kitchen flipping through the magazine with Oisín's face on the cover. He looked up when he heard her on the stair.

"Couldn't sleep?" he asked.

"Not so much. White wine and champagne equal sugar high," she said going to the refrigerator and pulling out some milk. Then, grabbing a small sauce pan she pointedly ignored her father's choice of reading material and moved to the stovetop.

"I plan on calling Martin in the morning, see if he got our notice tonight about booking his next available," her dad said, speaking of their usual go-to foundation expert.

"I submitted the request through the portal on the app as soon as O'Quinn signed the contract," she explained. "I'll follow up with the HVAC and then see about getting a drill for the new pilings and a lift for the beach house."

Her dad said nothing for a long moment. She heard the pages of the magazine turning and couldn't help herself. Twirling around, she crossed her arms over her chest and stared at him.

"What?" he questioned.

"I threw that away," she replied.

"Yeah? And? I pulled it out of the trash. It has an article on how to improve my golf game."

"Dad, come one, why on earth would you want to read about *him?*"

"Honey, listen, I'm curious about the other articles too, but I also need you to stop being so... rude to him. He's our client now. I know what he did was beyond wrong, but now, I need you to promise me you'll treat him like the client he is."

"Dad, I can safely promise you, I will treat him exactly how he deserves."

"That's my worry, honey," he sighed and walked over to her. "Look, any other time, I would be telling him exactly how I feel about him speaking to my little girl like that, but he just gave us sixty thousand dollars up front. This is huge for us and we can't afford to piss him off. Please, sweetheart, just for a couple weeks, play nice and you'll never have to see him again."

"Promise?" she asked though hated the tiny fluttering feeling of disappointment she felt. Oisín was like a vacation; enjoy it when it comes around, look at it, have fun, but never stay longer than expected and when you leave you are always a little disappointed.

"I promise," her dad answered rubbing her arms. "Can we get through the next fourteen weeks? Without you trying to kill him?"

She chuckled. "I'll do my best," she answered.

Her dad smiled and kissed her forehead. "You are so much like your mother," he said. "You know... she hated me when we first met. Said I was the typical American sailor boy and wanted nothing to do with me. But I pressed on. I found ways to be around her, talk to her... I slowly chipped away at her walls until she finally succumbed to my charms." His smile turned into a grin. "We had an amazing life. I can only hope for that to happen for you."

"Yeah, tried that remember? I found my husband in bed with another woman."

"Emilio was rotten from the beginning. He better not show his face anywhere near here or I'll take care of him. I was a soldier."

She laughed but smiled at her dad. "You were a mechanic, dad."

"Still learned how to hurt people."

She shook her head but patted his arm. "Thanks, dad. But Emilio is out of my life and I'm not about to replace him with an overpaid underwear model who, though hot, can't get it into his thick skull that I'm not interested."

"Hot, huh?" he teased.

"You tell him I said that and I'll move to Fort Lauderdale."

Her dad barked a laugh but winked and tapped the side of his nose.

"I won't say a word." He moved back to the island and closed the magazine. Picking it up, he tossed it into the trashcan, then headed up the stairs to his room.

Naomi stared at her milk, warming in the pot on the stove.

Oisín O'Quinn was not far from her thoughts. Maybe she should try to get along with him. *After all*, she thought. *I did almost hit him.* But then his words came back to her and how arrogantly he assumed she pulled out, nearly tapping him simply to get his attention. Could she put her feelings on hold so she and her dad could make some much needed money? She'd have to. But she'd be lying if she wasn't looking forward to the end of the project. And she'd be lying again if she said the thought of never seeing him again, made her happy.

Huffing a sigh, she poured the milk into a glass and carried it up the stairs to her room. Even after the warm milk and listening to the rain outside, morning came too early and as she groaned getting out of bed, her head pounding from lack of sleep, duty called. Day one of Oisín O'Quinn's renovation began. She would need caffeine and the patience of a saint.

After being on the phone for most of the day, Naomi looked over the names on her subcontractor list with pride.

"Eat your heart out, Emilio," she said.

Ever since her ex got back in town, he had set up shop as a general contractor and took several of her best sub-contractors. Though Naomi wasn't a vengeful person, knowing she booked Aron Jackson, the best electrician on the Emerald Coast, made her grin.

The grin was short lived as a knock came at her door and she looked up, then out the window of her office in the third bedroom of their house to see who was showing up unannounced. Her jaw dropped and hand clenched around her Bic pen so tightly it snapped, covering her hand in black ink.

"Shit," she muttered and grabbed some napkins from her desk that she kept from lunch deliveries.

Almost as if she had conjured him, her ex-husband knocked again.

"Do nothing, he'll go away."

Emilio was never a patient man and usually wouldn't wait longer than five minutes for anyone to answer the door.

"Ni, come on, I know you're in there," his voice, a middle range tenor with a hint of his original Brazilian accent called through the door. "I see your truck."

"Shit," she muttered again.

Instead of answering the door, she went to the window and, hating herself for it, checked her reflection in the glass. Soothing her hair back into a ponytail, she opened the second story window. She popped her head out and looked down. Emilio stepped back from the front stoop and looked up.

"What do you want, Emilio?" She demanded.

"Is that anyway to greet me, darling?"

"You don't get to *darling* me. What do you want?"

"We need to talk," he said almost sweetly.

"Anything needed said can be said to my attorney. By the way, you're late with your alimony… again."

"Tesouro, that's what I want to talk to you about."

"I'm not your treasure, and again anything about that can go to my lawyer."

"Invite me in," he prompted.

"No," she answered.

"Now now," he replied. "I heard you got a good contract today. I wanted to congratulate you," he lifted the gift bag in his hand. The long skinny shape of it along with the sparkly *congrats* from a pour of champagne told her what was in the bag. But what worried her more was his words.

"Who told you about that?" she demanded.

"I have ears on the ground, Ni."

"I want a name."

"And I want a kiss, but in the immortal words of Mick Jagger, *you can't always get what you want.*"

"Go away, Emilio. I have a lot of work to do."

"I could help with that, you know."

"I don't think so."

"Now, Ni, don't be like that. We always have fun don't we?" He looked up at her with those damn dark puppy dog eyes of his. Though tempted for a split second, she was instantly reminded of those eyes going wide as she walked in the see some blonde woman riding her husband and she immediately hardened her heart and mind to him.

"Go away before I call the cops."

"I'm offering an olive branch, *Caro.*"

"And I'm refusing. Goodbye, Emilio. Nothing you can do will ever win me back."

"Never say never, *tesouro.*"

She pulled her head in and slammed the window down. Hearing another truck pull in and the driver cutting the engine, she glanced out to see her dad stalk out of the car headed straight for her ex.

"Oh god, no," she mumbled seeing her ex grin at Bill but then his smile faltered when her dad shoved him and started shouting. Naomi needed no more inspiration than that and took off running.

Down the stairs, through the hallway, and out the door, her bare feet sinking into the white sand that lined her garden and driveway. She hurried to the two men ignoring her dad using language she hadn't heard outside the construction site. Throwing her hands between the two, she separated them.

"Enough," she shouted over her dad's shouts. "Dad, please, stop. Emilio, go. Neither of us want you here nor want to see you."

"Come on, babe," he tried.

"Go," she shouted.

Her dad took a menacing step forward but bumped into Naomi's hand still stretched out. Emilio looked between them, then scoffed.

"Fine, I tried to be nice, just remember that," he said.

"Go," she ordered again.

"I'm gone. Just remember what happened here today."

"Is that a threat?" her dad growled.

"A reminder," he said and walked away to his Ferrari sitting on the street.

Her dad stared after him, a murderous look on his face. He only relaxed when the break lights disappeared turning on I-98.

"What the hell was *he* doing here?" her dad demanded.

"God knows," she huffed. "He just showed up. He said something about knowing about our new contract. But I think he was just fishing." She spoke quickly.

"He better be," her dad grumbled.

"Hey," Naomi soothed. "Easy, okay? Please. I need you to not be hurt."

He melted in the plea from his daughter. "I really scared you when that happened, huh?" he asked softly.

Her eyes instantly filled with tears as she gazed at the buttons on his shirt where his heart beat beneath.

"I never want to see you clutch your chest like that again. I thought I lost you just like mom."

"Oh honey," Bill pulled her into him and embraced her tightly. "I'm so sorry I scared you. I'm okay."

"Swear to me you'll take care. Swear to me."

"I promise, sweetheart."

"Okay good," Naomi pulled back and looked up at him. "Oh shoot. I didn't marinade the chicken for dinner."

Her dad chuckled. "Well, what have you been doing all day? Playing kissy-face with a hot model's pic on a magazine cover?"

"Ugh, never. You can rest assured, if I ever kiss Oisín O'Quinn, I have gone insane and need to be put down."

Her dad chuckled again. "Sure honey, I'll remember that."

"Do, I swear to you. I'll never kiss that man."

"Understood," Bill said fighting a smirk.

"I'm serious."

"I know you are."

"Why are you laughing?"

"No reason."

"Whatever."

Her dad's body shook with laughter.

"How about Sharky's for dinner?" he asked.

She rose an eyebrow at him. "And how are we paying for this?"

"I got the check in from the Sanderson's and Oisín's money hit our account. Let's celebrate.

Naomi watched her dad, then grinned.

"I like the sound of that. We have a lot to celebrate. I booked Aron Jackson."

"Seriously? That's wonderful!"

"I know! I'm excited. He said his latest project ended early and he'd be happy to work on such an old building. I sent him the contract and got it back about an hour ago."

"Oh honey, that's wonderful news!"

"It is, so I'll definitely celebrate with you tonight. I may even get a Mai Tai."

"Fancy! Yes, two are needed, STAT."

Naomi grinned and squeezed her dad's arms. He locked eyes with her again and held her gaze.

"Are you sure you're all right, honey?"

"I'm fine, Daddy. Did I like seeing him? No. Am I going to cry into my pillow tonight? Definitely not. He's not worth it."

"No, he's not. Come on, I can practically hear garlic fries calling my name."

"And you know what you're going to say in response?" she replied.

"Get in my belly?"

"No."

"Awe, no fair, sweetheart. I've been good all week."

"Yeah, right. Leon told me he saw you chowing down on some Culvers two days ago."

"Turncoat," he grumbled.

"Tell you what… we can split a *small* side of garlic fries, *if* you don't have bacon on your burger."

"You drive a hard bargain, missy. Fine. I agree."

"Good, let's go then." She turned toward the garage and keyed in the code to open it. Turning on their golf cart they kept and used for short distances, she backed it out, as her dad closed the garage door and hopped in.

It had been a long time since she had dinner out with her dad. Food prices were high in Panama City Beach but as they shared a side of garlic fries and toasted their Mai Tais watching the sun set on the water, Naomi Moon wouldn't change it for the world.

Chapter Eleven

"And that's a wrap," the photographer called to Oisín as he pulled away from the female model joining him on the shoot. She was beautiful but Oisín never slept with other models, a message from his mother before he made it big.

Applause from the other side of the pier drew his attention. They had utilized the PCBPD to cordon off the left side of the pier for the shoot, but some spectators and fans had been allowed to watch from the gate and the beach below. Oisín had to admit he was surprised they had gotten away with it. He had visited Pier Park for dinner a couple nights back with Byron and even at sunset the pier was filled with fishermen and women, families, and drunk college students. One had even come up to him to whisper something about another guy's mom, but Oisín couldn't get over the rancid smell of sour beer and whatever else he'd been drinking wafting off of his breath. Not that he had gotten very close. Byron promptly shoved the kid away.

Kid. Jesus. He hit thirty and everyone younger than twenty-five looked like a kid. When did he start channeling his older brother? Lachlan was approaching forty-five and happily married to his second wife Corinne with two children and another on the way, but the veterinarian hadn't always been happy. After losing his wife and unborn daughter in a car accident fifteen years ago, he had become a curmudgeonly old man prematurely. But then, Corrie blew into his life... literally. His big brother was a family man, and it was Oisín's time to be the premature curmudgeon.

"Those shots look great, Osh," his agent walked up and pulled him from his thoughts. "I really think they're gonna turn out."

"Great. Any news about Metric?"

"Actually, couldn't wait to tell you. Got the call twenty minutes ago. You got it."

"Really?"

"Don't sound so surprised."

"No, I'm not just... wow."

"Got a lot to celebrate. Go back to the condo and enjoy. Check into the house in two days."

And with that, his agent left. Byron waited for him at the chairs as the model headed to her station to get into her street clothes. Oisín accepted his shirt from Sheila as he sat in his makeup chair.

Sheila said nothing as she splashed his hair with water, releasing the hairspray and gel she used to keep it the way the photographer wanted it. He took his phone and stared at it. Nothing. His brows furrowed.

"Okay, honey, what's wrong?" She finally asked.

He hissed when she gently spread aloe on his sunburned shoulders.

"What do you mean?" He asked.

"You're quiet. You are never quiet after a shoot wraps up. You're always telling me about your plans. So I asked again, what's up?"

"Honestly?" He questioned. She waited. "I don't know. I'm trying but I just don't feel... happy. Like I know I should. Something's up. I must be coming down with something."

"Not uh," she shook her head washing the remaining Aloe off her hands. "You are not allowed to come down with anything while you're on vacation. Get out, have a beer or six. You'll be fine."

"You're right," he grinned. "I'll snap out of it."

"Yes you will." She slid her hands coated with conditioner through his hair, massaging his scalp. "Go to the pool, lay out on the beach, drink some fruity froufrou drink and enjoy the Florida sunshine. You'll be fine."

"Fruity froufrou?" He questioned with a chuckle.

"Why not? Who doesn't love a little Sex on the Beach?" She winked naming a tropical drink.

"Only then you'll have Sand in Your Shorts," he replied.

"Followed by Sand in the Crack and Blue Balls."

"Never worry about blue balls for me, honey. That never happens," he winked back.

Sheila laughed and turned to wash her hands in the sink set up in the tent.

"Well, whatever you decide to do, text me, lover boy. I live vicariously through you in your sex life," Sheila said.

"Bollocks," he replied. "A gorgeous creature like you? You never have to wait."

"Tell that to the singles here. Haven't pulled in weeks."

"Shit, come with By and me tonight, we'll get you laid."

"I might have to take you up on that. But unlike you, I don't have a condo in one of the most exclusive resorts in PCB."

Oisín grimaced. "If I'm in the most exclusive, I shudder to think what any other is like."

"That bad, huh?"

"Not a fan of mold on the shower ceiling."

"Yikes."

"But the view is good, and the pool is pretty badass, so it makes up for it. I'm just happy to have the house soon."

"Looks amazing from the pictures you showed me."

"Oh you'll see it. I'm already planning a pool party."

"And what about the secret little place that only Byron and I know about?"

"That is getting a much-deserved update, soon."

"And who is in charge of that?"

"Wouldn't you like to know," he said coyly.

"Well, judging by the grin my question evoked from you, there's a story there."

"For a later time. Right now, some fresh shrimp and a beer is calling my name."

"Amen to that," she said. "You're all set. Change into your shorts and get you gone. Take care of my boy, By."

"Always," Byron said in his usual deep voice.

Sheila grinned and her cheeks pinked as she walked past him. Oisín's brow rose as he pulled off the glaring gold and black Versace swim trunks and into his usual white shorts and light blue oxford. Rolling up the sleeves as he slipped his tan dockers onto his fingers, he was still barefoot on the sand. Byron picked up the dark brown, worn leather duffel bag as he slipped on his sunglasses.

"Ready," Oisín pronounced.

"Let's go," Byron replied.

"Oh and by the way, Sheila thinks you're hot."

Byron's steps faltered for a moment but soon he righted himself. "Eh, um… Condo or pool?"

"Dinner, then pool. We'll see how tired we are after that."

"Sounds good. Where do you want to go?" Byron asked pulling out his phone.

"Pizza and shrimp, that's all I care about. Doesn't the restaurant on site have both?"

"Probably. Want to go there?"

"Sounds good."

As they headed out of the tent, the sounds of Oisín's fans grew louder. He puffed up his chest and told Byron to hold on a moment. Together, they walked over to the throng of people and Oisín greeted his fans with his million-watt smile.

Chapter Twelve

After sharing a large pizza and a shrimp appetizer, Oisín and Byron headed up to the condo to change for the pool but as soon as they walked in, Oisín sighed.

"Would you hate me if I asked to skip the pool tonight?"

"Not at all," Byron said.

"Thanks, it's all coming down on me now and I'm exhausted."

"With reason."

"What reason?" Oisín chuckled. "I stare into a camera all day getting my photo taken."

"You are in the sun all day waiting to be ordered into odd poses, being poked and prodded by sea life, sitting in a chair while someone murders your scalp and then having to put on happy smiles for fans who don't know the meaning of the words *personal space*. You have every right to be tired, Osh."

Letting out a heavy sigh, Oisín clasped his friend's arm had smiled. "You are the only one who understands me, my friend."

"Only because I see what it does to you."

"I appreciate it." Then, after a beat, he grinned. "Got any beer?"

"Had it stocked while we were out."

"I love you."

Byron chuckled.

"I'm going to change. Pull me out a cold one?"

"Wanna glass?"

"No." Oisín thanked him and headed to his bedroom. Looking out the balcony door he couldn't see much now that the sun had set, and the inky blackness was unnerving in its beauty.

Quickly ducking into his room and changing into his soft non-designer lounge pants and a t-shirt he picked up in Atlantic City, he padded through the condo living room and found Byron out on the balcony with a closed can of a Destin local brew on the table and an open one in his hand. Byron turned when he heard the balcony door slide open. Immediately assaulted with the sound of screaming laughter, waterfalls, wind, and the roar of cars from Scenic-98 a stone's throw from their condo, Oisín winced.

"Is it always so loud here?" He asked.

"Probably," Byron replied.

"I hadn't noticed it before." Oisín popped the tab on his beer and took a deep swallow.

"We haven't really had a quiet night in since we got here, Osh," Byron reminded him.

"Yeah, you're right," Oisín sat on one of the wicker chairs and propped his feet on the balcony railing. Taking a deep breath, Oisín closed his eyes and listened. The pool had four waterfalls that gushed water, covering the sound of the waves beyond. Several people were enjoying the late moonlit swim and their laughter and squeals were loud. Byron sat beside him in the other chair but said nothing. Oisín opened his eyes when the loud rumble of a truck in need of a new muffler barreled down the road. Taking a sip of his beer, he looked up at the night sky.

"There's hardly any stars here," he said.

Byron looked up too. "There's some, probably not as many as you're used to, country boy."

"Oh please, country boy. If either of us is country, it's you."

"Can't argue there. You ain't country until you've wrestled a twenty-pound gator, skinned a rattler, slept under the stars while eating said rattler, and falling asleep to the sound of crickets."

"I didn't understand any of that."

Byron chuckled. "Wouldn't expect you to. It was a damn fine childhood. Wouldn't trade it for the world."

"Mine neither."

Suddenly, a sound Oisín had never heard before echoed across the pool. The sort of short nonhuman burping sound had him sitting straight up in his chair.

"What the hell is that?"

"What?" Byron looked over at him. "The wind? Waterfall? Bullfrogs?"

"Bullfrogs?" Oisín nearly shrieked.

"Yeah, this was my lullaby growing up by the creek at my granddaddy's place," Byron said with a contented sigh. "This and crickets. Nothing quite like getting woke up by your family in the middle of the night to go froggin'."

"What the hell is frogging?"

"That's when you take a stick and go out and find 'em, then skewer 'em, then eat 'em. My cousin Zeke always had an ear for a good one croakin'."

"Zeke?"

"Yeah." Byron looked up and raised his beer to the sky.

"He's the one who died in the war, isn't he?" Oisín asked.

Byron nodded. "He was my hero. Joined up after nine-eleven. Didn't make it home."

"I'm so sorry, By," he said.

"It's all good. Great memories. Especially with them croakin'. Brings back the good ole days."

They were quiet for a long moment until Byron pulled out of his obvious memories. "So, what's the plan for tomorrow?"

"Pool, beach, drinks, hot women."

"So the usual?" Byron teased.

"Yeah, the usual," he grinned and leaned his head back after draining his beer. "It's going to be a good day."

Chapter Thirteen

It's a horrible day, Naomi thought as she walked to the construction site. The crew she had lined up for the landscape clearing to be able to get the heavy elements down to the beach called saying they were double booked and couldn't be out for another two weeks. And then the fiberglass company she ordered the pilings from, emailed saying they wouldn't have them available for delivery until next week. All in all it was not a good day. But as she parked her truck behind a supped-up Ram 2500, she put all other thought out of her mind.

She got out of her truck seeing Martin Knowles standing by the front stairs, looking at the foundation and shaking his head. She knew that look.

When he heard the door to her truck shut, he turned and gave her his smile. She always liked that smile.

"Give me some good news, Mart, please," she begged as she walked over to the man who had her teenaged heart. She still remembered their first kiss at prom and what happened *after* prom.

He pulled her into a hug. "Good to see you, Ni."

She took a deep breath of him and it calmed her. "I've missed you," she said. "Where have you been?"

"Oh, in and out. Had some maneuvers."

"You're reserves now. Aren't you supposed to not be doing anything like that?" She asked.

He grinned but as usual, didn't tell her anything more.

"Thanks for coming out," she continued as they walked toward the stairs.

"Of course, anything for you, Ni. You know that."

"I do, that's why you're my favorite expert."

He gave her the side eye and chuckled. "Well, you may not like me when you hear what I have to say."

"That bad, huh?"

"It's not great." He walked around the stairs to show her. "The stairs are pulling away. Normally, that wouldn't concern me, we tear them out, and repour. But what has me worried is this." He pointed to a large crack running from below ground up past the stairs. He took her up to the steps to show the crack extended on the porch and under the door. Naomi swallowed and took out the keys. Opening the door, she saw for herself the crack went just into the foyer.

"Okay," she breathed. "What else?"

"I want to see the basement."

"Yep, this way. Then, I need you to check the beach house."

"You want a full read on this place?" He asked.

"Yeah, we're gonna need it."

"Okay, give me a second. Let me get my equipment."

Martin headed back to his truck and grabbed his gadgets as Naomi waited. The foundation issue wasn't a shock, but she worried it may push their timeline back even further.

Three hours later, Naomi waved goodbye to Martin promising dinner one night and turned to look at the old house.

Fortunately, the foundation issues weren't as bad as they thought. But there was still a lot to do. Thinking back to the dinner Oisín took them to, she remembered how he seemed knowledgeable in renovations and hoped he would understand the slight set back. She was confident he would. With a smile, she headed to her truck and drove toward the condo reno her father was overseeing.

Stopping for the rare indulgence of Starbucks on I-98 she got her father a decaf latte. Since the heart attack he was limited on caffeine. And went bold for her; a grande caramel macchiato. The scent was heavenly and as she sipped, she drove toward the condo, passing the resort where Oisín stayed.

"One day," she said to herself. "One day dad and I will have a place there. Ours. No reno, just relaxation."

Seeing the waters of the Gulf always calmed her and, rolling down the windows, she took in the sounds and the smells, though most of the time all she could smell was gas, diesel, or burnt rubber thanks to all the joyriders that came down.

Stupid kids.

Dear God, when did she get so cynical and worse, old?

Shaking her head, she pulled into the parking space next to her father's truck. Taking the coffees, she headed up to the sixth floor, hoping it was going how they wanted.

Oisín lounged in the pool, leaning against the wall of the island in the middle. The foliage providing much needed shade for his fair skin. Beside him, Byron took in a deep breath and let it out on a smile.

"This is the life, eh?" he said.

Oisín agreed and grabbed his tumbler of some fruity froufrou drink from the restaurant bar Byron had their cabana server get him and leaned his head back.

"God, it's gorgeous here," he said.

"It is," Byron agreed, watching their beautiful server walk by.

"Does someone have a crush?" Oisín teased.

"What?" Byron looked back at him.

"I saw that look. Daniella may be our server, but she's bloody gorgeous. You should talk to her."

"Don't be ridiculous, Osh," he answered.

"Just saying. She told me she gets off at nine tonight. I'll hole up in the condo with a good movie. You deserve to have fun. Davis can babysit me," Oisín said.

"I'm too old for her."

"You're barely forty and you don't look it. You're just making excuses."

"I appreciate you offering, but no. I'm on the clock twenty-four-seven."

"Doesn't mean you can't have a little fun."

Byron said nothing only took a drink from his beer. Oisín shook his head. It was like pulling teeth to get Byron to drink while on duty. Getting him to go on a date, would be even harder.

"What about Sheila? "

Byron choked on his beer and coughed. A shit-eating grin lifted Oisín's lips.

"Ah," he breathed. "Good to know."

"Good to know what?" Byron rasped.

"Nothing," Oisín shrugged and looked up as the repetitive whirl of a helicopter caught his ear and he watched the machine fly by.

"That's the sixteenth one today," Byron said. "Not to mention the fighter jets."

"Those were cool though," Oisín teased. Feeling the walls of the condo vibrate that morning was a little daunting but as Byron seemed unaffected and walked out to the balcony to look out, Oisín had followed just in time to see two F-16s fly by and do a loop around the beach strip.

"These must be a tour," Oisín said looking at the helicopters. "I think I saw a flyer for it when I was at the pier. Speaking of, how about we go there tonight for dinner? I'm still too tired to do much nightlife but by tomorrow night, I'll want to hit up the nightclubs."

"I'll call ahead tomorrow and get you a reserved table."

"And I'm wanting to bring along some girls. It'll liven things up a bit."

"Never knew you to not want things alive," Byron shook his head.

Oisín grinned and slapped his shoulder affectionately. "You know me too well, my friend."

"Oh my God, you're Oisín O'Quinn!" One of the girls near him squealed and Oisín lowered his sunglasses to look at her then winked.

"Sure am, lass," he replied and ignored Byron's silent chuckle as he exaggerated his Irish, tinged with Scottish, accent. Having gone to university in Scotland, Oisín maintained a slight mixed accent, but always exaggerated it when impressing women.

"Oh m'god!" She squealed again causing everyone to look.

Byron's eyes darted around the pool, no doubt looking for an exit if needed.

"I have followed your career since you signed with Burberry." She swam over to him.

Oisín nearly chuckled. Burberry was a campaign two years ago, nearly three years into his modeling career. Granted, it was that cologne that launched him into the stratosphere of recognition, but the way the woman said it, made it sound like ten years ago.

"I appreciate that," he said.

"You are so damn hot!"

He chuckled. "Thank you."

"What are you doing here?"

"I'm on vacation."

"I saw you at the pier," another woman swam up, followed by two others. "You were doing some sort of photo shoot."

"I was, yeah, but now I'm on vacation," he replied.

"Oh wow," the first girl said. "I never thought to see you here. Oh my God, wow!"

"I'm really here. What are you lovely ladies doing here?"

"Oh my God, Oisín O'Quinn is talking to me!" She squealed. "Well, um," and then she did what every woman who flirted with him did, she lifted her voice to a squeaky tone and giggled uncontrollably. "I'm here celebrating graduation."

Graduation... shite, she's twenty-two at most, he thought.

Why was it, Oisín wondered, two months ago, he didn't care how old someone was so long as they were legal but now he was thirty, he didn't like the high-pitched giggle. He preferred the alto quality of Naomi's voice and anyone younger than twenty-five looked like a child. Naomi's face flashed before his eyes. She had never lifted the smooth timber of her voice and though he didn't know how old she was, she was clearly in her thirties. He sighed as her smile flitted across his mind but squeals from more sorority girls broke his concentration. He shook his head. He needed to get Naomi out of his mind. He needed to get laid. Any of the girls currently swimming around him like sharks in the water would do. Maybe all he needed was to drop a little blood in the water to see who bit. Figuratively and literally speaking of course. He grinned.

"That's a fantastic accomplishment. What was your major?" he asked and saw Byron shake his head.

Oh yeah, buddy, if all goes well, you'll be needing your earplugs tonight.

Chapter Fourteen

Naomi and her dad stopped for lunch around two that afternoon. The condo was doing well but they had lost another two guys to Emilio's company. Fortunately, they were ahead of schedule and the owners were pleased. Grabbing a bite to eat at a fast-food joint, they ate in the truck and then hurried to another meeting. They had been fortunate in the last month or so to have had referrals from previous jobs but of the four referrals, only one had accepted. The other three had gone to another contractor.

Emilio had a reputation of getting things done quickly but after a year or so his shoddy workmanship crumbled but Moon Construction, prided itself on quality work even if it took a hair longer. But in the climate of instant gratification, their approach, though appreciated, was hardly chosen. It made finding work hard.

However with a newly signed agreement in hand, Naomi dropped her dad back off at the condo reno and headed home to get everything started.

As she sat in traffic on Front Beach Road, she listened to her radio as an old early 2000s Britney Spears song played and looked out to the sand and surf. Just as she eased up a little in the traffic jam, she heard a laugh, more like a screech and looked over. A girl, she couldn't have been older than twenty-one, was screeching with giggles as a man wrapped his arms around her front from behind, tickling her. She faux fought him but looked more like she was rubbing her back to his front in anticipation of foreplay. Naomi rolled her eyes but froze as the man laughed and looked up toward the row of cars.

Oisín.

"Because of course it is," she muttered. "And what a splendid song to be playing." She cranked the radio up as the chorus began, calling the man a womanizer. Whether or not he heard over the other sounds she wasn't sure, but he looked toward her truck and his grin widened. His bodyguard stood to one side of him, closer to the road as if standing between Oisín and a stray car.

"Now there was an idea," she laughed, though she had nearly hit him already. The light about a block away changed and as she eased forward, her phone rang. Grateful for the distraction as Oisín nibbled at the girl's neck, Naomi answered.

"Naomi Moon."

"Oh my God, girl heeeey!"

Olivia.

"Liv, hey, how's it going?"

"So amazing. Listen, and you can't say no."

No, she wanted to scream.

"Scooter is with my parents this weekend and I'm a free gal. I need some fun time! I've already talked to Chrissy, Kristy and Stacie and they are in! But I need you, Ni! We are going to the pier for dinner and then clubbin'. You are so coming!"

"Not tonight," she said.

"Oh no! Saturday sassy day! Saturday night! It will be auh-maze-zing!"

Saturday Saturday please let me have something on my schedule for Saturday. She pulled up her calendar on her phone. Saturday was blank. No surprise there.

Shit.

"Hellooooo? You're coming. Eight o'clock, hot stuff. The Pelican Snout. Girl time and drinks!"

Naomi sighed but decided, why not? She hadn't gone to a club in years... Decades really. But the club at Pier Park had amazing bands and really good food. It was also close to other shops so if she needed to go outside for some fresh air she had places to go.

"Okay," she agreed and had to pull the phone away from her ear as Olivia screamed her excitement.

"Where something sexy! We're prowling dawlin'." She giggled and reminded Naomi so very much of the girl in Oisín's arms. "See you Saturday!"

"See you Saturday," Naomi muttered after Olivia hung up.

Her phone chirped and as she was only a block further down the road than she was ten minutes ago, again stuck in standstill traffic, she looked at it.

Ocean (Asshole) O'Quinn: Thought that was you. Recognized the truck. Wanna come make a fourth?

Naomi: No, thanks. Quick question though, is she even legal? Gotta make sure to cash your check before you're carted off to jail.

Ocean (Asshole) O'Quinn: Oh, she's legal all right. But had to say, the song you played was very apropos.

Naomi: Apropos? That's a big word for you.

Ocean (Asshole) O'Quinn: Not just a pretty face in an eight pack.

Naomi: Well, at least not just an eight pack.

His reply was an emoji GIF of a man saying *Ouch*.

Naomi: Truth hurts.

Ocean (Asshole) O'Quinn: Nah, I'm used to it. I'm not everyone's cup of tea.

Wow that took a turn…

Ocean (Asshole) O'Quinn: But I'd like to show you what I can do with a cup of tea. *winky face emoji*

…And he's back.

Naomi: I don't drink tea.

That was a lie, but she wasn't going to tell him the truth.

Ocean (Asshole) O'Quinn: Oh, you wouldn't be drinking it.

She shook her head and put her phone away as the line of cars began to move. Once she pulled onto her street, she found a car sitting in front of the house.

"You have got to be kidding me."

She popped open the door of her truck as the driver side of the car opened and her ex stepped out

"What the hell are you doing here again, Emilio?" she demanded.

"I heard you had some trouble with a couple of contractors today cancelling on you. Thought I could offer my help," he said.

"No thank you," she walked past him and headed up the steps. "You need to stop coming round here."

"Come on, babe," he walked up behind her, and she whirled around.

"One, I'm not your babe. Two, you are not welcome here... ever. Three, if I find out you had anything to do with my guys not showing up today, you will regret it."

"Come on now, you just need to take a breath and calm down. You know I would never do anything like that."

"I don't. You *would* do something like that all the time when we were married, or have you forgotten?"

He huffed a sigh. "Look, I know I screwed up. I'm sorry. What more do you want me to say?"

"Nothing. There's nothing else to say. I don't hate you, Emilio. Hate does nothing but hurt me and you did enough of that for the both of us. But that doesn't mean I want to see you. I don't. But I also know you. You would do anything to make me feel like I had nowhere left to turn but to you."

"Babe—"

"Stop calling me that," she growled. "Leave now, before I call the cops."

He huffed but threw his hands into the air and turned, tossing over his shoulder, "this isn't over, Ni. Just remember what happens here on out is on you."

"Is that a threat?" she followed him.

"A promise." He cut her off and slid into his Ferrari.

She watched as he revved the engine and peeled out of her street. Wrapping her arms around her, she growled at the feeling of tears on her cheeks. She wiped them away and turned back to the house. She never cried over him. She never would. But she would cry over her father's business if it failed.

Her phone buzzed as she grabbed her handbag and headed up to her room. A text from her dad and Oisín.

Ocean (Asshole) O'Quinn: La Playa Blanca is lit!

He sent a dark selfie tinged with blue lights and a strobe.

Ocean (Asshole) O'Quinn: Come on out?

Another selfie of him pouting and Naomi shook her head, instantly smiling at his antics. She wanted to toy with him.

Naomi: Surprised you didn't go to the Double Rainbow. A good Irish lad like you?

Ocean (Asshole) O'Quinn: The Double Rainbow? Is that an Irish pub?

Naomi: I think you and Byron would enjoy it.

She bit her lip. It wasn't an Irish Pub. It was PCB's premier gay bar. She and a few friends had gone many times in college when they didn't want to get hit on at the meat markets that were at PCB's nightclubs. Was it evil? No. Would she laugh at his face when he found out? Hell yes. She was just sorry Byron might get caught in the crosshairs.

Ocean (Asshole) O'Quinn: Fun! Love to try the local Irish pubs. Thanks!

Now she felt a small – small mind – twinge of guilt. But she said nothing.

Ocean (Asshole) O'Quinn: You're seriously not going to come out and join me?

Naomi: From what I saw earlier, you have things well in hand.

Ocean (Asshole) O'Quinn: Not yet, but very soon.

Naomi groaned and clicked out of his text message chain to the one from her dad.

Dad: Getting dinner. Don't cook!

Naomi: Sounds good thanks!

She didn't have the heart to tell her dad about Emilio's visit, his heart couldn't take much more stress. And it worried her. With the threat of Emilio and her guys pulling off the jobs, she didn't need her dad to worry. She could worry enough for both of them.

Pulling out of her work clothes, she placed her beer on the small table by the tub. Instead of starting to work on the next project timeline, she turned on the water to hot then tested and adjusted the temperature. As the tub filled, she lit her pineapple and hibiscus scented candle and turned on some soft meditative music on her phone. Once the water was high enough, she dropped in her favorite bath bomb, also hibiscus scented and stepped into the bath. Sinking into the water she let out a soft sigh and leaned back resting her neck on her bath pillow and closing her eyes. That was heavenly. She took a deep inhale of the scent and smiled. But oddly, as she relaxed, she only saw one face smiling down at her.

Opening her eyes and sitting up quickly, she sighed. "Nope, no no no no no, not happening. I am not daydreaming about Oisín O'Quinn.

"Honey?" Her dad called from the other side of the door. She squeaked in surprised. "You in there?"

"Yeah dad."

"Okay, I brought Lucky's over. I'll keep it warm for you."

"Thanks, you go ahead and eat. I won't be long," she called back.

"Take your time."

She held her breath for a long moment then let it out between pursed lips and leaned her head back. Forcing her mind to anyone besides Oisín O'Quinn, she closed her eyes again with a smile.

Chapter Fifteen

Oisín smirked as he read back through the text chain with Naomi. Sitting in one of the most exclusive and popular nightclubs in PCB, he refused to think of any reason why he wasn't enjoying himself. The two girls he asked out were currently dancing together on the dance floor, giving him a show, but instead of watching or joining in on the sweat fest, he was waiting for the three little dots to show Naomi was texting him back.

The waiter covering the table service walked over and asked if he would like another bottle. The top shelf tequila was going to his head, but he wasn't too far gone just yet, considering he wasn't even planning on being out that evening.

"Not yet, but we'll take a bottle of your best champagne."

"Of course, sir." He nearly bowed as he walked away.

Oisín took another shot of tequila and savored the smooth taste of the alcohol. Byron stood stoically beside the couch. No matter how much Oisín tried, the six-foot seven-inch former marine wouldn't touch a drop of alcohol at a nightclub. He claimed it was because of all the other distractions around them and if he added alcohol to it, it would dull his senses.

But even as Oisín set his phone down, miffed slightly that Naomi had stopped responding, he looked over at the two girls... Women... – *No, girls,* he thought – dancing together trying to give him a show. He watched. He should feel a lot more than he did and his miffed attitude slowly led to upset, then boredom. Suddenly, the lights were too much, the music was too loud, there were too many people, it was too hot, and the tequila soured in his stomach. All he wanted, was to head back to the condo and sit on the balcony.

His eyes caught the two dancing girls. He was bored of them within ten minutes at the pool, but he'd be damned if he didn't get to enjoy their... enthusiasm.

His phone lit up and he reached for it eagerly, hoping Naomi was responding. But when he saw the name, he sighed. Not that he didn't love his family, there were too many of them not to love, but sometimes they were overwhelming. And ever since his big brother had gotten remarried and became a father, he took it upon himself to treat his kid brother like a son too.

Lachlan: Hey man. Aoife found some pics online and shared with the family. The shoot looks great! Are you wearing enough sunscreen?

He typed out a curt reply.

Oisín: Yes, daddy. I made sure to cover up like a good little boy.

As soon as he said hit send, he felt guilty. Lachlan didn't deserve his ire.

Oisín: Sorry.

Lachlan: Ooookay... What happened? What's going on? Are you okay?

Oisín: Just... frustrated about something.

Lachlan: I can see that. Want to talk?

Oisín: Can't. Sorry. Shouldn't have taken it out on you.

Lachlan: It's okay. I've got big shoulders. I shouldn't have asked you about the sunscreen. I just worry about you.

Oisín: I know and you're a doctor. I get it.

Lachlan: I'm your brother first.

Oisín didn't realize how much he missed his family until that moment. He hadn't been home for nearly a year and a half. He wouldn't be surprised if they didn't even remember him. But they always made an effort to reach out to him. Right then, he wanted nothing more than to be home with his family and revel in their love.

The champagne bottle arrived and the two women hurried to grab a glass. They kept eyeing him to the point he said, "screw it" and turned to Byron.

"Cash out the tab?"

Byron nodded and headed to where their waiter stood.

"Want to get out of here, ladies?" He asked the two

"Oh, yes please," one winked as the other grinned and giggled uncontrollably.

Oisín took the bottle of champagne and filled up three glasses then chugged his. It was good champagne, but he wanted to leave. Needed to leave. Byron parted the crowd as he returned from closing out the tab and, seeing him standing, Byron gave a quick nod. They were ready. Oisín kept the two women tucked under his arms as he followed his bodyguard out of the club. Seeing Davis waiting with his SUV, a little further away, Oisín breathed a sigh of relief. The two women started talking and Oisín's headache grew.

Wading through the people trying to get into the club, Oisín distractedly looked at his phone, so when screams and shouts of "gun!" rose around him, he looked up confused. It wasn't until he felt Byron's calloused hands on the back of his neck and upper arm forcing him down into a crouch, racing him into the SUV, did it become real. That, and the *pop pop pop* of gunfire.

Byron bundled him into the SUV and slammed the door shut. "Drive," he ordered. Davis threw the car into gear and peeled away.

"What... What the hell happened?" Oisín demanded, his hands shaking as much as his voice.

Byron's face betrayed his displeasure. "No clue. But we're going to find out." He pulled out his phone and began typing.

Oisín looked around. "The girls?"

Byron shook his head. "They skedaddled as soon as the screaming started."

"What the hell?"

Byron put his phone down and turned to look at him. "Breathe, Osh," he said. "You're safe."

"Do you think I was the target?"

Byron's jaw ticked.

"You do! Why?"

Byron glanced at Davis who met his eyes in the rearview mirror. "There's been some... Letters."

"Letters?" Oisín question.

"Hate mail, social media posts, voicemails left on the agency's phone that sort of thing. Tony let me know and I've been keeping my eyes open," Byron explained.

"Why didn't Tony tell me?"

"He didn't want you paranoid."

"How long has this been going on?" Oisín demanded.

"About a month now."

"A month?!" Oisín shrieked.

"The language got worse over the last week or so, hence Tony joining you onsite and getting you out of New York," Byron went on.

"Who is it? What are they saying?"

"Does the name Jackson Hester mean anything to you?"

"No," Oisín shook his head. "Is that who was doing this?" He pulled out his phone and searched for the social media posts Byron had mentioned.

"You won't find anything. The lawyers had them all removed."

"And you think this Jackson Hester tried to shoot me? Why? What does he have against me?"

Byron hesitated and again met Davis his eyes in the rearview mirror.

"Apparently, he says you slept with his fiancée."

Oisín stared at him. "I sleep with a lot of people. How am I supposed to know if they're in a relationship?"

"Look, no one blames you, Osh. I just caution you. I don't know if this guy was the creep who fired the gun but even if he isn't, his threats shouldn't be ignored."

Oisín finally nodded slowly. "I wish you had told me about all of this."

"I was asked not to. Honestly, they only brought me in during the last pier shoot," Byron confessed.

Oisín said nothing for a long moment, but then he sighed and turned to his bodyguard. "Is it safe to stay here? Should we leave?"

"Yes and no. Yes, it's safe, no, we do not need to leave. When we move to the house tomorrow, that place is locked up tight, and anyone you invite over will have a full body scan. You don't need to worry about anything. I've got you."

Oisín knew that was true, but it didn't help much. He could have been killed that evening. And to add salt in that particular wound, all he wanted to do at that moment was call Naomi Moon.

That morning, Naomi walked down the stairs and into the kitchen. Her dad wasn't there but instead of going out and meditating as usual, Naomi poured a cup of coffee and wandered into the living room.

"Mornin', Dad," she greeted him, but he sat frozen staring at the television. "Everything okay?"

"Hm?" He looked up. "Oh, yeah, I hope so." He looked back at the TV.

"Oookay," she breathed. But then her eyes caught the familiar headshot and her ears tuned to the anchor.

"And now to our top story. International male model Oisín O'Quinn was rushed out of La Playa Blanca last night after a gun was seen and three shots fired. It is uncertain if he was the intended target, but witnesses at the scene described a short Caucasian male pulling out a gun and aiming it in Mr. O'Quinn's direction. Fortunately, no one was injured but the gunmen fled before police arrived. The PCBPD is asking for anyone with information to please contact the number on screen. Mayor Sheridan and Commissioner Matinez spoke in a news conference just a few minutes ago saying such violence will not be tolerated and have expressed their deepest regrets to Mr. O'Quinn and his agency. Reporting live from La Playa Blanca, I'm Florence Whitman, WHGN Panama City Beach."

Naomi didn't wait. She grabbed her phone and dialed Oisín's number. When he didn't answer, she hung up and texted him.

Naomi: Just heard the news. Are you okay?

After she hit send, she told herself she would be worried about any client in that situation.

She stared at the screen willing three little dots to show he was texting her back.

"Have you heard from him?" She asked her dad.

He shook his head. "I'm sure he's fine," Bill said. "The news said he was rushed out. They wouldn't say that if he was hurt."

Naomi nodded slowly. "You're right. I'm overreacting. Sorry."

"It's okay, sweetheart. I was worried too. As annoying as he is, he's become a friend of sorts. I'm glad Byron was there. He's in good hands. I think I heard earlier he's going to have a press conference later today to allay any fears."

Naomi nodded and turned her phone to sleep mode and pocketed it in her pajama shorts. Taking a sip of coffee, she headed into the kitchen to get some cereal. Once finished eating, she went upstairs to her office and sat at her computer. She needed to get her thoughts off Oisín O'Quinn and the best way to do that, was work. She needed to finish the schedule for the newest client and then head to the mansion to meet the surveyor.

She wouldn't think of Oisín at all... for the next two minutes.

Chapter Sixteen

Oisín stared at the text from Naomi for the sixth time in fifteen minutes. He sat in the back seat of the SUV… The SUV with bullet holes in the side door. Fortunately the thickness of the frame saved them from being hit.

It's not as if he didn't want to text her back and say he was all right, it was that he knew he needed to keep his distance.

After the shooting the night before, Byron had Davis drive around for over an hour to see if they had a tail. Once they got back to their complex, Byron bustled him up the stairs and into the condo. Latching, chaining, and bolting the door, Byron held his sidearm to his thigh.

Once he was comfortable, Byron turned to him and holstered his gun.

"I don't want you in the room tonight. We're going to camp out on the sofas."

Oisín didn't argue, simply nodded. He felt numb as he asked, "can I shower?"

Byron nodded and walked into his room to check it before letting Oisín in. Showering had never felt like that before. Standing under the hot spray, he closed his eyes. He was so very tired. Scared and tired. For twenty years he had never let fear take over him. He never wanted to feel helpless like he did back when he was ten and Connor Gregory had called him a *bodach,* or pig in Irish slang and pushed him down on the playground as his friends laughed. But one scare and he quaked like that ten-year-old again.

Granted a nine mil versus a ten-year-old bully was definitely more intimidating. But as he soaped his hair and body, his hands shook. Taking a deep breath, he turned off the spray and grabbed a towel. Once dry and in a clean pair of boxer briefs and sweats, Oisín headed out to the living room.

Byron had pulled the drapes and fixed the old lumpy leather pullout couch with the spare sheets and had moved the pullout loveseat to the opening of the hallway as the first line of defense. His bodyguard was on the phone having a security talk but when he saw Oisín, he nodded to him and told whoever it was on the phone that he was back, and that Byron would call later, asking for any updates to go to his cell as a text and hung up.

"Who was that?" Oisín asked.

"The security firm. They're flying a few more guys out to cover us until the threat is handled," Byron answered.

"Oh," Oisín replied, his eyes on the sofa bed.

"Tony also called and thinks it would be a good idea to have a press conference tomorrow. Show you won't be intimidated by a freak."

Oisín looked over at him. "But I am intimidated."

Byron sighed and walked over to him. Placing his hands on his shoulders. "I know. But hey, you're safe. Nothing will happen to you under my watch. Understood?"

Oisín nodded slowly. "By," he asked softly. "Could I have died tonight?"

Byron didn't react, only looked at him more intently. "It is... possible."

Oisín swallowed hard. "I – ehm – want to call my folks. They shouldn't hear about this from the news."

Byron squeezed his arms. "Okay. It's, what, seven in Ireland? Call them now."

Oisín pulled out his phone and spent the next two hours assuring his family he was safe and fell into a fitful sleep, woken only by Byron's insistence six hours later, needing to check out of the condo and into the house down by Pier Park.

After a whirlwind of police, the mayor, governor, and owner of La Playa Blanca all offering their apologies, Oisín wanted to go to the new house they had rented and do absolutely nothing. But that was not in the cards.

He stared at the text from Naomi as he sat in the SUV heading to the press conference.

He was about to text her back when three little dots popped up on the feed. He waited to see what she typed but after a few seconds, the bubbles went away. Letting out of breath, he didn't realize he was holding, he typed out a quick reply, but his usual wit was nonexistent.

Oisín: I'm all right. Thank you for asking.

Hitting send, he turned the phone to sleep and looked around to see where they were as the car came to a stop. The building was fairly nondescript but the press in front swarmed the SUV, taking pictures of the bullet holes and trying to take a picture of him behind the darkly tinted windows. Every fiber of his being wanted to tell Davis to drive away but seeing Tony and his PR manager, Nic waiting at the front door, he slid on his sunglasses and nodded once to Byron.

As soon as his bodyguard opened the door, the reporters began the barrage of questions while snapping a thousand pictures. Oisín stayed close to Byron's back as he pushed through the crowd, the additional security team flanked him. Without replying, Oisín got to the steps and Byron bustled him into the building. While hearing Tony and Nic calm the reporters down, Oisín waited just inside the entry.

"Ladies and gentlemen, you will get a chance to ask Mr. O'Quinn all of your questions at the press conference. Until then, we ask you to respect his privacy during this frightening time," Nic, the PR Rep who had been with him for a little over six months, said.

The doors opened again and Oisín turned his back to the cameras. Byron subtly stepped in front of him, blocking their view. Once alone and before any of them spoke, a uniformed police officer, who stood in the hallway, stepped forward.

"Mr. O'Quinn, I'm Officer Perkins. I've been tasked with making sure you and your bodyguard have everything you need.

We have a room set up for you all prior to the conference. If you'll follow me? There's also coffee, tea, water, and some snacks."

"Thank you," Oisín said, and they all followed him down the hall.

Once they were in the room, Tony and Nic stepped forward.

"You all right, kid?" Tony asked.

"I'm alive thanks to Byron."

"Terrible thing to happen." Nic shook his head.

"When were you going to tell me about the threats?" Oisín questioned.

"We didn't think they had escalated enough to warrant telling you."

"Escalated enough? I could have been shot. Byron could have been shot. The people I was with could have been shot. When did you think to tell me about this?" Oisín shouted.

"Let's not make a scene, Osh." Tony said. "It sounded like some blowhard blowing off steam. We had no way of knowing it would escalate so quickly. We've prepared a statement for you to read for the cameras. You're not to admit to sleeping with anyone in a relationship if that question pops up. Stick to the facts, flash your award-winning smile, get through this, and get on with your vacation."

Oisín growled but agreed and studied the statement to make it sound less stilted and scripted as Nic went to find the officer to let him know they were ready.

Good news," Tony saddled up to him. "I heard back from the casting director on that Pearl Harbor movie. You are in the top three for the part."

"Jaysus," Oisín breathed. It had been nearly three months since he had auditioned for the part of the Irish American Medal of Honor recipient featured in the new war movie. He had honestly forgotten about it.

"They said it's down to you and two other actors."

Oisín scoffed. "So that means I won't get it."

"It doesn't mean that at all. You're third, that means they liked you."

Oisín gave Tony a skeptical look. "Always the optimist, Tony."

Before Tony could reply, Nic and the officer came back into the room.

"They're ready for you, Mr. O'Quinn," Officer Perkins said.

Oisín stood, folded the statement into his jeans pocket and took a deep breath.

"They'll ask some questions after you finish your statement. I'll come up after a suitable time and finish it out. If there's any question you don't want to answer, look at me and I'll come help," Nic said.

Oisín nodded as they approached the door. Looking back for Byron, Oisín saw his friend behind him. Officer Perkins locked eyes with him and after his nod, opened the door for him.

Cameras clicked with flashes that blinded him for a moment. But Oisín stepped on stage, stood behind the lectern, and pulled out his statement.

"Good afternoon," Oisín cleared his throat. "Thank you for being here. I also want to thank the governor of Florida, the mayor of Bay County, the police commissioner, and the owner of La Playa for their help, support, and assistance in this matter. Last night, I was enjoying a wonderful evening of Florida sunshine, sand, and surf, along with a couple of friends. When we left the club, there was a shout of a gun and shots fired. I am very grateful to my security firm and personally to my bodyguard for getting me out of that perilous and scary situation. The Panama City Beach police have been scouring the city speaking with witnesses, looking for the gunman. At this time they have not informed me of an arrest, but I urge the public to do whatever they can to assist the police in this matter. Whoever the gunman or woman was, they are dangerous. There is no evidence to assume I was the intended target as it appears they fired toward me but there were others around. I ask anyone with information to please reach out to PCBPD. I am pleased to note that no one was injured and hope everyone will continue to exercise caution in these sorts of situations. With that, I will take a few questions."

Everyone spoke at once until Oisín called on one of them.

"Mr. O'Quinn, PCB News at 10, is it true that there are bullet holes in your SUV? And if so, is there any doubt as to you being the intended target?"

"As I mentioned earlier, there is no evidence to show I was the intended target. The person fired into a crowd," Oisín explained, then called on another.

"You mentioned your bodyguard got you out of the situation. Can you expand on how or what you were feeling at that moment?"

"Confused. Grateful," Oisín said. "My security team is one of the best and my personal guard is a former marine and I've never felt safer than when I know he's there. He's my friend as well as my guard and I'm damn lucky to have him."

He called on another reporter who spoke next.

"Mr. O'Quinn, is there any truth in the accusations leveled against you by Mr. Hester that you knowingly slept with his fiancée?"

Oisín froze. "I was only made aware of the accusation yesterday."

"And is it true," the reporter went on. "That he may be the one responsible for firing those shots at you?"

"I'm not going to comment on that except to say I have every faith in the PCBPD to see that this person is brought to justice."

"So you have no knowledge of sleeping with Mr. Hester's fiancée?" the same reporter questioned.

"As I mentioned, I was only just made aware of the accusation—"

"Yes, but you would know if you slept with her."

"Look, I know my reputation, but I can assure you, I would never *willingly* sleep with another man's fiancée. That's not how I was raised. I respect the sanctity of a relationship. *If* however, Mr. Hester's fiancée did not disclose her relationship status to me at the time I met her, which I have no name so I do not know if I met the woman or not, then I can hardly be held accountable."

"So you are saying it's possible?"

"I'm saying no. I would never willingly do that."

But the reporter wasn't done. He continued, "do you have any comment on your sister-in-law's friend the Marquess of Garvey and his recent questionable behavior?"

"What?" Oisín asked confused.

"The Marquess has recently been seen holding hands with his supposed best friend Peter Carlisle while the marchioness was seen in the company of another man, her previous beau, Derek Nevers. I was wondering if you had any comment on their apparent affairs and if you have any knowledge if the Marquess is gay or not."

"That has nothing to do with me and is not relevant. If my sister-in-law's friend is seen with his best friend that is not something new. As far as him being gay, I don't care one way or the other."

"So would you agree that having an affair with someone in a relationship with someone else is, possibly, a family trait?"

Oisín stared at him for a long moment. "Piss off," Oisín stated and walked off the podium, ignoring the shouts around him. He headed for the door; Byron and the other guard's falling into step next to him.

Nic and Tony hustled after them as soon as Nic ended the conference.

"What was that about?" Oisín whirled around on Nic, his eyes scathing.

"We have had reports of Geoffrey Ainsley and his wife have been carrying on with their previous relationships. It has been going on shortly after their second son was born, three years ago. Apparently, The Marchioness was dating Derek Nevers before her marriage, and it has been made clear that Peter Carlisle is staying with Geoffrey as often as he can make it over to England. The photos that were taken showed them eating ice cream together and holding hands as they walked down the road while on vacation in Cabo alone together."

"And you didn't think to mention that to me so I had a heads up?"

"We didn't think—"

"What do I pay you for?" Oisín bellowed.

"I'm sorry. I didn't think they would make the link between you so quickly," Nic said.

"No, clearly not. Maybe you figured this one out. You're fired." He turned to his agent. "Get me someone better." Tony nodded.

Oisín stalked away, Byron and the other guards following.

Chapter Seventeen

"Piss off," Oisín spat and then walked out of the room.

Naomi let out her breath as soon as the anchor reappeared on screen.

"That was a set up job if ever I saw one," her dad said. "I mean what the hell business is it of Oisín's if his sister-in-law's friend is seeing other people?"

"Notice the title they used? Marquess. He's aristocracy. You know how *royal news* crazy Americans are," Martin said from beside her. They had just finished with the surveyor to get a clearer picture of the Riparian Rights when Martin arrived to give his estimate on the sagging floors and foundation issues. The press conference had dinged on her phone, and she pulled up the news feed. Oisín looked tired. He looked good, just tired and Naomi was about ready to throttle the reporter who asked such a stupid question. How would he know if the woman was engaged? Naomi knew from personal experience people didn't always disclose their relationship or even marital status to someone they wanted to sleep with. The memory of finding Emilio in bed with the buxom blonde riding him entered her mind.

To the blonde's credit, she freaked when she found out Emilio was married and apologized profusely. Naomi thanked her for sleeping with her husband because without it, Naomi would never have known what a lying cheating scumbag he was.

Shaking her head to rid it of those thoughts, she pocketed her phone and turned to her dad and Martin.

"Let's get started. The crew is set to arrive any minute and I want to make zones so we know where they're going to be," she said.

"Good idea," her dad agreed.

"Do you want me to stick around?" Martin asked. "I'd be happy to help."

"So nice of you, Martin," her dad said. "We could probably use an extra set of hands. Demo of the kitchen is on the docket for today, right?" He paused. "Honey?"

Naomi looked up startled. "Yeah, sorry, yes, kitchen demo as soon as the guys get here."

"Ah, we don't need 'em," her dad grinned. "How about it, Martin? Wanna help me swing a hammer?"

"You'll be swinging your own hammer, Mr. Moon," he winked. "Sounds too personal for me to be involved."

Her dad laughed and slapped Martin on the back as they walked into the main house.

As the kitchen demo began, Naomi refused to acknowledge the face she saw every time she swung her hammer. The reporter.

Two hours later, they finally heard the rumble of a truck coming down the drive. Naomi pulled her mask down and took off her thick gloves. Heading to the front door, she stopped when she saw the three guys waiting.

"Where are the others?" She asked. The one man she recognized as the foreman of the crew, stepped forward.

"We're it," he said.

"What do you mean? I ordered a crew of eight and more tomorrow."

"I know, but the rest of my guys got offered another gig paying twice as much early this morning. That's what took so long. I was scrambling trying to get these two."

"Offered another gig? Where? By whom?"

"All I know is, one of my guys made contact with another GC last night and called around to the rest of my guys and next thing I know, I'm waking up to guys calling off. As soon as I know who stole my guys, I'll be speaking to them. Meanwhile, these two guys are loyal and hard workers. We'll get the job done, just might take a little longer."

Naomi knew exactly who had stolen her guys. That bastard ex of hers.

"Well, I appreciate all of you. You'll be getting time and a half for your troubles." The crew beamed and thanked her. "I'll find us a couple more guys but I'm sure the homeowner will understand the delay. I'll talk to him. Let me get you guys set up and show you where you'll be working, then I'll call around."

There had been times where Naomi had issues with a renovation but none quite so much as Oisín's property. With only a four-man crew, thank God for Martin sticking around, Naomi made the call to focus on the kitchen and dining room attached. But as soon as they started ripping up old tiles and demoing the kitchen/dining room wall to make a half wall serving place, rot was found behind the stove and termite damage weakened the floorboards.

The entire plan needed to be reworked and Oisín wasn't answering his phone. By the time the sun went down, Naomi and her dad called it a day and thanked everyone for their hard work.

Though the kitchen and living room looked as if a bomb had gone off, they were able to make a plan. All the furniture had been moved carefully to the temporary storage shed and Martin had worked his magic on getting new floorboards at half the cost from his brother who owned a lumber yard.

The problem was, they needed permission from the owner for the added expense and extra two week turn around and still, Oisín wasn't answering.

Naomi called her dad and put him on speaker as he pulled off on their road and she continued straight.

"Where are you going, honey?" He asked. "Thought you were right behind me."

"I was, Dad. I'm going to Oisín's new rental. He sent me the address earlier. I'm going to see if I can talk to him so we can get that processed first thing."

"Oh, okay, sounds good. If you do get a chance, tell him we're both rooting for him."

"Will do. I'll be home after that."

"Sounds good, just be careful. It's Friday night, you know how crazy traffic is."

"I will. Call you later if I need anything."

She hung up and drove toward Pier Park where Oisín's new beachfront house rental stood. Even if she didn't have the address, she would have known which house was his. The extra security wasn't the only give away, the sound of pounding music and squealing girls was the main one.

For some unknown reason, the sound of the pool party angered her instantly. She had no idea why. But pulling up to the security shed, she rolled down her window.

"Can I help you?" The security man asked.

"Hi yes, I'm Naomi Moon, Oisín O'Quinn's contractor. I need to speak with him regarding his property renovation."

"Do you have your ID on you, Miss Moon?"

"I do." She grabbed her wallet out and handed him her driver's license.

"Thank you. Any firearms in the car or on your person?"

"No."

He turned to the computer and entered her ID. Then, clicked around before looking up at her and waving her through. "Mr. Marcus approved you, Miss Moon."

"Mr. Marcus?"

"Byron, Mr. O'Quinn's bodyguard."

"Oh of course, sorry I didn't know his last name."

"Quite all right. Please pull forward and park anywhere on the grass or gravel." He handed her ID back.

"Thank you, I won't be long."

She pulled forward and parked her car, finding the front door by seeing the two security team members standing on either side. They opened the door, and she was instantly motioned through a metal detector and to the stairs leading down. She followed the sounds to the pool and hot tub but took a moment to acknowledge the beauty of the view and architecture. It was a massive beach house but well designed and decorated in deep blues, greens, and eggshell white.

There were about a dozen people there. She didn't recognize any of them. Finally, she found her way to the hot tub and instantly recognized Oisín. He was lounging on one of the sides, staring right at her. But his arms were around two women, one looked vaguely familiar, but Naomi couldn't place her. The other, she'd never seen before and yet another glided across the water to sit on his lap, but his gaze never wavered. Byron stood near him.

"Come to join the party?" He drawled.

"I tried calling you... all day in fact."

He shrugged. "I've been busy." His fingers caressed one of the girl's arms.

"Yeah, I can see that," she replied and crossed her arms over her chest.

"If you're not here to join in... What can I help you with?"

"I need to speak with you about the renovation."

Oisín waited.

"You want to do that here?" She asked.

He shrugged again. "Good a place as any."

"Okay, well, the crew has been poached. You have rot and termite damage. The price has gone up about ten grand and without the proper crew we're looking to be adding an additional two maybe three weeks."

Oisín stared at her for a long moment. "Your contract is to finish in fourteen weeks not sixteen or seventeen. We signed a contract. Get it done."

"I just explained why I can't. I was hoping you would understand."

"I understand… If you go over the agreed time, you're in breach of contract."

"Look, I'm sorry about that. But there's nothing I can do about it."

Oisín shrugged again. She was really starting to hate that shrug. "Then you're in breach of contract. I'm sure there are recourses I can take."

Her jaw dropped. "Are you threatening to sue me?"

"If that's my only recourse. Get it done and we won't have to have that conversation."

He turned away from her and gave the woman in his lap a feral smile effectively dismissing Naomi. Her heart hardened and she crossed her arms over her chest.

"And to think," she started, her voice hard. "I worried about you today with that reporter. I didn't realize *you* were the asshole. I hoped you had changed after our first meeting, but I see you're never going to change. You're just going to use and abuse.

I'll get your damn reno done on time but that's it. I don't want to talk to you. I don't even wanna look at you. You need something, you call my father. Don't text me. I'm done giving you chances and having you prove me wrong. Thank you for your understanding, Mr. O'Quinn. We'll get it done, no thanks to you."

With that, Naomi turned and walked away. Part of her, the foolish part she called it, hoped he would call her back and say he was sorry. Why she wanted that so desperately, she didn't know. Why tears threatened her eyes, she hated the answer to. She had gotten a glimpse of the true Oisín O'Quinn and she felt like it had been ripped away, replaced with the unfeeling guy lounging in the hot tub with three women.

She reached her car before she heard anyone call to her. Turning, ready to give him a piece of her mind, she stopped abruptly when Byron hustled up to her.

"Naomi, wait, please," he called.

"What is it, Byron?" She questioned.

"Look, he was a jerk to you in there. I know. But he would never do that. He's had a very… difficult few days and a horrible day today. I've seen it before. His coping mechanism is to shut down and exert his authority. Believe me. But he doesn't mean it. Hell, I'd be fired ten times over if he did. Please just give him overnight to think about it. I swear to you, he will regret it in spades tomorrow."

"Yeah? Well, I don't have time for him to regret it. If I can't get a crew out there to help without my damn ex stealing my guys, my dad is going to work himself into another heart attack and I will not let that happen."

"Is Bill okay?"

"He's fine now, but he had a heart attack three years ago because a couple of our crew got poached and he tried to do too much. I will not let that happen again."

"No no, of course. Look, I can help. I've got some experience. Osh has more bodyguards now because of what happened. Give me a hard hat and goggles and I'm your man for carrying heavy things and demolition."

"That's really sweet of you but you are not certified in Florida. I can't. Just keep him away from me or I won't be held accountable for my actions."

Byron sighed, put his hands on his hips and nodded. "Okay, but listen, if you need me, I'm here. okay?"

"Okay, thanks. We'll be there around nine if you..."

He nodded and reached around her, opening the car door. "And please, don't lose faith in my boy. He's a stupid ass but he's also the best friend anyone can have."

"Have to take your word on that." She slid into the truck and let him shut the door.

"I'm serious, Naomi," he said through the open window. "Give him another chance? I know Oisín O'Quinn, he'll be up all night thinking about how he treated you."

"Oh, he'll be up all night all right, but with those women pawing at him. It won't be because of how he treated me." With that, she put her seat belt on, started the car, put it in gear, and headed out of the courtyard, leaving Byron standing in the middle of the drive.

Oisín writhed beneath three sets of lips and six hands touching him everywhere all at once. It was a damn good distraction from the events of the day... the last couple days.

Opening his eyes, he looked at the women. He had already forgotten their names, but that didn't matter. One woman licked her way over his chest and to his washboard abs. Grinning, he watched, but when her brown eyes met his, he froze. Her face morphed in his mind's eye and instead of her blonde hair, he saw the dark haired dark eyed Hawaiian beauty with the sassy mouth he yearned to taste and a body his hands itched to touch. But her image faded from the amorous look he desired to see, to the hurt shock from earlier that evening. He had put that look on her face. He had said those words to her, making her worry and then hate him. He had driven her away. He closed his eyes at the memory of her shoulders shuddering with a silent sob as she hurried out of the house. He had done that. It was his fault. And he felt horrible.

The women whined at his lack of response to them, but it felt wrong. It shouldn't feel wrong.

"Sorry ladies," he sighed as he pulled out of their nest of arms. "It's a no go tonight. I guess the fear of everything has me vulnerable." He had no idea what he was saying but their combined "awe" along with a few "we'll help you forget, baby," soured his stomach.

He sat up and pulled on some sweatpants. Without another glance at the three of them, he took his whiskey glass and walked to the balcony off his room. The stairs to his left, lead down to the main deck and the pool and hot tub.

Slowly walking down the stairs, he kept his eyes firmly focused on where Naomi had stood earlier that evening. It was a clear night and the sounds of the surf crashing against the beach was calming. Looking over to his right, Byron looked up from the deck chair where he was reading, his eyes on him.

Oisín waved him off as he walked to the railing and looked out. The deck was just tall enough to overlook the sand dunes with a clear shot of the water. Now completely dark, the Gulf was nothing but a large black void with the occasional rhythmic waves caped in white. A tiny speck of light glided slowly on the horizon. A ship, maybe.

Oisín took a sip of his whiskey and sighed. He felt Byron's eyes on him, and he knew why. His bodyguard had front row tickets to the shitshow that had unfolded with Naomi. Oisín even remembered him racing out after her. Not sure why that caused a quiver of jealousy to run through him, Oisín didn't look over as Byron walked up beside him. Leaning his forearms on the deck railing, Byron took a sip from his water bottle.

"What has you out here, Osh? Thought you'd be busy with one of those blondes in your bed by now," Byron said.

"I had all three in my bed at once," he snapped then again, instantly regretted it.

Byron didn't reply right away. "They ignore you?" He teased.

"No, but I couldn't... I couldn't... *enjoy* myself when I was thinking about what an arsehole I was to someone else."

"Someone else?" Byron question, still calmly looking out at the inky blackness.

"Don't pretend like you don't know. I saw you run out after her."

"Well yeah, she was upset. You acted like an ass. She needed a friend."

"She was upset…"

"She had tears in her eyes, and I have a strong feeling that woman doesn't cry for just anything. I truly think she cares for you… or did."

"It's only been a week, what… How… Why?" Oisín floundered.

"Do you really think she would come over to check on you after a televised press conference just to tell you some bad news about the house… Which, I'll be helping out with by the way so there will be a change of your security detail during the day."

"You're helping out on the house?"

"She needs guys. Her dad can't lift all the heavy stuff. Her ex is stealing her guys off her jobs. She needs help. I can help. I'm not going to let Bill have another heart attack."

"Another?" Oisín felt the color drain from his face. "Oh God…" He pulled out his phone and dialed her number. It went straight to voicemail as if she had blocked his number. He hung up and clicked on the text chain.

Oisín: I'm beyond sorry, Naomi. I would try to say something about stress but that would just be an excuse and you don't deserve excuses. I was and am an arse. I'm so sorry. You did not deserve how I treated you. You did not deserve what I said. Please know, nothing I said was true. I respect you and your father. If there is anything I can do, please don't hesitate to ask. You take as long as you need to fix the houses and any additional expense is fine. I can't thank you and your dad enough for working on this for me. I will respect your wish to not speak to me and I will stop trying to reach out. But please know I will always regret how I spoke to you and how I treated you. Forgive me, please. I do not deserve it, but I hope you can find it in your heart to forgive me.

He sent the text and saw it was delivered. Hoping to see the three bubbles pop up, he stared at the phone for a long time but when nothing happened, he closed his eyes and pocketed the phone.

"I've lost her."

"You never really had her, Oisín. But you could have. Had you been real. The man I know. The one who I call friend. Not the public persona. You let your guard down around her. I saw it. But as soon as the going got tough, you reverted to the celebrity."

"That's who I am." Oisín turned to look at him.

"Bullshit," Byron shook his head. "That's *what* you are."

Oisín searched Byron's face, then his shoulders slumped.

"I'm so tired of this. I'm tired of not knowing who I am."

"Then change." Byron leaned on the railing and looked at him. "You have the power. Only you. If you want to be the kind of person who attracts friends and good people like Naomi and Bill Moon, then only you have the ability to do that."

"I don't know how."

"Sure you do. Stop messing with the Cheries, Candies, Kimmys, and Ashlies of the world. Stop with the one-night stands, they're degrading to women and to you. Stop with the arrogant *can't touch this* shit. Be a human. The man who defended his brother's girlfriend when she was kidnapped. The man who helps his family every chance he gets. The man who, dammit, I'm proud to call my friend. Be that guy. Have fun, yes, play, yes, but be serious too. Yes, you have an image to maintain but you have much more to give than your body, your face, or your name. You have your heart and soul, a damn good personality, and everything else you had before this," he waved at his face, "got famous. Remember that."

Oisín stared at him for a long moment. "I hardly remember that guy anymore."

"He's not gone. I saw him many times the last few days. And I see him now." Byron clutched Oisín upper arm in a brotherly squeeze and walked away, leaving Oisín with his thoughts and the rhythmic sound of the waves hitting the shore.

Chapter Eighteen

Naomi looked at herself in the full-length mirror in her bedroom. The little dress she purchased that afternoon was a way of getting back at Oisín with its mini skirt and scoop neck. But as she looked at the open sides crisscrossed with fabric ties she began to second guess herself. It was way too far outside her comfort zone and even the color of dark deep red was a far cry from her usual black or olive green.

Still, the memory of his indifference, and the echo of the words he spoke so apathetically, and the reminder of the concern she had for him, all culminated in her mind cementing the decision to walk out the door and into the limo Olivia had rented for the night.

Fortunately, as she walked down the stairs, her dad had left to check on their neighbor Mrs. Kirkpatrick so he wouldn't see what she wore. She may be thirty-six, but she respected her dad enough to not want him to see the very physical manifestation of her anger at Oisín.

Clutching her small purse by the gold chain, she hurried out the door and to the waiting limo. Her phone safely tucked away with Oisín's unread text message. She saw it early that morning but couldn't bring herself to read it, nearly deleting the entire chain before stopping and deciding to wait.

"Gurl!" Olivia squealed. "You look hawt! Oh my gawd! Who are you and what have you done with Naomi Moon?"

"Just thought I'd give something a little different a try," Naomi said looking around and seeing the other women wearing dresses equally as... clubby.

"Well, it's hot!"

"Thanks?"

"Did you hear Oisín O'Quinn got shot the other day?" Olivia asked and poured a glass of champagne for her. "I mean, we were just talking about him."

"Shot *at,*" Naomi corrected. And why the idea of him being shot twisted her stomach, she didn't know.

"Well, excuse me, Oisín's girlfriend," Olivia giggled. "I didn't know you were so up to date on a certain lion." Her eyes twinkled.

"No, I'm not. I saw the press conference, like anyone."

"Oh and didn't he look good enough to eat?" Another of the girls, Stacie said.

Naomi never could tell Chrissy and Kristy apart, but Stacie had been the nicest of the four *mean girls* in high school. Why they suddenly wanted to hang out with her was beyond her understanding. She took a sip of the cheap champagne and looked out the window while the women talked about what they would do if Oisín O'Quinn gave them a chance. The constant vulgar talk gave her a headache and by the time they pulled into Pier Park, the best shopping experience in Panama City Beach, she was ready to go home.

Byron hated seeing Oisín moping, Oisín knew that, but it didn't help. He had screwed up royally with Naomi and felt even worse about the entire situation. Byron had left early to help with the construction, leaving him alone with the new security guards. Though Oisín had used them a couple of times when Byron needed an extra set or when his bodyguard went on a much needed vacation, he hadn't gotten to know them and they kept mainly to themselves.

By the time Oisín finished his early morning run on the beach, his two guards following a clip behind and had tried to enjoy the fresh fruit and omelet his private chef prepared, he was well and truly shattered. Naomi hadn't returned his text, probably hadn't even read it, and to make matters even worse, his little episode at the press conference had been blown way out of proportion, the media referring to it as his breakdown. They also began speaking of Geoff's relationship and making a family connection when there wasn't one.

Oisín pulled out his phone while E! was on commercial and called his brother Lachlan, who answered on the third ring.

"Hey, how's Florida?" Lach asked.

"Beautiful. How's everything?"

"Good good, yeah, all good over here."

"You saw the press conference, didn't you?"

Lachlan sighed. "Yeah, we're in London staying with Geoff. It's not good, man."

"What happened?"

Lachlan sighed again, then his voice muffled like he was speaking to someone and covered the receiver.

"Hang on," he said to him. After a beat, he continued, his voice a little louder. "Geoffrey and Winifred have had a marriage of convenience for years."

"We knew that."

"Aye, but no one else did. Apparently, Winifred's boyfriend Derek and Peter have been living with them on and off since the lads were born three years in. The lads are from those two years where they were together to, 'do their duty' as Geoff calls it. Then, they talked, and she encouraged Peter to come back, and he encouraged Derek to live with them. In the eyes of society, Geoffrey and Winifred are married and happily, but in private they were nothing but friends. Now, Geoff and Peter... well, we've always known there was something there. They didn't mean to be found out."

"What's the media doing? How are they going to spin it?" Oisín asked.

"We're not sure right now," Lachlan said. "Geoff's father is coming over. We're thinking he's going to try to do some damage control but it's very likely he will disinherit Geoff and name Geoff's first-born son as his heir, skipping Geoffrey completely."

"As far as I remember, their relationship is not a good one, but didn't Geoff not want it anyway?"

"He didn't, but it's his birthright. I don't know, man. Peter's really shook up about it. He grabbed Geoff's hand after they left the ice cream shop that's when the picture was taken."

"It's not his fault," Oisín ignored the true reason behind him defending Peter's actions.

"No one here blames him. Geoff has said over and over again that it wasn't his fault but it doesn't make him feel any better."

"No," Oisín said softly. "It won't. Only he can. He has to accept what his actions caused and know Geoff will always love him."

Lachlan was quiet on the other end for a long moment, then, "what's going on?"

Immediately, Oisín wanted to say *nothing*, but as he debated, his mouth opened and everything began pouring out. Naomi, the shooting, the press conference, Naomi, the house, the internal struggle... Naomi. Everything. After he was done, he waited. His brother stayed quiet for a long moment, no doubt gathering his thoughts. Either that or he was upset Oisín dumped it all on him while he was still dealing with everything else. Oisín was about to apologize and tell him not to worry about it, when Lachlan's cautious voice began.

"I've never seen you like this, Osh. Are you... Are you falling in love with her?"

"No! I can't be, it's only been a week. There's no way... There's no..."

"Lightning?" Lachlan asked calmly.

"What?" Oisín was breathless.

Lachlan took a deep breath. "Do you remember how our Grandpa Orin always talked about how he felt lightning strike him when he met our grandma? Either his first or second wife?"

Oisín thought back to his grandfather. He had only been in his teens when his grandpa died but he did remember how Orin always used to say that after his first wife passed, he never thought he would marry again, until he met Deirdre. Oisín vaguely remembered hearing the older man say it felt like lightning had hit him where he stood when he first saw her, and it felt like his heart started pumping again.

"Aye, I remember."

"I can tell you from firsthand experience it doesn't take long to fall in love when you have experienced the lightning," Lachlan explained.

Oisín thought back to when he first met Naomi, her instant concern that she had hurt him, not knowing who he was, her sweetness tinged with some fire, then his idiotic statement and offer to take her back to his condo. He could have found any contractor in the greater PCB area. Why did he pursue Naomi after she had made it clear she wanted nothing to do with him? Could it be? Did he feel a sort of... Lightning? And that's why he had to pursue her? Could it be that he threw up his barriers because she was burrowing deeper than anyone ever had before? Could it be? Could he be in love?

Oisín swallowed audibly. Lachlan chuckled. "I see you've already come to that realization," his brother said.

"Wh – what do I do?"

"Stop being an arse for one. For two, don't let her get away."

"I've been so... horrible to her."

"You are under stress and, let's face it, scared. She'll understand if you talk to her."

"I tried to call her. She didn't answer. I texted her but... nothing. What do I do?" Oisín paced.

"Give her and it time. And if she reaches out to you, don't be pushy. Be understanding and patient she may need more time. You apologized. Now show her you've changed."

Oisín nodded. "I can do that."

"Good. I like seeing the old you coming back. I want to meet this woman," Lach said and Oisín could hear the smile in his brother's voice.

"Thank you," he replied. "I know you're busy but thank you for taking the time."

"You're my kid brother, Oisín. I'm always here for you. Be careful and stay safe. Let me know what happens."

"I will. You too. Give my love to Corrie and the kids and let me know how it all works out with Geoff and Peter."

"Will do. Love you, brother."

Oisín smiled. "Love you too, you old sap." He hung up hearing Lachlan chuckle.

Turning to look when he felt eyes on him, Byron stood in the doorway looking a bit sweaty but back from the construction site.

"How is she? What happened?" Oisín hurried to him.

Byron shook his head. "She wasn't there. Her dad directed everything. Apparently, she's going out to a club tonight with some friends."

"A club?"

"Yeah it's called The Pelican Snout. It's a lounge."

Oisín swallowed hard. "She's going clubbing?"

Byron nodded.

"I didn't get the impression that was her scene."

"Neither did I," Byron replied.

"She's pissed."

"Probably," Byron shrugged.

"What do I do?"

Byron shrugged again. "I'm heading to the shower."

"Wait," Oisín called him back. Locking eyes, they stared at each other. "Thank you for sticking with me. I'm sorry I've put you in some tough situations. And I know you've wanted to tell me to sod off many times. But you stuck with me. Thank you."

"You're welcome." Byron turned. "Oh," he turned back. "We have a reservation at The Pelican Snout for nine. Might want to change."

Oisín grinned and hurried to his room. "I have to make a quick call first."

Chapter Nineteen

The second Naomi stepped into the club she wanted to go home. It just wasn't her scene, and she didn't like all the stares. Granted, she had gotten the dress for the stares, but she just felt exposed. One hour later, she desperately needed to leave. Weaving her way through the throngs of moving sweaty bodies, she found Olivia dancing, more like grinding, against a large man with a goatee.

"Mimi!" She shouted and held out her hands. "There you are! Dance with us."

Like a siren call, guys began crowding around her and a couple sweaty hands landed on her exposed sides. Pushing away, she threw her best fake smile and turned to Olivia.

"I'm gonna head out."

"No!" Olivia whined. "It's not even ten o'clock yet."

"What does that have to do with anything?"

"Um hello? My birthday?"

"You're... seriously? Why didn't you say anything?"

"I didn't want you to feel obligated to get me anything. I know money is tight for you right now."

Her cheeks flamed red. "I would have. Not a problem. But I do need to get some fresh air. It's stuffy in here."

"But you'll be back?"

"Yeah, I'll be back." Naomi hated lying but she needed to leave.

"Okay, hurry back! They're bringing birthday cake shots!" Olivia went back to grinding against the guy behind her and Naomi pushed her way through to an exit she had seen next to the restrooms.

Coming out in an alleyway, between the club and another building, she tried not to gag when the smell of rotten fish mixed with garbage hit her nose. The alley was dimly lit but she could smell cigarettes near her, and movement caught her eye.

Immediately, she heard a catcall followed by, "I see you Momma. You're hot, baby girl."

More than one voice had spoken. Finally, she found the men, three in total gathered to her right about fifty feet away from her. And they were walking over to her.

"Not interested," she replied and began walking the other way, hoping it wasn't a dead end.

"Don't be like that, baby girl."

She walked faster. So did they.

"We just want to talk."

"Yeah, we want to see you, baby. Why don't you come over here? We'll get to know you better."

"No," she muttered and picked up the pace.

"You rude, baby girl?"

"We're just wanting to talk to you."

They were gaining on her. The heels were not helping as she tried to hurry away.

"Hey, bitch, we're talking to you. Be nice and talk back, ugly ass bitch."

The end of the alley was in sight, and she raced to the corner glancing back to see the three men had nearly caught up with her.

Still moving even though she wasn't watching where she was going, she ran right into a large chest and hands came on her arms to steady her. Whipping her head around to see who had grabbed her, she breathed a huge sigh of relief and threw her arms around him.

"Baby," she said loudly. "There you are!" Then, quietly in his ear, she said. "Three guys have been following me. Please help."

Oisín's arms tightened around her waist. "Always."

The sound of the men still calling out to her reached her ears as they rounded the bend.

"You know how much I love your curves in that dress, baby," Oisín grinned then his eyes trailed up to three men just coming round the bend. "Friends of yours?" He asked.

"Hardly," she replied.

The men looked at both Byron and Oisín as Oisín pushed Naomi behind them. She still held his upper arm, grateful to have him there, even if she was still angry at him.

"Giving my girlfriend problems?" Oisín flexed and Byron crossed his arms over his massive chest.

"Nah, nah, man, we're cool," one said.

"Why don't you call me what you called me earlier?" Naomi felt stronger with both of them there.

"Nah, we're good, baby girl," another one said.

"Never call my girl baby girl. That's a derogatory term and I won't stand for it," Oisín said.

"Not as derogatory as the other name they called me," she muttered.

"You insult my woman?" Oisín took it the menacing step forward. And Byron widened his stance.

The three guys took a step back and then ran away as fast as they could. Once they were alone, Oisín turned to Naomi.

"Are you okay?" He asked.

"Yeah, I'm glad to run into you… again."

"You can run into me anytime. I'm just glad to have been in the right place at the right time."

"What are you doing here?"

"Is it weird to say I came to find you?" Oisín asked.

"Why?" Naomi took a step back. "Want to tell me more about how you're going to sue my dad and me? Or maybe how you don't care that my dad is breaking his back to help start and finish your home? Or I know, you want to wave the fact you have a new girl or three every night and care nothing for anyone else."

"I have no defense, none. I am so very sorry. I know there is nothing I can say to make up for what I said to you but please let me assure you I would never... could never sue you or your father and when Byron told me about your father's heart attack, I felt even more horrible. Please, I want you to know, take as long as you need. There is no need to make it to the deadline. I'm happy to sign an addendum to the contract so you feel safe."

Naomi stared at him for a long moment. It took a lot of effort for her to remember why she was angry at him but when she did, she took another step back.

"Okay, good. I'll have the addendum written up and get it to you. I'm going to head out now. Thank you for your help. Sorry to bother you."

"Please don't go," he reached for her. "Please, I can't say how sorry I am."

"I understand. And thank you. But I should go."

"Can I have Davis drive you home?" Oisín offered.

"I'll call an Uber." She took in his outfit, a sheer black shirt and silk pants. "Besides, it looks like you should be in there." She gestured to the club.

Oisín grinned. "Actually, I was on my way to The Double Rainbow. You mentioned it the other day and I thought I'd give it a try."

Her eyes widened. "You can't go there."

"Why not?" He asked. "You said it's an Irish pub. I'd love to try it."

"No, you can't go there dressed like that."

"Why not? It's Balenciaga." He slid a hand down the front of his shirt.

"It's not the outfit, it's…"

"What?" He was fighting with grin.

She stared at him for a long moment. "Asshole, you know already, don't you?" She couldn't help her grin.

"Know what? That you set me up thinking Double Rainbow is an Irish pub when it's clearly a gay bar? No, no idea." He beamed. Naomi breathed a laugh.

"Okay guilty. Though not sorry. You were being a complete—"

"Jackanapes bastard?"

"Yeah, sounds about right."

They stared at each other for a long moment.

"Truce?" He offered.

She huffed the sigh and nodded. "Truce," she replied.

Oisín couldn't stop his grin from spreading across his lips. For a moment, he had thought he was being the pushy his brother warned him not to be but when she smiled and laughed he let out a silent breath. He was damn lucky.

"But that doesn't mean I'm going to be jumping in bed with you," she stated.

"Understood," he replied. "Thank you for giving me another chance."

The corner of her lip ticked up as she watched him.

"I don't know why, but you've…"

"I've…" He prompted.

She looked away. "Nothing. I'm just glad you were here." She looked back at him. "But don't be an ass again."

Byron chuckled silently.

"Scouts honor, Miss Moonbeam," Oisín said.

"Oh yeah sure, like I've never heard that before." She rolled her eyes.

Oisín beamed. "I was pretty proud of myself for that one."

"Well, don't be. It's not that original." But her face lit with the grin.

"Can I make it up to you?" He asked after a long pause.

She hesitated. "What did you have in mind?"

"Have you eaten?" He asked. "Let me take you to dinner?"

She stared at him for a long moment. His hands instantly grew sweaty.

"There's a good brewery just down the main stretch," she said. "Wanna check it out?"

"Definitely," he breathed.

"I'll need to change," she motioned to her handbag.

"Yeah, okay."

"What, no silly come back about my dress? And wanting to see me out of it?"

"I think you've had enough of guys objectifying you tonight."

Her face froze at his words, and he wasn't sure what he'd said wrong. But then she nodded and instantly, she looked away.

"Thank you." Was all she said.

Chapter Twenty

The brewery was closing but Naomi seemed to know everyone and when the owner came out from the back she gave the older beefy guy a big hug, one that stirred some jealousy, but the man didn't act like they were anything more than friends.

"I haven't seen you for months, darling," the guy said. "What have you and Billy been up to?"

"You know dad hates it when you call him that," Naomi said.

"That's why I do it," he winked. His eyes traveled to Oisín and a flicker of recognition flashed in the depths. "Ni, what are you doing with Oisín O'Quinn?"

Oisín gave his award-winning smile. "Pleased to meet you. Naomi told my friend and I about this great place and we decided we'd love to check it out."

"And how do you know our Naomi?" The guy placed his arm around her shoulders. She rolled her eyes but leaned into him. Oisín watched the movement.

"Well – ehm – you could say we... Bumped into each other," Oisín replied. "I've hired Moon Construction to renovate a property I just recently acquired."

"Oh yeah?"

"He bought the old Bay Tree property," Naomi said.

The man's eyes widened. "Well, isn't that kismet, eh honey?"

"Sorry, what?" Oisín asked.

"Ni has been after that property ever since she was a little girl. Always said it was her dream to dance in that ballroom."

"Really?" Oisín looked at her. "She never mentioned that."

"Nah, wouldn't imagine she would even remember it. It was back when pigtails and Disney princesses were all the rage for her. You know, a couple of years ago." The man winked and kissed her cheek.

"Uncle Kei..." She breathed.

"Sorry," he grinned. "Force of habit." Then, turning back to Oisín, he stuck out his hand. Keimoni Kekoa, Naomi's uncle."

Oisín chuckled, realizing his mistake. "Oisín O'Quinn, my bodyguard Byron."

"Hau'oli kēia hui 'ana o kāua."

"Pleased to meet you in Hawaiian," Naomi translated.

"Go raibh maith agat," Oisín winked. *"Thanks* in Irish."

Naomi's uncle looked at Naomi and smiled. "I like him."

"Uncle Kei," she breathed.

"What? He's better than that *okole* you married."

"And divorced," Naomi corrected.

"Yeah, because you found the asshole in bed with another woman," Uncle Keimoni stated.

"I'm sorry?" Oisín question.

"Nothing. Uncle Kei, can we get some pints and a pizza please? I can lock up."

Her uncle pursed his lips together but nodded. "Sure thing, honey," he said. "What will it be?" He looked at Oisín.

"Whatever Naomi is getting," Oisín said.

Uncle Kei turned to Byron.

"You're drinking. I won't hear anything of it," Oisín ordered.

"A lager then," Byron said.

"Good choice, we have one with a hint of Florida orange," Uncle Kei stated.

"That sounds wonderful." Byron took a space near the door as Oisín and Naomi took a four-topper out of the way of the closing team but not near any windows.

Naomi's uncle placed the pints before them with a wink.

"Pizza will be out soon. Any dietary restrictions?" He asked.

"None," Oisín replied.

"Good. It'll be out soon."

When Uncle Kei left the room to check on the food, Oisín's phone rang a notification. He pulled it out of his pocket, checked the text, and smiled.

"Something good?" Naomi questioned, taking a sip of her beer.

"Aye, I think it will help. I'm sorry for checking the phone."

"Help?" She asked waving him off for checking his phone during their conversation.

Oisín just grinned and lifted his beer glass toward her.

"Remember what they say."

"No, what?"

"If you don't look someone in the eye when you toast, it means seven years' bad sex," Oisín said making a show of looking her in the eyes.

"Seven years bad sex?" She shook her head after drinking. "Maybe that's the answer."

"Answer?" Oisín asked.

"I forgot to look my husband in the eyes on our wedding day toast and that's why it's been years of truly god awful sex."

Oisín chuckled. "What did you see in him? You had to see something, or you wouldn't have married him. You're an intelligent woman. I can't see you being taken in by a fake."

Naomi sighed and took another drink. Uncle Kei brought out some breadsticks for them, then went to talk to Byron.

"Sorry," Oisín replied. "You don't have to tell me. It was rude of me to ask."

"No, no. Truce, remember?" She replied. "It's just, I did see it. I saw him for the fake he was and thought I could change him."

"That's admirable."

"It's dumb. No one will change. They are who they are. And no amount of love or begging from me would change him."

"Sometimes people put up a front. They become someone different because they feel like society won't like the real them. Or maybe the real them is too shy to put themselves out there and be rejected.

Naomi stared at him for a long moment. "Emilio was... he was like no guy I ever met. He was handsome in an exotic way. He made me feel like I was the most beautiful woman he ever saw. He was kind, in his own way. But he only seemed to talk down to me. Acted like I didn't know anything. He would compare me to other women, even flirt with others while standing next to me. When I confronted him about it, he blamed his hot Latin blood. He's Brazilian. But I knew that wasn't right. Still, he made it to where I needed him or at least *felt* like I needed him. My dad and I grew apart.

"I was at work when my dad had his heart attack. Dad was rushed to the hospital. Once Dad was stable, since I couldn't get a hold of him, I hurried to our condo to tell my husband, hoping for comfort and to have him join me at the hospital. But as soon as I got home, I could hear them. My husband was in our bed... *enjoying* a busty blonde. Since then, I moved back in with dad and Emilio has set up his own general contracting company half a mile down from us. He gets things done faster and cheaper. He has no pride in his work, only taking clients from my dad and me."

"I'm sorry," Oisín breathed. "He's an idiot. To throw away you and your trust," Oisín shook his head. "He's got to be the biggest eejit this side of the Atlantic."

"I think so too."

They locked eyes again and simply stared at each other.

"And besides, if he doesn't know how to satisfy you, he doesn't deserve another thought."

"And I suppose you think you do?"

"Well… yeah," Oisín grinned.

Naomi burst out laughing just as her uncle brought out the pizza.

Oisín walked beside Naomi, up the sand path to the front door of their house. A single light was on in the front room.

"Looks like Bill waited up for you," Oisín said.

"Always does," she smiled.

"My folks did too when I lived at home. I'm sure they would still if I stayed with them."

"Parents, huh?" She said.

"We were blessed with a couple of great sets," Oisín stopped on the stoop.

"We sure were," Naomi held her keys in her hand. "I'd invite you in, but—"

"Yeah, it's late," he agreed. "Thanks for sharing your uncle's place with me. It's a great spot. Glad to know it's so close to the house."

"Yeah, Uncle Kei is great."

"He is."

They stared at each other for a long while.

"What time are you guys going to the construction site?"

"Tomorrow?"

"No, no, Monday. I mean, I assume you get the weekend off? As your boss, I demand you not work on my houses tomorrow."

Naomi chuckled. "We usually start around nine-ish," she explained.

"Could I – I mean – would it be okay if By and I join you?"

"You want to work construction?"

"Yeah, why not?"

"I don't know, you could get a splinter or break a nail or something."

"The only thing I will be breaking is a sweat. Come on, I could use a manual labor workout. And I don't want your dad to do it all alone. I'm strong. I can help."

Naomi thought a moment before nodding. "Okay. On one condition."

"Anything."

"Bring coffee and breakfast. Enough for the guys helping out too."

"Done, any dietary restrictions?"

"An array would be good."

"Can do." He grinned. Naomi had trouble looking away.

They were quiet for a long moment.

"Thank you for... helping me tonight with those guys."

"Absolutely, always. I'm glad I was there."

"And for the truce... I had a great time tonight."

"Me too," Oisín said softly. "Thank you for giving me another chance."

"Thank you for being persistent."

Again, they just stared at each other. Oisín leaned forward just slightly then pulled back.

"You should probably get inside. I'll see you Monday morning," he said.

"Okay."

Why she kept her eyes on him as she shut the door and why she watched him walk slowly back to the SUV through one of the windows on the side of the door, she didn't know. And she definitely wasn't going to think about why she went to bed disappointed he didn't kiss her when he leaned forward.

Chapter Twenty-One

Monday morning finally rolled around. Oisín woke at three then tried to fall back asleep. When next he opened his eyes, it was five o'clock. Groaning in frustration, he got up and went to the restroom before trotting down the steps to seek out the kitchen.

The coffee was programmed to start at six so it would be hot when Byron woke but there was still some left from the two guards. Nodding to the night guards sitting at the table, one watching the outside and the other watching him, Oisín grabbed an orange from the fruit platter his chef had out. He walked over to the window. As the first rays of pre-dawn began to lighten the area around them, he could see the water and sand.

He turned back to his guards who stood and walked over to him.

"Can we open the door? Go outside?" He asked. The two looked at each other and one of them spoke into their cuff asking the outside team if the coast was clear. After confirmation, the other guy opened the door just enough and slipped out onto the second story deck. The pool and hot tub were below them.

Oisín waited for the all clear, and once it was given, he stepped out into the early Floridian morning. The air was not as humid and the breeze coming from the Gulf was heavenly. He took a deep breath, filling his lungs with salt air.

Peace. Serenity.

All day Sunday, Oisín wondered what Naomi was doing but he gave her some space and only texted her a good morning text which led to a fun conversation over the course of the day.

Oisín: Good morning! I hope you slept well. I had the door of my room open and fell asleep to the sound of the waves. It was wonderful.

Naomi: Good morning! I slept very well. My uncle's pizza always puts me right to sleep. *food coma*

She followed it up with a sleepy emoji and Oisín chuckled.

Oisín: It was such a good pizza. I may have to order it every day. Not sure how my agent will react when I look like this.

He found a GIF of *Pizza the Hut* from the movie *Spaceballs* and sent it.

Naomi texted back and the laughing crying emoji and Oisín laughed.

But with Monday morning in full swing, he itched to text her.

A loud crash in the kitchen had him jumping and his two guards whirling around, grabbing their guns. When they saw the chef had just dropped a pan and waved to say sorry, they relaxed.

His chef made the best buttermilk biscuits and quiche, so Oisín had put in an order for extra to take with him. He also asked for extra bacon and sausage. He knew from running his own business, how hungry physical labor could make people and the key was carbs and protein in the morning.

Thinking about his former business with his friends always brought a jolt of guilt. He had dissolved the company as soon as he got his modeling contract and had left a lot of his friends high and dry. Fortunately, they weren't the kind to hold grudges... Not all of them anyway.

You can't buy your friends. Callum, his best friend and former business partner had told him over the phone one day. Callum was right of course, and it would have been easier and possibly cheaper if he had just kept the business open. But he was blinded by stardom, something he recently started to realize wasn't all it was cracked up to be. But now, hopefully, he had a chance to make it up to them.

One of the guards tapped his ear and listened before giving the typical response.

"Roger, standby," then, he turned to him. "Three men are at the gate, sir. They are saying you're expecting them."

Oisín pulled out his phone. They weren't supposed to be there until seven o'clock but, as he looked at the phone, several text messages popped up, each one made him smile.

Callum: Let us in, you bastard. It's damn weird just waiting here.

Denis: Where are you, ya huir? I need some coffee if you're gonna drag me out of bed at this god-awful time of day.

Willie: Let us in, ya mucker. I ain't got all day. There're some hot girls in need of my special Irish attention.

Oisín grinned and looked over at the bodyguard.

"Aye, they're supposed to be here."

"Next time, sir, please inform us of any visitors."

"Sorry, sorry, Byron knew they were coming. They weren't supposed to be here before seven." They turned back to the kitchen.

The guard gave the okay for entry, and soon the front door opened and all hell broke loose.

"Where is he? The gobshite?" Oisín heard Callum call.

"Damn," Denis said and whistled low. "This place is great!"

"Yeah, the eejit at least has taste," Willie said.

Oisín's cheeks began to hurt from smiling too much. Rounding the bend, the three friends all locked eyes with him.

"Heya lads, thanks for coming," Oisín said.

Their eyes traveled to the two guards flanking him.

"I'd deck ya if I was sure these two numpties wouldn't draw on me," Callum stated.

One of the guards stepped forward. Oisín stopped him.

"Easy, he's just playing,"

Callum and Oisín stared at each other for a long moment. No one moved or spoke, even Byron as he walked down the stairs was silent. Finally, Callum's face split into a wide grin.

"Ah, get over here, ya shitehawk," Callum and Oisín embraced tightly. "How the hell are ya?"

Thumping each other on the back, they laughed and all the tension in the room evaporated. Oisín made his rounds embracing his old friends.

"You lads have no idea how amazing it is to see you," Oisín said.

"I could scarce believe my eyes when I saw your name pop up on my phone," Callum replied. "Let alone hearing you ask for help."

"Aye, I know. I was a right arse to you all," he said. "But it's urgent or I wouldn't have begged. I am sorry by the way, lads. Truly. I was blinded by the opportunity and the cash. I know I put a lot of you in a tough space. The others still aren't talking to me?"

"They're still pissed. These two were the only ones who would listen as soon as I said your name." Callum gestured to the two men beside him.

"Willie, Denis, thank you."

"Never been to Florida, thought I'd give it a chance, like," Willie said.

"Beach, sun, girls, a little manual labor, what's not to like?" Denis questioned.

"What's the job?" Callum asked. "All you said on the phone was that you bought a place."

"Aye, it's beautiful but in need of a heavy reno."

"Did you get a contractor or something? You can't be doing it all yourself," Callum said.

"Aye. I have a local but... Let's head out to the deck. Want some juice?"

He turned to the chef who had been working quietly and who had a tray of different juices freshly squeezed. Once they

172

were all served, Oisín looked back at Byron who nodded once and spoke low to the two guards from earlier. Motioning for the men to head out to the deck, Oisín hung back and waited. Byron was at his side almost instantly.

"You called your friends to help Naomi?" Byron asked.

"And her dad. I remember being devastated when my grandpa passed away from a heart condition, I won't let Naomi lose her dad. He means the world to her. If that means she needs extra hands to help, that's what I can give her."

"Oisín," Byron said nothing for a long moment as he stared at him.

"What?" Oisín questioned.

Byron shook his head. "Nothing, just… I'm proud of you."

Oisín grinned but didn't let how those words affected him show. "Awe, gee, thanks, pa," he teased in an atrocious southern accent.

Byron winced and chuckled. "Get on out with your friends, Ope."

"Who?"

"Oh dear god, son," Byron shook his head.

Oisín grinned again and they both walked out to the deck where Oisín began explaining the situation to his men.

The lads all stared at him for a long time before Willie asked a question.

"Why haven't you just slept with her and get her out of your system?"

"It's not that easy."

"Refuse you, did she?" Denis asked.

"I like her already," Callum replied.

"I don't want to just sleep with her. She doesn't deserve that. She's been through a lot and if you lads can't respect her, then I can call my pilot and get you on a flight home tonight."

Everyone stared at him. "What?" He found himself asking a second time in thirty minutes.

"Damn," Callum stated.

"What?" Oisín said again.

"Shite man," Willie replied.

"What?" He felt his blood pressure skyrocket.

"Mate," Denis began. "Are you... like... in love with her?"

"What? No! I mean... I don't... I—"

Oisín looked helplessly at Byron who, helpful as ever, said nothing. Oisín's breathing sped up as he thought of Naomi Moon. Her smile, her wit, her sharp tongue, her... everything. Only one answer came to mind. But he'd be damned if he told them first. "I care about her, yes."

"Damn!" All three said at once. Byron only smirked.

"Oisín O'Quinn has finally had a woman catch his eye?" Denis cheered.

"Now, we got to meet her," Callum replied.

The whole while Willie was dancing around them singing *Oisín and Naomi sitting in a tree.* Oisín rolled his eyes but laughed so hard at his friends' antics, tears gathered in his eyes. Then, he sobered. Not all of his friends were there, and some would probably never speak to him again.

As the other three kept talking to each other about Oisín's perceived relationship status, Oisín walked to the railing and set his now empty glass of orange juice on the railing and looked out past the sand dunes to the water. Byron walked up to him, silent as ever. But at that moment, Oisín reveled in his friend's silence and comfort.

"I'm really not a good person, am I?" He mumbled.

"What are you talking about?" Byron questioned.

"I left my friends high and dry, taking away their source of income simply because I was blinded by the possibility of wealth and fame. Those same friends won't talk to me and for the longest time, I blamed *them* for not speaking to me, not forgiving me, taking it too far. I mean, who does that? It wasn't their fault I left. Dev was getting married at the end of the year and they had to postpone because he couldn't afford it once I left. I had people counting on me and I failed them. What right do I have to ask for their help? What right do I have to be happy? What right do I have to any of it? When people like Dev, and Naomi, you, and everyone who has been affected by me are struggling? I don't have any right to be happy."

Only after he spoke, did he realize his friends had stopped talking and were standing in a huddle listening.

"Oisín," Byron said and for the first time, his accent didn't change his name. "You are a good person. I've seen you care about your family. You share your good luck by setting your family up for life. You have helped more people on this security detail than anyone knows. You think of others. I've seen you, when a photographer poses you in a pretty provocative pose, you ask permission from your shootmate to make sure she's okay with everything. To make sure she's comfortable. You have every right to be happy. You can talk to them. You understand it now. Acknowledge the fact that you screwed up, apologize to them, explain to them you know what you did was wrong but you have to leave it up to them after that. But you recognize their struggle. You just need to reach out to them. Bear your soul. So you've seen you need to change, you want to change, so what are you going to do now? How are you going to change?"

Oisín was quiet for a long time. Callum, Willie, and Denis hovered but said nothing.

Finally, Willie spoke up. "While you were out living the good life, I was struggling to figure out how I could pay ma and da's bills. I was the sole breadwinner for them. When you left, I couldn't make the payments. They nearly lost the farm. How do you think that made me feel? It hurt. I depended on you. My family depended on you."

"What can I do? Do you need money? I can help—"

"No, see, that's the answer you always give. I don't want your money... I want my friend back. The one who thought of other people and how his actions affect other people. That's who I came to support. You could have more money than Midas but I still wouldn't want it. All I want is a heartfelt apology. One I don't second guess a hidden meaning behind. I want to look in your eyes and hear you say it."

Oisín stared at Willie, the full understanding of his selfish actions dawning on him. Stepping up to his friend, he kept his eyes on him.

"I'm so sorry, Willie," he said, his voice catching slightly. "I know my actions caused more pain than I ever knew. And I know, no amount of money could never bridge the gap I caused by not taking you and your family into consideration. It was selfish and hurtful. And I am so very sorry."

Everyone was quiet for a long moment, then Willie offered his hand.

"Forgiven," he said.

"Thank you," Oisín replied, truly touched by his grace of acceptance.

Denis offered his hand too. "Just be our old friend again, Oisín. We've missed you."

"I've missed you guys."

"I don't know about you, lads but I want to meet the woman who has caused this change in him," Callum said with a wink at Byron.

"Naomi exacerbated Byron's quiet help," Oisín replied. "I may care deeply about her, but it really was By who helped me through everything."

Byron's soft smile lifted the corner of his lips.

"It was By who has been on the receiving end of my woes more times than I can count."

"Dude, good to finally meet you. Anyone who can put up with this eejit for more than a week gets bonus points in my book," Callum said, offering his hand to Byron. "Had to live with the guy for two semesters at uni... never again." He winked.

"So what's the plan?" Denis asked. "You said we'd be helping out?"

"Aye, Naomi needs guys. I don't want her dad doing heavy lifting. She'll give you your assignments when we get there. But please keep an eye on her dad."

"We will. Is he cool?" Willie asked.

"Very," Oisín replied.

"Why do I get the feeling she doesn't know we're coming?" Callum asked.

"Because I haven't told her."

"I knew it. Trying to impress her, eh?"

"Something like that," Oisín said.

"Well," Willie started. "What are we waiting for? Let's see this woman who's caught our baby deer's eye."

Byron quirked an eyebrow and looked at Oisín.

"Don't ask," Oisín said.

"*Oisín* means little dear. When the lads found out, it was the running joke," Callum explained.

"I thought Oisín was a God or something in Celtic mythology," Byron said. "A poet or something."

"Yeah, but if we call him the *greatest poet of all time,* it will only go to his head. Besides, this guy tried poetry to get into a girl's knickers and it backfired, so we steer clear."

"I was sixteen, what the hell did I know?" Oisín asked.

They all chuckled as they headed inside, the wondrous scent of breakfast filling the air.

"We all ready chef?" Oisín asked.

"About ten more minutes," the chef said. "The van is already packed with the extras. I'll follow behind you."

"Excellent, thank you." Oisín turned to Byron. "Just enough time to change. I'll be back."

"I've gotta talk to the guys staying here. I'll meet you right here," Byron said.

"I won't go without you." Oisín winked and hurried up the stairs.

Chapter Twenty-Two

Naomi woke in her bed with her laptop and notes surrounding her. She had stayed up late Sunday night researching the little project she wanted to surprise Oisín with. She was going to convert the basement with its original brick and exposed ductwork into an Irish pub with a dash of Floridian motif.

Sucked down her usual rabbit hole of research, she found so many ideas before she passed out at four in the morning.

Rolling over to look at the time, she blinked away sleep to see nine-thirty reflected on her phone.

"Crap," she sat up and swung her legs over the edge of the bed. Unlocking her phone, she had a text from her dad.

Dad: I'm heading to Bay Tree. Didn't want to wake you. Come when you can, sweetheart.

Naomi jumped up and gathered her notes. She was supposed to be there at nine, she had told Oisín. She stopped. Why did that matter?

Shaking her head to clear it, she placed her notes and laptop on the small desk in her room before racing through a shower and pulling her wet hair into a low ponytail.

The mascara brush was halfway to her left eye after brushing on her right, when she stopped herself.

"What the hell am I doing?" She questioned out loud. She never wore mascara on a job site. Looking at her lopsided makeup job, she huffed and completed brushing on the dark makeup. It would look silly if she only had one eye done and she didn't have time to wash her face again and reapply her moisturizing routine.

She dressed in her usual jeans and steel toed boots but debated on her top. Usually wearing a black tank top, she eyed her collection and decided on a yellow one at the back of her closet. It looked great against her tan skin and since she would be more focused on directing the beach house team, she didn't have to worry about getting it too dirty. She grabbed her tool belt and hard hat and hurried to the front door.

As she was placing everything into the back of her pickup, she heard a car door shut.

"Miss Moon?"

She turned to see the foreman who had walked off a job three months ago head up the drive to her.

"Tim?" She questioned.

He wrung his hands and glanced back to the three other men in the truck.

"Is something wrong?" She asked. "I'm in a bit of a hurry."

Though she hated that he had walked off a job, she knew better than to make enemies, even if she would never use him again.

"Me and the guys just want to apologize for walking off the Ardsdale job. That's not like us, and we know what a tight spot it put you in," Tim said.

"Thanks for the apology. But as I said, I'm in a bit of a hurry." She moved to the driver side door, but Tim moved too.

"I know it's a long shot, but we wanted to offer to make it up to you. We'd be happy to work for you again."

"Aren't you working for my ex-husband, Tim? What happened, not enough projects coming in? Somehow I doubt that as he's stealing my clients."

Tim paled and wrung his hands again.

"Look, you're a good foreman, but I don't trust easily in this business and when you break that trust, it's over. I'm sorry. I could use you all, but I just don't trust you. Excuse me." She opened the door of her truck and slipped into the driver's seat. Tim was at the window.

"Please, let me, let us prove ourselves to you again. You won't regret it. We'll work for half time. Just please… give my guys another chance. They need this. I lead them astray, blame me not them. Please."

Naomi took a deep breath and let it out slowly, watching his eyes. She had a feeling she would regret it. There was something in his eyes she didn't trust but, she needed guys on

Oisín's project and if she could just use them for manual labor it would be fine, right?

"You are not the foreman. You will take orders from the foreman without complaint. I'll pay you three-fourths salary as a test for three weeks. If you and your guys prove useful and trustworthy I will raise your salary to full for the remainder of the project. If you put a toe out of line, you will be relieved and the *verbal* contract we have will be null and void. Is that clear?"

"Yes, thank you," Tim smiled. "So, what's the job?"

She hesitated again but plowed ahead. "You know the old Bay Tree mansion?" Tim's eyes grew wide but he nodded. "Follow me there."

Tim hurried back to his truck and climbed in. Naomi prayed she hadn't just made a huge mistake.

Her phone rang as she turned onto Front Beach Road. Answering it and putting it on speaker, she didn't recognize the number.

"Naomi Moon of Moon Construction, how can I help you?" She answered

"Miss Moon?" A vaguely familiar young man's voice said in the receiver.

"Yes? Can I help you?"

"I don't know if you remember me, but my name is Bobby. We met at the restaurant that you and your... friend stayed at for a couple of hours a couple of weeks ago?"

"Oh yes," she finally remembered the young man. "Bobby. Of course, how are you?"

"Not really all that great," he said. "As you know I'm trying to save up for college."

"Yes definitely, how's that going?"

"Not great. They just cut my hours, something about the season wrapping up. I don't really know what to do."

"Well, didn't we talk a little bit about that?"

"We did," he said, his voice so shaky it endeared him to her instantly. "I just was wondering if you actually meant what you said. Do you think you may have a job for me?"

"Oh do I ever, Bobby. How much construction have you had? You said something about your dad's shed?"

"Yes ma'am," he said. "I helped my dad build a shed I'm pretty handy too. I've got my own tool belt."

"Well, that's all you need," she smiled. "Why don't you meet me at the old Bay Tree mansion. You know where that is?"

"Yes ma'am."

"Good, can you meet me there sometime today?"

"Yes ma'am, I can bring my schedule too. I'm only working half days on Monday, Wednesday, and Friday."

"That's perfect. We'll discuss your salary and hours when you get there. Happy to have you on board."

"Thank you so much! Thank you, really thank you."

"Of course. Now, get on over to Bay Tree mansion when you can."

"I could leave in about thirty minutes?"

"That would be great. See you then. If you don't see me, talk to one of the guys, they'll know where I am."

"Yes ma'am."

"Oh and Bobby?"

"Yes ma'am?"

"Do you have boots and a hard hat?"

"Boots, yes ma'am, hard hat? No, I don't think so. Is there somewhere I can buy one?"

"I'm sure we can find one for you. Not to worry. See you soon."

"Yes ma'am, yes ma'am, thank you, thank you so much."

Naomi hung up the phone and smiled to herself. The kid, Bobby, was such a sweetheart. She knew what it was like needing to save up money and help pay the way through college. She would help anyone she could in the same situation. And she needed guys.

Pulling off the main road to Bay Tree Lane, Naomi followed the winding dirt road until her dad's truck, the foreman's truck, two black SUV, and the grounds crews' truck and trailer came into view.

Pulling in behind her dad's truck, she gaped at all the people in front of her. There were two good looking, well-built guys hauling lumber in grey tank tops and jeans, walking the two-by-fours to the side of the house. Another guy she'd never met before stood next to her dad as Byron, stripped to a black tank top, carried two eight-foot ladders, one under each arm, his smooth muscles bunching and clenching under his milk chocolate skin. Her dad stood near what looked like a buffet table, a cup of coffee in his hand, and gesturing to the front of the house with the hand holding a bacon, egg, and cheese biscuit.

Oisín was nowhere to be found, but the guy standing next to her dad caught her gaze through the windshield and yelled over his shoulder away from her so she couldn't catch what he said. But a moment later, Oisín hustled down the steps of the stone patio off the ballroom. His face split into a wide breathtaking grin as he hurried over to her truck. She slowly stepped out and met him as he approached.

"Good morning," he said brightly.

"Morning," she said surprised, still looking around. "What's going on?"

"I pulled a few strings and got a few friends to help from Ireland."

"Friends?"

"Yeah, might surprise you. I do have a few."

"No, I mean... uhm... I'm just surprised."

"Yeah? Well, surprise," his smile turned blinding, and Naomi had to consciously stop herself from leaning into him. "Are you hungry? My chef prepared some amazing food."

She breathed a laugh. "You know when I said bring food, I didn't think you'd bring a chef."

"Why not? His food is delicious." Oisín walked over to the table, and she glanced behind her to see her foreman approach Tim and his three-man crew. Happy they were going to be supervised, she turned back to the table.

"Morning, honey," her dad said. "Isn't this great?"

"Amazing," she replied. "Still a little surprised though."

"Aye, whatever our Oisín puts his mind to, god help anyone standing in his way," the man standing next to her dad said.

"Ni, this is my best friend, Callum O'Grady. We worked together at my... *a* moving company. That's Willie and Denis, also friends of mine," Oisín introduced.

The two men he named hurried over and stuck out their hands to her. Oisín seemed to be holding his breath for some reason but as soon as the two said hello, and offered their help, one commenting on how pretty she was, he let it out. They were called away, leaving Naomi and Oisín alone.

"This is amazing," Naomi said.

"I hoped it would help." Oisín shrugged. "Callum, Willie, and Denis are great lads and Byron, along with three of my security team offered to pitch in. I hope that's okay."

"Okay? It's amazing," Naomi grinned.

"Yeah? I just didn't want your dad to have to do any heavy lifting. The lads are going to help watch out for him."

Naomi's face softened. "You really are full of surprises, Oisín O'Quinn."

Oisín didn't respond but turned and gathered a muffin and a slice of quiche from his chef and offered it to her.

"We're here, use us," he said. "But first, eat."

Naomi, feeling emboldened, took a forkful of quiche and locked eyes with Oisín slowly removing the fork from her lips. Her eyes fluttered close as the burst of flavors danced across her tongue. Finally, she opened her eyes to find Oisín watching her, eyes hooded and his stare hot.

"This is very good," she replied, her voice husky even to her ears.

Oisín swallowed hard and licked his lips.

"I'm glad," he whispered. "I could watch you eat all day."

"Let's not," she smiled. "I'd get too full."

Oisín breathed a laugh. "So ehm, where do you want me?"

"What a loaded question, O'Quinn."

He chuckled. "I'm trying to be more of a gentleman, Miss Moon but if you want the bad boy back, give me a minute to switch brains."

"I like your brain."

"Which one?"

She chuckled softly.

"Hey, you two," Callum called from the front steps. "Are you going to work or flirt the day away?"

"Shut it, ya wee gobshite," Oisín called back in an affectionate tone but never took his eyes from hers. "What's on the docket today, Miss Moon?"

"Pilings were here Friday, so I want to work a bit on the beach house, as those set over the weekend."

"Great," Oisín said. "We can split the team since there's enough of us."

"Good idea. I also have another guy coming in about half an hour. Know anything about decking?" She asked.

The corner of Oisín's lip tipped up. "Only as much as my civil structural engineering degree gave me."

Naomi blinked and surprise. Oisín winked. "See? Not just a pretty face."

"Why didn't you say anything before?"

"Would you have believed me?"

Naomi debated. "Probably not."

"Mmhm, didn't think so."

"Okay so, you know construction."

"I know a bit."

"Well then, let's get started. Dad," she called. "You good here? I'm going to take a team and get started on the beach house deck. Oh and I've got another guy coming in about half an hour. Come find me when he gets here."

Bill stuck his head out of the window opening where he and Callum worked on replacing the front windows and gave his daughter a thumbs up.

"By," Oisín called. Byron glanced over. "I'm going with her. Do you want to stay here? I'm comfortable being alone."

"Just a few more loads and I'll come find you. Until then, take Bragstad." Byron motion to one of the two guards standing nearby Bragstad, a former Navy SEAL stepped forward and nodded once. Oisín thanked him and turned to Naomi.

"Oh the problems with fame."

"Is he going to wipe your butt for you too?" She winked.

Oisín barked a laugh. "I don't pay him *that* much."

Taking two of Tim's guys and Willie, Oisín and Naomi walked down the duckboard to the dunes and the beach house beyond.

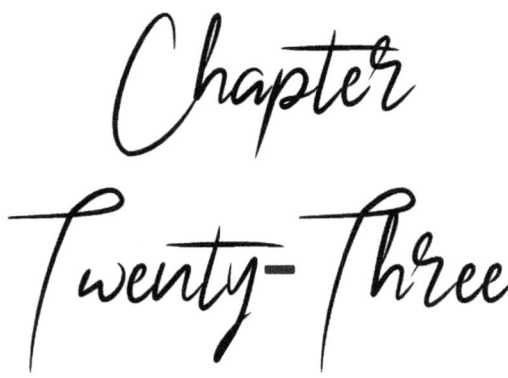

Chapter Twenty-Three

It was just after midday when Naomi called a stop. The decking was going very well but Oisín's arms ached with the use of muscles he hadn't used for a long time. He groaned as he stretched his back and wiped his forehead with his t-shirt.

"Sore?" She grinned.

"Really sore," he replied.

"Let's go up and get some lunch. I can smell it from here." Naomi headed down the steps. Oisín jogged up beside her.

"This is really looking good," he said. "I love the openness of the main floor."

"Yeah, it's going to look amazing. We get to pick out backsplash and paint color soon," she teased.

"Hey, just because I'm a guy doesn't mean I don't like shopping."

"I'm curious about your tastes. I have some ideas too. I love decorating on the beach."

"Why don't you and your dad live on the beach?"

"It's a dream. You know how expensive it is. We just can't afford it. Not right now. Maybe one day though."

"I'm sorry," Oisín said.

"For what?"

He shrugged. "Making you decorate a place you've always wanted."

"It's a dream come true. I would hate you going to anyone else."

"At least you added that last part and didn't stop at *hate you.*"

She chuckled. "Truce, remember?"

"Ah, of course."

"Honestly, it's such an amazing property that I—" she broke off as soon as they left the copse of trees and saw the red Ferrari parked in the circular drive. "What the hell?"

The driver's side door popped open and a man Oisín had never seen before stepped out. He disliked him instantly.

"Hey there, *Tesouro*," he said looking at Naomi. "So this is where you've been hiding out huh?" He whistled low. "Must be costing a pretty penny getting this place up and running."

"What are you doing here, Emilio?"

Emilio, so he was who Oisín thought he was. The arsehole who cheated on Naomi.

"I wanted to see what you were doing. I know you're in way over your head with this one, Naomi. Does the owner know you won't be able to finish this on time?"

"And let me guess, you could?" She demanded.

"With time and money to spare. Come on, Ni, you and I both know you're in over your head. I wonder if this," he pulled out a piece of paper and squinted at it. "Ocean O'Quinn knows just who he's gotten into bed with, figuratively speaking of course. Besides, what kind of name is Ocean?"

"Irish," Oisín said beside her. "And it's pronounced Oh-Sheen. Nice to meet the man who I will *not* be using on my property. Literally and figuratively, you're a bastard. Now," he walked over to him. "Get in your flashy car and get the hell off my property."

Emilio's face had drained of color as soon as Oisín spoke up and he took two steps back toward his car before a shit-eating grin lifted his face.

"Mr. O'Quinn, I'm afraid you caught me. I'm sorry for the insult. I'm just not used to Irish names. Please, allow me to apologize and please let me introduce myself."

"Emilio, the cheating ex-husband and piss poor general contractor. Yeah, I know who you are. I looked up local contractors when I purchased this property, but you should really take a look at your Yelp reviews. Shoddy work, overcharge for little things to make up for using shitty materials. I wasn't going to touch your company with a ten-foot pole. Now, as I said before, get off my property."

Emilio stared at him for a while. Then, he turned to look at Naomi and then to Tim, the worker Naomi had brought with her.

"Thanks for the tip, Tim. You'll get double pay on the next job," Emilio called.

Naomi whipped around to glare at the man. Oisín could see the anger curling around her.

"You," she spat. "I gave you another chance and you were a spy?"

Tim shrugged. "He promised to pay me more."

"I doubt you'll see a dime," Naomi replied. "You're done. Take your guys and go."

The men who came with Tim gathered their things and headed to their truck. Emilio still stood next to his car.

"I'll see you soon, Ni." He opened the door to his car as Oisín took a menacing step forward.

Once the dust settled, Oisín turned back to Naomi who wrapped her arms around herself trying and failing to make it look like she was crossing her arms. Oisín wanted to do something. Take her somewhere private. Comfort her, but there were people everywhere. Sighing, he touched her arm gently and offered a half smile.

"I want to say something to help but I doubt *your ex is a douche bag* will really help."

Naomi let out a harsh laugh. "Not really, no, but you're not wrong."

They were quiet for a long moment but then Naomi let out a frustrated groan and heaved a sigh.

"Let's get some lunch, then get back to work."

That gave Oisín an idea. "Can I take you to the pier for lunch? I know we have a lot to do here, but I'd love to have you join me. We'll be back soon and can finish the deck then."

"It won't get completely finished tonight but at least the frame will be up. That's what I wanted to accomplish today."

"Is that a yes?"

She stared at him for a long moment. "Yes," she answered.

He beamed. "By, we're going to the pier," he called to his bodyguard standing near Bill, eating a barbecue rib. Byron made to move to join them when Oisín held up a hand.

"I think I can manage lunch in my own. You deserve a break."

"Osh, no, they still haven't caught the guy who shot at you. I don't feel comfortable leaving you alone."

"Then I'll take Davis."

"Davis stays with the car. He doesn't get out of the car."

"Fine," Oisín turned his back on Byron and looked at Naomi rolling his eyes. "I love him but damn, he's like a mother hen sometimes."

Naomi chuckled. "He's trying to protect you."

"I know," Oisín sighed.

Byron walked over to them. "Davis is pulling the car around."

"Super," Oisín's voice betrayed his displeasure, but he was grateful Byron didn't say anything about it.

Soon, the SUV kicked up dust as Davis expertly maneuvered the vehicle between trucks and machinery. Oisín and Naomi scrambled into the back seat as Byron took his place up front.

"Where to, boss?" Davis asked.

"Pier Park," Oisín replied. "There's a place I want to try, looking out over the water."

"Sounds good."

"I'll call ahead," Byron said pulling out his phone. "Which one is it?"

Oisín gave the name and saw Naomi smile.

"Good choice," she said, then settled back for the twenty-minute drive.

Chapter Twenty-Four

Lunch at the pier overlooking the beach past Front Beach Road was... nice, Naomi thought. They were ushered to an outside table on the upper deck. The constant helicopter flights ferrying tourists down the beach, was a bit annoying but having lived near there almost her whole life, she was able to tune it out. After they finished eating, Oisín and Naomi walked out of the restaurant and turned down the sidewalk. Oisín took her hand then dropped it like it was on fire.

"Sorry," he looked sheepish. "I don't know why I did that."

"I don't mind," she said.

"Really?" He questioned.

"Truce, remember," she replied.

"Right." He took her hand again. "Wanna walk for a bit?"

"We should get back but... you haven't experienced Pier Park yet, have you?"

"What? Is there more than the constant golf carts filled with horny teenagers blasting their rap music?"

Naomi giggled. "Much more, grandpa. Come on."

Though Naomi knew they needed to get back to the construction site, there was just something about the palm tree lined main strip with its boutiques and restaurants that called to them. After stopping in an ice cream parlor with an insane number of choices, Oisín and Naomi walked down the main thoroughfare hand in hand. They visited different boutiques and shops. Oisín had bought a pair of sunglasses for himself with plastic palm trees framing the lenses which made Naomi laugh. He also bought Byron a t-shirt with a funny saying that she knew he would never wear. And then he purchased a necklace for her that had a shell and flip flops that she fell in love with.

The niggling feeling of it being wrong to fraternize with the client entered the back of her mind, but she suppressed it... for now. There was only so long it would last or could last.

They walked back toward the pier where Davis waited with the car but before they got much further than the information booth, Oisín stopped outside another shop.

"The Spice and Tea Exchange?" Oisín asked her.

"Oh, it's one of my favorites," she gushed. "They have all these spices, salts, teas, and trinkets from all over the world. Things I couldn't find anywhere else."

"Can we go in?"

"You don't have to ask me."

He grabbed her hand and walked through the open door.

"Afternoon," a man called from the back counter.

"Heya, how are you?" Oisín ask jovially.

"Doing fine, doing fine, anything I can help you find?" The man was tall with a runners' physique and a kind smile.

"Just stopping in, never been here before."

"Oh welcome! We—" his eyes lightened on Naomi. "Miss Moon!"

"Hey, Lance."

"Oh my goodness, excuse me, sir," he said as a side to Oisín and walked over to her to give her a hug. "I haven't seen you in forever. How's your dad?"

"He's doing really well."

"I'm so pleased. I had lunch with your uncle a week or so back and he let me know he was ill."

"A cold, nothing else thankfully. But that tea and soup mixture you gave us was amazing," Naomi said.

"I'm so pleased." He beamed. "Honey!" He called, tilting his head back to aim his voice to the back of the store. "Naomi Moon is here."

Lance's wife, a lovely woman in an apron with her name tag saying; Sandra, walked out of the backroom wiping her hands on her apron.

"Naomi, sweetheart, so good to see you." She gave her a quick hug. Her shoulder length blonde hair caught a soft breeze from the open door.

"Good to see you too. I was just showing Oisín around."

"Oisín?" Lance asked then his eyes lightened on the model standing off to the right, watching. "Oh, where are my manners? I am so sorry. What can I do to help?"

"Just looking around."

"Of course of course, let me show you around." Lance and Oisín walked to one side of the store and Lance began opening sample jars, having Oisín smell all the amazing spices on display while telling the story of how he and his wife came to own part of the franchise.

Sandra stood beside Naomi, silent but watching and when Oisín laughed at something Lance said and looked over at Naomi with happiness and… another emotion Naomi refused to name, Sandra softly elbowed her to get her attention. Naomi turned to look at the proprietor. Sandra's eyebrows bounced and eyes sparkled.

Naomi shook her head. "He's a friend and a client. Nothing more."

"Whatever you say," Sandra teased.

"I'm serious Sandie," Naomi replied.

"Mmhmm, I know you are."

"He's arrogant, egotistical, selfish, narcissistic—" she cut herself off realizing deep down the true Oisín O'Quinn was nothing like that. He looked over at her again, his smile faltered for a moment as his brows quirked in question then his grin returned, and he winked at her. "Oh god," Naomi groaned. "Oh god no, Sandie tell me no."

Sandra shrugged but looked lovingly smug like she had figured out a secret first. Naomi looked over at Oisín again and groaned softly seeing his dimples pop as his smile widened. "Oh my god, I love him."

Sandra huffed out a pleased sigh and someone cleared their throat behind her. She froze when she heard Byron. Slowly turning around, she saw a small smile tugging at his lips.

"You can never breathe a word of this to him, okay?" She ordered.

He pantomimed zipping his lips, locking them, and tossing the key over his shoulder.

"Ugh, how could I have let this happen?" She pressed the heels of her hands into her eyes and massaged. "I swore it wouldn't. I didn't want it to. I never wanted to fall for him. Especially after Emilio... and, and, he's so much younger than I am."

"Six years, not much," Byron said.

"He'll never want me like that are you kidding? He could have anyone he wanted. Why... ugh!"

Fortunately, there was the sound of the children's train ride honking right outside the door so Oisín couldn't hear her, but she stared at him as he listened and asked questions. Lance was in his element as he explained all the fascinating ways they smoked the sugars and blended the teas.

Naomi's head pounded with the truth. It was almost as if she spoke the words into existence and couldn't stop it. She took in the curve of his back, the way his hair glinted when the sunlight pierced through the shop, the carefree way he threw his head back and laughed as if he had just heard *Who's on First* for the first time. His thoughtfulness in bringing his buddies over from Ireland to help her. The way he opened up to her. The way he took time with the people who recognized him but didn't ignore those too shy to speak to him. The bad boy/playboy persona he gave off at their initial meeting wasn't him. None of it was. Under that fake exterior lay a man who cared about his friends, family, even strangers. She finally saw the man Byron told her about. And she liked him... she loved him.

The shrill ring of her phone startled everyone, and they turned to look at her when she nearly shrieked. Looking at the name, she blew out a sigh of relief, not caring who it was so long as she could step out and take the call. Byron walked outside with her and stood on one side of the door.

Answering the phone, she heard the wail on the other end.

"Liv? What's wrong?"

"Oh it's horrible! Absolutely horrible! Why?" She wailed. "Why did this have to happen to me?"

"What?" Naomi questioned not understanding her. "What happened? Calm down, talk to me."

"It's ruined! It's all ruined!" She wept.

"Olivia Nicole Harrison, calm down and tell me what the hell happened."

Liv sniffled on the other end and there was a muffled crinkled sound as if she was wiping her eyes with a tissue.

"The venue for the reunion..." she began again after a moment. "A pipe burst, flooded the entire place. The reunion is cancelled. It's all ruined. They said it'll be months before it'll all be cleared up. The reunion is in four weeks. What are we going to do? All the decorations are in my garage there's nowhere else."

"Have you called around? Any venue open? We live on the beach, Liv there's got to be a place. Even if we need to drive to Destin."

"They are not giving back the deposit in time. We can't afford anywhere else. It's over," she cut herself off on a sob.

"It's not over don't be so dramatic. Listen," she sighed. "I can look around, call in some favors. Give me some time."

"Really?" She sounded so hopeful.

"Really, now, I need to go and get back to... work. I'll call you when I have news. Hang loose, okay?"

Olivia sniffled. "Okay."

"Okay good, we'll talk soon." Naomi hung up with a *don't worry* and *bye* then stared at her phone.

"Problem?" Oisín's voice behind her made her jump. "Sorry," he grinned.

"No no, it's okay," she turned, but couldn't look at him. Instead, her eyes caught the three bags in his hands filled with spices, teas, sugars, salts, and trinkets. "Did you buy them out?" She teased and bit her lip.

"Almost," Oisín laughed and offered her one of the bags. "Lance said these were yours and your dad's favorites."

"Oh, wow, you didn't... have to..." she gingerly took the bag.

"I know but I wanted to thank you. You guys are working so hard, and I know I've not made it easy."

"You've apologized enough," she answered finally looking up at him, surprised he didn't look any differently to her. After her big realization, she thought for sure he would look different, but he didn't. Still handsome, still... Oisín O'Quinn.

He shrugged. "I just wanted to…"

"To what?"

"Make you smile?" He offered.

She stared at him for a long moment, then a smile lifted the corner of her lips. "You do."

He let out a breath and grinned. "Good. Come on, let's get back before I go back in there and buy more."

Naomi laughed but popped back in to wave at Lance and Sandra. Sandra winked at her, and Lance gave a big thumbs up. With that, Naomi and Oisín walked back through the throngs of foot traffic to Davis waiting in the public car park.

Chapter Twenty-Five

Once at the construction site, Oisín handed one of the spice bags to his chef who took it like he had just offered him the Holy Grail. His chef cleaned up the remaining food, which wasn't much and packed the tables and warmers away in the van he drove. Willie volunteered to help. But once the chef was gone, Willie came back grinning holding two six-packs of beer.

"I tell ya," he tossed a beer to each of them. "If I wasn't straight, I could kiss your chef. Still might. That man can cook *and* brings beer? Marry me."

Denis laughed. "You'd miss boobs."

"That's not all he'd missed," Callum called.

"Lads, come on," Oisín said with a glance at Naomi, her dad, and the young man named Bobby who looked at the beer skeptically.

"You're one to talk, O'Quinn," Naomi called back. "I think it's brave Willie put himself out and proud proclaiming to be straight."

"I *am* straight," Willie winked.

"Oh, sure you are, big boy," Naomi winked. "That's the story we're going with, got it."

Oisín, Denis, and Callum all burst out laughing.

"You can't deny it!" Oisín called.

"Sure I can!" Willie protested.

"Ah, it's okay, Willie, this is a safe space. No judgment," she said.

The lads laughed so hard Oisín felt tears on his cheeks.

"Whatever, ya gobshites. I'll remember this and as for you Miss Moon… I bow to your banter," Willie winked.

Naomi's grin eased Oisín's worry.

"Who is for watching the sunset on the deck of the beach house?" Oisín offered.

"Can't," Callum said after taking another long drink. "I got a date."

"A date?" Oisín questioned. "Since when? With whom?"

"Never you mind," he tapped the side of his nose, finished his beer, and mock saluted. Then, he piled into the second SUV with Willie and Denis.

"You lads leaving to?"

"Hey, what can I say? I'm exhausted," Denis said. "And I gotta keep Willie away from your chef."

"Sod off!"

"All right then, night lads," Oisín said. "Thanks for all your help today. I really appreciate it."

"Night!" They all called but Oisín didn't miss the quick glance between Callum and Byron and his bodyguard's subtle smirk and nod. It was strange, almost as if Byron put him up to it. *What is that about?* Oisín wondered.

"Bill, join us?" Oisín asked Naomi's dad.

"Oh, I need to talk to Byron for a minute then I think I'll head home. Start dinner," Bill explained.

"Okay, Naomi?" He asked.

"Um… I should probably help dad."

"No, honey, I got it. You stay. Enjoy your beer and the sunset. You always said it's your favorite."

"Sun*rise*, dad."

"Still sun related," Bill teased. "Byron, about that thing you wanted to talk to me about…"

Byron and Bill walked over to the trucks and began speaking in low tones.

"I guess it's just you and me, huh?" Oisín asked.

Naomi looked nervous and Oisín still hadn't figured out why. She was so quiet on the drive back from Pier Park, he wasn't sure if he had done something wrong. He didn't think he had. But then he remembered the phone call she had received.

As they walked down the duckboard, Oisín brought it up. "Everything all right with that phone call?"

"Hmm? Oh… yeah not really."

"I'm here if you need to talk."

She smiled softly. "Thanks. I'm helping plan our eighteen-year high school reunion party and the venue had a pipe burst. The organizer was frantic. She's crazy on a good day. Today wasn't a good day."

"Oh man, I'm sorry. I have to say, I've never heard of an eighteen-year reunion."

"Yeah it was Liv's idea. Something about how we've been out of school the same amount of years we were old when we graduated. I don't know. It sounded really stupid to me, but she's all for it."

They walked up the steps to the new deck of the beach house.

"Sounds fun," Oisín said. "I missed my reunions both sixth year and university. I was in Taiwan on a shoot."

"If it's anything like our reunions in the US, you didn't miss much besides corny games, bad punch, throwback music, and the hot guys from school have a potbelly and receding hairlines."

"Is that where you met your husband?"

"Ex-husband. And no. I met him college. But Martin, who you'll meet, was my high school sweetheart."

"Why would I meet him?" Oisín helped her sit on the edge of the deck since there was no railing up yet. And he hated the slight twinge of jealousy he felt when she mentioned her high school sweetheart.

"He's the foundation expert. He'll come back to inspect everything before the end of construction," she explained.

"Oh, and you still... with him..." He sat beside her, their legs dangling over the edge.

"No! No, we're friends. Only friends, will always be friends but no, nothing like that. Once, a long time ago, but no."

"Oh, okay good." They were quiet for a long while just watching the sunset dance on the water. "Why don't you have the reunion here?"

"What?" She questioned.

"It's not like I don't have the room. Do you think we'll be done with it in time?"

"Here? Like at your home?"

"Yeah, it's got a ballroom for god's sake. Do you think we'll be done with the reno in time?"

"It would be amazing but... I don't know. It's in four weeks. We'd have to put all our manpower into the mansion. And this," she looked around the beach house. "Would have to be put on hold."

"I wouldn't mind. I'm renting the house I'm currently in and the end date is open. I can move into either beach house or plantation when they are ready. But if it helps, use the mansion. It would be nice to have it lit up with a party to christen it."

"It would be amazing. Let me talk to dad about it. But we can't lose anymore guys. If we do, then it won't be done in time."

"My lads are here for as long as you need them. The other ones helping you out seem pretty loyal to you and Bill. Bobby is a great kid. Eager to please and knowledgeable. Callum took a shine to him and wants to help him. Reminds him of his kid brother."

"That's sweet."

"Reminds me a bit of my younger cousin Killian. Though I haven't seen him for years."

"Why not?"

"Not sure. He's a great car mechanic and took over his dad's business when Uncle Emmet retired. But every time I'm home, he's busy. Sometimes not even in Ireland. But I have no idea what he does." Oisín chuckled.

"Ooh could he be a spy," she teased.

"Ha, doubtful. The kid's as honest as they day is long. Like I said, reminds me of Bobby. But you know, your guys are loyal."

"Yeah but for how long?" She sighed. "You heard Emilio. God, I can't believe he showed up here. Spied on me." She drank from her beer.

"I know things are rough there, I'm sorry."

"I appreciate it, but he just doesn't understand me. It was always like that. I turned a blind eye to it."

"There must have been something you loved about him, right? Did it just progressively get worse overtime?" He asked.

"Yes and no. We were married after my mom died and I was looking for stability. She had met him and seemed to like him, so in my warped grief-stricken mind, that meant she had given her blessing. I really wanted to be with someone she had met. It was like I had part of her there since she knew him. But then, there were these little petty arguments. He would say random stuff about starting a family, having kids, just random things like that. We'd be watching TV, right? And a commercial comes on for diapers and he turned up the volume claiming he wanted to learn just in case. And then he paused and continued by saying, in case his sister had a baby because he knew we wouldn't."

"Do you not want kids?" Oisín asked taking a sip of his beer.

"Oh, I, um – I can't have any."

"I'm sorry. I didn't know."

"No, it's okay. I've come to terms with it. But he knew about my condition before we got married. I never hid it from potential long-term relationships."

"Then he's a bigger arse than I thought."

She chuckled. "Yeah he is."

They were quiet for a long time. Then, she turned to him. "Thanks. For not asking why."

"Why what?"

"Why I can't have kids."

"It's none of my business. I figured if you had wanted to share you would. But I'm not going to push. There's no need for you to deal with that on top of everything else today."

"It's been so long since I was first diagnosed, I forget sometimes that people don't know. And it's tough, you know? Hearing the *when are you going to get married again? When are you going to have kids? You're getting pretty old, you should think about starting a family.* I used to get it so many times when we went back to Hawaii with family members. Granted, they used to not know but they would ask even after I told them. They would conveniently forget and every time I had to go through it again. It got old really fast. It got to the point where I just forced a smile and shook my head. I'm a master at changing the subject."

"I bet."

"But then I'd go to the bathroom and cry my eyes out silently. I've always wanted kids and to know I cannot have them due to something I was born with and have no control over, it's tough."

"And you hoped your family would understand," Oisín said. "We're not living in the ancient times where women are measured by how quickly they can get a husband and have a couple of kids. You are a strong, successful, beautiful woman and that is what the world should judge you by, not by the contents of your ovaries."

Naomi was silent and Oisín worried he overstepped. He turned to apologize and was stunned by the tears in her eyes.

"No one has ever said that to me."

"Then it's high time they did. You have so much to offer and they're eejits if they can't see you for who you are. A truly remarkable woman."

Naomi stared at him for a long time, then, slowly, she leaned toward him. Ever so slowly, he leaned toward her. Time stood still as the setting sun's rays danced across the water and the Gulf breeze caressed their faces. Oisín cupped her jaw and gently pressed his lips to hers.

The kiss was sweet, exploratory, innocent. It was unlike every other kiss he had ever experience. Even his first kiss was a prelude to a heavy make out session in his dad's old Range Rover with a village lass. But the first kiss with Naomi was beautiful. And he wanted it to go on forever.

But suddenly, Naomi pulled back with a gasp and pressed shaking fingers to her lips.

"No," she breathed. "Oh, no no no no no no no no no. Not good. Not good." She stood quickly, nearly losing her balance. Oisín caught her arm but she pulled away.

"Naomi?" He asked.

"Oh no no no no no. This can't happen. This can't. No. Not good. You're a client."

"I'm your friend too, I hope." Even as he said it, his stomach clenched.

"You're a client," her voice was final. "You're... you, and I'm... me. No, this can't. Do not do this to me. Don't ruin me for all other guys. It's not fair."

Oisín had a surge of jealousy race through him at the thought of other men kissing her. Touching her. But he didn't have time to think about it. Naomi hurried across the deck and down the steep stairs. Oisín tried to follow but she had a quicker step than he did and was on was in her pickup truck before he reached the mansion.

"Naomi!" He shouted after her, but his voice was drowned by out by the cloud of dust and the roar of the old engine as she drove her truck down the dirt drive to the main road.

Oisín stood staring after her. What the hell did he do now?

Chapter Twenty-Six

Naomi weaved in and out of traffic to put as much distance between her and Oisín O'Quinn as possible.

She still felt the tingle of his kiss against her lips. The sweetness of his hands cupping her jaw, the gentleness of his eyes, and the passionate words he spoke in her defense. All of it meant more than she was willing to say.

Tears threatened but she swallowed them back. She didn't want to get hurt again. The image of her husband with the blonde morphed into Oisín in bed with any of the faceless, nameless women she had seen him with and a sob broke from her lips. Pulling into the drive of her house, she put the truck in park and gave in. She wept harder than she had before. She never shed a tear when Emilio cheated. She never shed a tear when the divorce was finalized but then, she wept. *Why?* She questioned.

Unsure how long she stayed in the truck, she startled when the driver's side door opened and her dad's worried voice spoke.

"Honey? Was wrong? What happened? Are you okay?" He wrapped his arms around her at an awkward angle but she buried her head into her dad's chest, breathing in the familiar comforting scent of him and let her tears fall.

Bill, fortunately, said nothing, just let her cry and gently stroked her back. When she finally had her tears under control, she pulled back and looked up at her dad's concerned face.

"I love him, Daddy. I love him and I kissed him."

"Honey, that's okay," he said. "He's a good guy. Why are you so upset? Did he do something else?"

"No, he... he's a client, daddy. I can't – I—"

"Honey," he interrupted her. "It's okay. It's not the end of the world. So you kissed him, big deal. Did he kiss you back?" She nodded. "Okay, that's good."

"It's not good, he's going to hurt me. I know he is."

"Sweetheart, you don't know that. You cannot judge every guy as Emilio. Oisín isn't like him."

"It doesn't matter. I freaked out and ran away."

"Oh now come on," he soothed. "It's not the end of the world. Did you tell him you loved him?"

"No!"

"Okay, why didn't you say anything?"

"Because he's him, and I'm me." She said again.

"Yes, correct me if I'm wrong but he being him is who you fell in love with, right?"

"It's not that simple."

"It really is, honey. Ask yourself what it is about him you fell for? Then, think would that change after you kissed him or is it the foundation of why you kissed him. Now, come on honey. Let's get you inside. There's nothing wrong with this. You're adults, both single. It's okay."

Naomi didn't resist when her dad helped her out of the car and walked with her tucked under his arm to the house.

Oisín couldn't sleep. He tossed and turned but couldn't get Naomi's horror-stricken face out of his mind. To kiss her was heaven. She was soft and sweet, yet he felt the fiery passions that lay just under the surface. If he could just coax it out, he knew he would never want to let her go again. But he didn't know what to do. He was falling in love, and she ran away from him. He wasn't a bad guy. He had learned his lesson speaking with his lads about it. Why was she so... horrified?

With a frustrated groan, he tore the sheets off him and pulled on a pair of shorts. Stuffing his feet into his running shoes, he snuck past Byron's closed door and down the stairs to the main floor. His night guards looked up from their chess game to see him. He waved at them.

"Just waiting on Byron," he said hoping his bodyguard wouldn't get in trouble, but he needed to be alone. They seemed content with his explanation and went back to concentrating on their game.

Oisín let himself out to the deck quietly and, without a glance back, hurried down the steps to the private boardwalk over the dunes and then he was free. Taking a precious moment to inhale the salt air tinged with the smell a fish and the sharp musky scent of the sand, he let the healing power of the beach wash over him. Then, he was running. The freedom of running alone for the first time in five years made him smile. He loved Byron's companionship but there were times where he missed being alone. Pre-dawn of a beautiful day was one of them. He cleared his mind of Naomi, his feelings, his job, everything that caused him to think too hard and simply focused on putting one foot in front of the other.

Looking out to the water, he saw something jump near the horizon. He looked closer and saw it again. Dolphins. He grinned. They were playing and seemed to follow him, though Oisín knew they were too far away to see him. He still ran. Unsure how far he had gone, he pulled up near a small river feeding the Gulf. He panted as he pulled his shirt up to wipe his face. The sun peeked just above the horizon, and everything was calm... for a moment.

Then, he heard it. The roar of an ATV. Looking around, he saw the vehicle, looking like a souped up three-wheel motorcycle and its helmeted and tinted visor wearing operator. The ATV drove right toward him, kicking up sand as he approached.

Oisín watched. The operator twisted the handlebars and spun around him in a circle, revving the engine as he went. Sand kicked up all around him making a cloud. It all happened so fast, but for a fleeting moment, Oisín was truly scared. The operator pulled something out of their pocket and pointed it at him. Only then did Oisín see the glint of a barrel of a handgun.

"Oisín!" He heard a deep voice bellow. The operator stopped spinning around him and looked over their shoulder. Pocketing the gun they took off driving the ATV as fast as they could down the beach.

Another vehicle pulled up beside him and Byron jumped out. "Get after him!" He shouted to the second vehicle as he grabbed Oisín and pushed him low like he did at the club that night and bundled him into the back of the other vehicle.

"Drive," he ordered Davis who whipped the vehicle around, leaving his own cloud of sand and raced back to the house.

Byron did not speak on the drive back and did not look at Oisín. Only after they climbed the deck stairs to the main floor did Byron's barely controlled anger explode.

"What the hell did you think you were doing!"

"It was stupid, I know," Oisín replied.

"Stupid? Stupid! It was idiotic! Do you have a death wish? Tell me now so I can find a new job."

"I didn't know," Oisín tried.

"You didn't... oh that's rich. You knew we didn't know the identity of the shooter. You knew not to go out by yourself. And to tell Nelson and Badger you were waiting on me? Then, sneak off on your own? Thank God I woke early. Do you have any idea..." he huffed out. "Damn it, Oisín!" Byron shouted.

For a man who hardly spoke loudly enough to be heard over the base at a club, all of the shouting was new.

Oisín stepped toward him. "I'm sorry. I just wanted a few minutes alone. Like I used too."

"Is my company too much for you? Tell me and I can assign someone else."

"No, I wouldn't want anyone else. I'm sorry, By. I didn't think. My head's all over the place and I just needed some time to think."

"Never. Again."

"I promise."

Byron stared at him for a long moment, then nodded once. Turning to the other guards still in the kitchen, he spoke. "Call the others see where they are with the perp."

"Yes sir," he answered and called their code names over the closed-circuit walkie.

"How did you know where to find me?" Oisín asked.

Byron pulled out his phone. "HQ got this off social media. They masked their IP address so it's of little use, but it was enough for me to get a call and thank God I did. Another minute you would have been shot."

Byron passed his phone over and Oisín looked at the tweet. A photo of him running on the beach with the caption: *I hope you die.*

Oisín swallowed as a shiver raced up his spine. "Who is doing this?"

"I don't know. But I will find out. I promise, Osh."

Oisín nodded. "I need... I need to take shower."

"We're heading out to the site by nine."

"I... I don't know if she'll want me there."

"Why? What happened?"

Byron looked genuinely concerned and Oisín sighed.

"I kissed her and she ran away."

Byron sucked his teeth for a moment then shrugged, "she's not one to run easily."

"She claims I'm her client and it's unethical or whatever. I don't know. Emotions were high. I think I should steer clear. I'll stay inside, leave one of the guys with me. You go. She'll need you."

"If you're sure."

"Yeah. Feel it out for me? Ask Bill if I did something wrong?"

"I'll talk to him."

"Thank you. You are a great friend, By."

Byron's lips tipped up in a half smile. Oisín stopped on the third stair and turned.

"Oh, by the way, could you do me one small favor?"

"Anything."

"Could you find out who's organizing the eighteen-year high school reunion for Naomi's high school? And get me her number. It's Liv something."

"Olivia Nicole Harrison. Naomi said the name when I stepped outside with her. I'll get her number. Anything else?"

"Just keep an eye on Naomi? I hate to think I hurt her in any way."

"I'll watch for her."

"Thanks." With a dejected smile, Oisín trudged up the stairs to his master suite and jumped in the shower.

Chapter Twenty-Seven

Two weeks. It had been two weeks since Oisín and Naomi had kissed, and she still hadn't seen him. She was pretty sure she scared him off. Every day she would wake up, attempt to meditate, drive to the construction site, see Byron, Callum, Denis, and Willie all there but when she looked at Byron hopefully, he shook his head. Her chest felt heavy, like a cinder block was weighing her down. She could no longer deny she missed him and part of her hated that, the other part nearly sobbed when yet another day went by and he wasn't there.

The mansion, which was the sole focus of their attention, was coming together nicely. The kitchen was nearly complete, the sagging floors had been jacked up, and the couple broken tiles from settling had been replaced. The new footers in the basement had been poured and the columns covered in reclaimed wood from an architectural salvage yard in Panama City.

The ballroom fireplace had a new mantle installed to match the ornate turn of the century style. The crumbling ceiling had been scraped away and new beams installed. The recessed fresco had been restored by a local painter and the alcoves had fresh velvet curtains replacing the old moth-eaten ones. The music room had been deep cleaned, the ornate piano shined and tuned. The master bedroom had been completely remodeled, Byron helping pick out furniture from a catalog for Oisín's bedroom. Without him there and her calls and texts going unanswered, Naomi threw herself into the secret Irish pub project in the basement. Getting some pointers from Callum who had stumbled upon her idea while looking for her. It had become their little secret.

Another two weeks and still nothing, Naomi grew angrier by the day. Then, as she stood in the completed pub in the basement, four weeks after their kiss on the deck, placing the last trinket above the mirror over the bar, her anger morphed to loss and sadness. Tears slipped down her cheeks again and she groaned in frustration wiping them away, she stared at the little trinket, a double rainbow pin, an ode to their banter. But the name of the pub she had waffled on for weeks and as the custom tin sign glinted in the dim light, she hoped he liked it.

Chasing after Moonbeams.

"Honey?" Her dad called as he walked down the steps. "Oh wow, this looks great!"

"I hope so."

"It really does. I feel like I'm in Ireland."

"Good. Do you think he'll like it?"

"I do. I really do."

"Good." She wrapped her arms around herself. "I wish I could see his reaction."

"I'm sure you will. But hey, the caterers are here."

Naomi nodded. She had gotten the updated invite from Olivia three weeks ago and knew the reunion was taking place at Oisín's home that evening.

"What time is it?"

"About five," her dad said. "Why don't you go home, honey? Get ready for the reunion."

"I'm not going."

"What?" He gasped. "You absolutely have to!"

"No, I really don't. And I don't want to. I'm not in a partying mood."

"Honey," her dad rested his hands on her arms. "We're sponsors. You need to represent. Please?"

Naomi sighed. She hadn't thought of the business just her own pain. Nodding once, she agreed.

"That's my girl. Go on home. I'll finish cleaning up."

She took one more look at the space she had created for Oisín O'Quinn, the man she realized too late she loved and walked up the steps.

She was numb as she headed to her truck, numb she drove home, numb as warm water sluiced down her body in the shower and numb as she zipped up her black formal A-line, asymmetrical gown. Pulling on her strappy black pumps, she looked in the mirror. The reflecting image made her ache even more. She looked like her mother. Tears gathered in her eyes, but like a breath on the wind, she felt her mother's soft hand on her cheek.

"Shh shh, darling. You look beautiful. And Oisín is an idiot if he doesn't see it." She heard her mother's voice, and it made her laugh through her tears.

"I love you, Mama."

"I love you, too, Ni. Now go knock 'em dead."

Opening her eyes once more, her tears stopped, and she took a deep breath. Wiping the tracks away, she stared at herself again.

"Come on, Moon," she pep talked. "You don't need a man, never have. Yes, it would be nice but if he was easily scared away, he's not the one for you. Let's knock 'em dead." She grinned as she used her mother's words. Gripping her clutch, it was time to go.

Checking her phone as she walked to the door, she saw a text from Byron.

Byron: Davis is outside. Oisín asked him to pick you up.

She blinked in surprise at the words. But then replied.

Naomi: Oisín asked, huh? Why do I get the feeling it was your idea and you're simply giving him credit?

Byron: I never lie, Naomi. Though I thought about it, Oisín asked me to make sure you do have a car. He wants you to enjoy yourself tonight and didn't want you to worry about drinking and driving.

Naomi: If he did think that, why didn't he text me?

Byron: He has his reasons. Please, enjoy yourself.

Naomi: Will you and the lads be there?

Three dots popped up as if he was typing, then disappeared. Then popped up again, then disappeared. When they didn't pop up again and no text came through, she huffed and walked to the kitchen door. Locking up, she turned to see a black limo and Davis, Oisín's driver, standing next to the door. When he saw her, he smiled and opened the door for her.

"Good evening, Miss Moon," he said.

"Hello, Davis. Thanks for picking me up."

"Of course, happy to, miss." He held the door as she slipped in. He shut the door and hurried to the driver's side. Once in and the car was in gear, he looked in the rearview. "May I be so bold as to say you look lovely tonight, miss?"

"Thank you, Davis."

"Mr. O'Quinn made sure there was champagne on ice for you. I opened it as soon as I saw some movement. Please feel free to pour yourself a glass."

"Thank you." A glass of champagne did sound good. Taking the bottle, she poured a full glass and took a sip. It was crisp, cold, and delicious.

She looked out the window watching the sunset on the Gulf of Mexico.

"Would you like some music, Miss Moon?" Davis asked.

"No thanks," she answered.

They were quiet for a long moment before Naomi spoke again.

"Have you seen Oisín?"

Davis' eyes flashed in the rearview again, but it was only for a moment before they were back on the road.

"Yes, I just left him."

"Is he... okay?"

"As okay as he could be after the second attempt on his life."

"What?" Naomi shrieked sitting up.

Davis winced. "I'm sorry, I don't think I was supposed to say anything."

"Is he okay? Is he hurt? What happened?"

"Miss, I—"

"Tell me!"

Davis licked his lips and sighed. He launched into the story of how Oisín snuck out of the house for an early morning run and he was nearly shot by a person driving an ATV. That person was not found.

Naomi's heart beat so fast she worried she would need a hospital. She grabbed her phone and shot off a text.

Naomi: I know you don't want to talk to me, you've made that clear, but I would have hoped you thought enough of me to be my friend and to tell me that you were nearly killed again. I'm glad you're okay but I would much rather have heard it from you.

Pocketing her phone, she drained the champagne glass and watched the scenery change as Davis pulled into the dirt driveway. She looked with pride over the hedgerow and trimmed trees. The gate was no longer falling off, the new wrought iron held a scrolled design and was etched with the crest of the O'Quinn name. It looked posh but tasteful.

Davis pulled around the fountain and to the door. She waited until he opened the door for her, and she took in the mansion for the first time as a visitor instead of a contractor and pride flare deep in her belly. It was beautiful.

"Have a wonderful evening, Miss Moon. When you're ready to return home, please text Byron and he will call me," Davis offered.

"Thank you," Naomi said and walked up the steps to the doors which were open with two liveried footmen on either side.

"Welcome, Miss Moon," one said, and they bowed, extending their arm through the door in welcome.

Music played from somewhere inside and the whole place was lit with light and laughter. Moon Construction's banner was proudly placed near the door and the reunion banner was strung up on the stairwell overlook. Balloons were placed around the area and Naomi took a moment to remember what it looked like when she and her dad had first walked in.

"Dear God, you look stunning."

She whipped around but her smile fell instantly, then she forced a smile back on her lips.

"Martin, hi," she said. "Thanks."

"Wow, I've not disappointed you that badly before."

"What? Oh, no no, I am happy to see you."

"You can't lie to me, Ni," he replied.

"Oh yeah, I forgot you put those freaky skills to use in the military. What branch was it again?" She teased.

As usual, Martin's lip ticked up but he said nothing about his military service. He did however move closer to her and speak low.

"That and I know you. I know everything about you. I could always read you, Ni."

"That was a long time ago, Mart," she said.

He softly stroked her arm. "It doesn't feel that long ago to me." But then, like the spell he was under broke, he dropped his arm and smiled sadly. "Who was that smile for, Ni? It's okay. Our time has been over for nearly two decades. I get it. Who's caught your eye, now?"

"Umm…"

"Ah! Oh my God, Mimi!" Olivia's screechy voice screamed. "You're here! You look auh-maze-ing!"

Naomi forced to smile and was about to return the compliment when Olivia continued.

"This place! I nearly fainted when Oisín O'Quinn called me to personally offer his place and told me you and your dad would have it ready! He insisted on using your name, not his as sponsor. I can't believe you held out on me!" She slipped her hand through Naomi's arm and walked with her toward the ballroom. "You have to tell me everything! You know he's my dream come true. What's he like? Is he single?"

"Oh – I don't really…" she and Liv had reached the ballroom and Naomi stared. It looked beautiful. The chandeliers glistened, the two-tone tiles were polished to perfection. Everything was perfect. Except one thing. Oisín wasn't…

The crowd parted and the very man she was thinking about ambled through as if her mind had conjured him. He was dressed in a traditional tuxedo with one minor change. The suit pants tapered just slightly to show his polished black silver buckled shoes. He was there. He looked amazing.

And he was staring at her like he wanted to devour her whole.

Staying away from Naomi Moon for four weeks was the hardest thing Oisín O'Quinn ever had to do. It was harder ignoring her texts and phone calls. He begged Byron and Callum, Willie, and Denis to keep an eye on her. But it wasn't like physically being there.

He had stayed away for two reasons, firstly, he wanted to give her space after their kiss. Secondly, after nearly being killed, he wanted to keep her safe. But every day, hour, minute that went by where he did not speak to her was torture. And as he watched her, he realized how much he missed her.

"You're here," she breathed.

"I'm here," he confirmed.

She stared at him for a long moment. He wasn't sure if he needed to apologize, but thinking back to her last text, he knew he should.

"Naomi, I owe you an—" He couldn't continue. His Little Miss Moonbeam grasped his lapels, yanked him forward, and slammed her lips against his.

Grunting due to the sheer force of her kiss, he quickly corrected and clutched her to him, kissing her back with every passion inside him. She was it. She was his woman. He just had to convince her.

Naomi pulled back and stared up at him. His lips quirked as he watched her. She looked at him with such happiness but that soon morphed into something he couldn't discern. Then, he felt a slight sting against his cheek.

He couldn't help himself, he burst out laughing. She had slapped him.

Their relationship had come full circle.

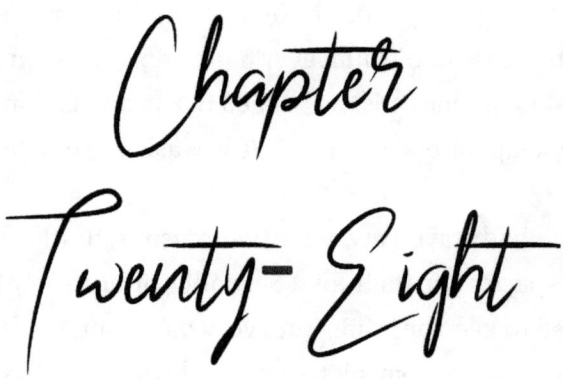

Chapter Twenty-Eight

Naomi couldn't believe she had done that. She had wanted to kiss him but to slap him? Listening to his chuckle, she was grateful he seemed all right with everything. Maybe she should apologize.

"Hello to you too," he grinned.

"I'm sorry."

"No, you're not," he winked. "And it's... what did your uncle call it? Kismet?"

She laughed but leaned into his touch as he slipped some hair behind her ear.

"I missed you," she said softly.

"I missed you too."

"Why did you shut me out?" Her eyes pleaded with him.

He sighed. "I needed to protect you. I didn't want the person who is after me to come after you too. And I thought you might want space."

"I know it seemed like that with how I reacted. I didn't need space. I freaked because of how... how I feel about you. I've never liked a client before."

"You renovated my house. You didn't treat me any differently than I treated you." He cupped her cheek. "And this place looks amazing."

"You like it?"

"I love it."

"You haven't gone into the basement yet, have you?" She questioned.

"No, why?" His lips widened into a grin.

"Just don't. Not without me."

"Okay," he agreed. "Right now, I would like to make one of your childhood dreams come true." He offered his hand. "Naomi Moon, will you dance with me in the Bay Tree mansion's ballroom?"

Her heart couldn't swell any larger as she took his hand. "You dance?" She asked.

"I dabble," he winked. "I won't step on your toes, if that's what you're asking."

"Good, I like these heels."

Oisín chuckled and Naomi decided it was one of her favorite sounds. He led her to the dance floor as the music started a slow song from the fifties. Holding each other close, they swayed to the music, dancing together to the tune of *Fly Me to the Moon*.

"Appropriate," he pronounced.

"Did you plan this?" She asked.

"I may have had a word with the DJ."

Naomi giggled.

"It is my house," he winked.

"Yes, it is."

"It really looks amazing, Ni."

"With the extra help it was easy to get everything done that was needed in time. The rest of the house isn't finished but the important parts are."

"I can't wait to see it completed."

"The beach house still isn't done."

"I didn't expect it to be," he said.

"Have you seen your room?" She asked.

"I did. It's perfect. I intend on sleeping here tonight."

"Good," she answered, then decided to be bold and went on. "Want company?"

He sighed a sigh she couldn't discern.

"Yes, but," he started. Her heart soared, then crashed. He pressed his forehead to hers. "I want to give you and I this. Please give this to me? One perfect night where sex isn't the end goal? I want you more than my next breath, but let's be together without *being* together. I will come to regret it, I know I will. But I respect you more than anyone or anything I've ever had or wanted. I… I've fallen in love with you, Naomi Moon."

Her breath caught in her lungs as his words washed over her. She had heard three men say that to her. One of them was standing on the side of the room. She had cared about Martin in high school, he was her first. She thought she was going to die when he left for boot camp and then war, but she never actually *loved* him. She knew that now. The second man to tell her that had been her ex-husband and the only image she saw when she thought of him was the one with the blonde. She had loved him enough to marry him, but she realized she never truly *loved* him. The third man to say that to her was holding her in his arms and never in her life before had she ever so confidently replied with; "good. Because I love you too, Oisín O'Quinn."

And the feeling that filled her heart at his instant bright reaction, told her all she needed to know. He kissed her once more and held her tightly. She reveled in his warmth, scent, and love.

After their dance, Oisín grabbed two glasses of champagne and met her back at the side of the room. They toasted each other and drank.

"And three... two... one," she mumbled into her glass.

"Mimi!" Olivia screeched and hurried over to her. "You never said a word! You know you're my hero, right? Oisín O'Quinn? I mean, how?"

"By being genuine," Naomi said smiling.

Olivia's grating laugh resounded through the room.

"Just remember our deal," she grinned at Oisín, then the song changed. "Oh yes! This is my jam! Come on, Dave let's dance."

As soon as she was out of earshot, Naomi looked over at him. "What deal?" She asked.

"To keep everything a secret and to change the plans at the last minute," he began. "I promised to name my first-born daughter Olivia."

Naomi choked on her champagne. "You what?" She gasped.

"Considering I have no intention of having a child, it was an easy agreement to make to ensure you were surprised and to make sure this went off without a hitch."

"Oisín," she breathed then laughed. "Wow."

He shrugged and drank more of his sparkling wine.

"Naomi?" Martin's voice distracted her and she looked over at his soft eyes and even softer smile.

"Martin," she replied. "Have you met Oisín O'Quinn?" The men shook hands as she continued speaking. "Martin is the best foundation expert in the city and my old high school flame."

"Och aye, Naomi's mentioned I might be meeting you. Thanks for your help on this place and the beach house."

"Oh no, it's my pleasure. I'm happy to meet you finally. I've come out a couple of times over the past few weeks and you weren't here," Martin said, and Naomi heard the slight challenge in his tone.

"Yeah, I had some personal issues to work through," Oisín replied.

"I saw the news. Glad you're okay for our Naomi's sake."

Martin glanced at her but seemed to see the look of warning in her eye. "Well, I'll leave you two alone but Ni, save me a dance? It'll be prom all over again." He winked and walked toward the group of their old friends.

Oisín looked at her, an amused look in his eye. "Prom, huh?"

She blushed slightly. "We dated through eleventh and twelfth grade."

"Good to know him," Oisín said. "And I respect a man who wants to make sure the guy who is dating the girl who he cares about is a good person."

"You men and your secret code language." Naomi chuckled.

"We're fluent in many languages," he winked. "But now, I was promised a view of the basement?"

Naomi's hands instantly grew sweaty, but she took another swallow of her champagne and set the empty glass on the tray of a passing waiter.

"Okay, but you have to promise that if you hate it, you'll let me redo it."

"I could never hate any design of yours."

"Even still."

"Okay, if I hate it, I'll tell you and let you redo it."

With that promise, Naomi took his hand and walked him through the door to the music room where the photo booth was set up and down the short hall to the basement door.

"Certain places speak to me and tell me what it wants to look like. This is what this told me. She opened the door and led him down the stairs not turning on the lights until they were both on the flat surface of the basement floor. Then, turning on the lights she spoke, "welcome to Chasing After Moonbeams Irish Floridian pub."

Oisín stared, his expression unreadable.

Chapter Twenty-Nine

Chasing After Moonbeams Irish pub, his own slice of home with a Floridian flare. He took in the crushed shell bar top, the Guinness plaque and taps, the old flags lining the ceiling, Ireland and his favorite football team, the padded stools, the dart board, the whiskey mural painted on the red brick, the pictures of his family, the lads; Callum, Willie, and Denis, the pins in the cork board of an Irish and American flag, *Keep Calm and Irish On*, and a small double rainbow pin that made him smile.

It was perfect.

Naomi had created the most perfect place for him and he absolutely loved her for it.

"Do you like it?"

"Like it? Ni, it's amazing!"

"Really?"

"Really," he grinned. "You did all of this for me?"

"I like to do a surprise project in a space for the homeowner that reflects their personality. Since we had no plans for the basement, I saw this and wanted to bring it out."

"Thank you, this is beyond anything I could have dreamed of," he hurried to her and scooped her up into a twirling hug eliciting a fit of giggles from her. Her arms wrapped around his shoulders and her body pressed to his, he slowly set her down and kissed her gently.

"Thank you," he breathed pulling back slightly and resting his forehead against hers.

"You are so welcome." Her hand stroked the short hairs on the back of his head as her right hand clutched his bicep. "Pour a drink?"

"I'll pour you one first."

"Okay," she grinned and stepped away as he lifted the flip up counter and stepped behind the bar admiring the glassware, wine cooler, taps, liquor, all high-end if not top shelf.

"Ni, this is amazing. Like absolutely incredible."

"I'm so glad you like it. Callum caught me down here one day working on the bar and he offered to help, at least after he called you a lucky sod."

"I'm sure he did. I see a couple inside jokes of ours around."

"Really? He offered a few pins, and he knew your favorite soccer team."

"*Football* team."

"In America, we call it soccer." She winked.

Oisín chuckled. "I know. Never understood why."

But he grabbed an imperial pint glass emblazoned with the Guinness logo and flipped it up catching it with his other hand. Naomi gasped a *woah* and laughed. She knew, he saw it in her eyes, she knew he was trying to impress her, but he didn't care. He grabbed the familiar black and gold tap handle and smiled.

"You know, have you ever been told or shown how to properly pour a pint of Guinness?" He asked pulling the handle to hear the satisfying nitro sound.

"Can't say I ever have," she answered sliding onto the barstool directly in front of him. "I usually drink beer out of a bottle or can."

Oisín chuckled. "Guinness is a very unique beer. There is none like it in the world. At least, none as good."

"Think you might be a bit biased?"

"A wee bit," he winked. "But it's a Nitro stout which means the bubbles look like they're sinking versus rising. It's an illusion but it makes it unique to watch." He stopped pouring about three-fourths of the way to the top of the glass. "And when you pour, you need to leave it just here," he set it down and leaned across the bar top. Naomi leaned forward too. "For one hundred and nineteen seconds."

"Why one hundred and nineteen seconds?" She asked breathlessly.

"Because that was the exact amount of time of the first kiss Arthur Guinness shared with the woman of his dreams." Oisín's voice went husky even as he whispered. They were so close, they shared air between them. Oisín's eyes stayed on hers but he leaned even further toward her.

"You made that up," she breathed.

He shrugged. "Doesn't make it any less of a good story."

She laughed quietly as he pulled back. Taking the glass in hand again, satisfied with how it settled, and finished pouring, swirling the glass at the end, a shamrock shape embedded in the foam.

"There," he set the glass before her. "The perfect pour for the very first pour of my new place. That's lucky you know."

"Is everything lucky with you?"

"I'm Irish."

She laughed but took the glass as he poured another. She held it and didn't drink. At his questioning gaze, she spoke. "Aren't I supposed to wait until we toast? And be sure to look me in the eye, O'Quinn, I'm not about to risk seven years bad sex again."

He tossed his head back and laughed but finished pouring and raised his glass to hers.

"May you always walk in sunshine, Naomi Moon. And with luck, I can walk beside you too." It was bold, but he had to say it.

"I look forward to it."

She clinked her glass to his, keeping their eyes locked and then drank.

Chapter Thirty

Oisín woke to an incessant buzzing in his ear. He groaned and slapped his phone. There was no way it was time to get up, it was still dark out. Instead instantly, the memories of the night before came back to him, and he smiled sleepily. He and Naomi had finished their beers and spent time at the basement bar so she could show him everything she had done, then they joined the reunion upstairs.

Olivia and a man named Dave Prince were crowned king and queen of the reunion and Oisín saw their... dance. It was clear they were going to leave together that evening.

Oisín and Naomi danced again and then grabbed some of the finger foods from the passing waiters. As the evening wound down, Oisín had Byron, who was standing off near the door to the patio watching them, call for Davis. His driver met them out front and Oisín walked her to the limo. She had kissed him once more and made him promise to never shut her out again no matter what.

With that promise, a *good night, thank you,* and *I love you,* Naomi slid into the back seat of the limo and Davis drove her back to her house. Oisín went up to bed thanking Byron for everything, showered, and fell into bed thinking of his Hawaiian beauty.

But to be woken by his phone buzzing at... he squinted... four in the morning, he nearly shut it off until he saw the name, Tony. His agent was desperate to get ahold of him. Before he had a moment to think, Byron entered his room and flipped on the light switch. Oisín's eyes watered and his eyelids spasmed attempting to filter the light.

"He's awake," Byron said on the phone. "Yes, sir." He hung up.

"What the hell is going on?" His first instinct was Naomi. "Is Naomi okay? What happened?"

"Naomi's fine. Call Tony back, now," Byron ordered.

The look on his bodyguard's face was enough motivation. Oisín dialed as fast as he could.

"What the hell have you done?" Tony's voice came over the phone sounding ragged.

"What?"

"Social media is blowing up. Your sponsors need a statement. Metric has already pulled the plug. What the hell did you do?"

"What?" Oisín's sleepy brain only comprehended some of what he was saying.

"Turn on the news." Tony gave him the call sign news whose early morning show was re-airing a previously recorded interview. Oisín grabbed his TV remote and switched the flat screen on. Finding the news station, he turned up the volume.

A woman sat in a comfortable chair, tears in her eyes, a ratty tissue between her fingers. The name on screen read, Molly Haywood.

"I don't know what to do," she was saying. "All I can say is, he's a predator."

"Do you want to see him in jail?" The news anchor asked.

"If that's what the courts decide. It's just so difficult seeing him everywhere knowing what he... did to me. And to know he could be out there right now doing it to someone else."

"If you could see your attacker, what would you say to him?"

"I'd say, please come clean. Don't hurt anyone else. I don't want money or an apology. I just want to make sure he can't hurt anyone else."

"You don't want an apology?" The reporter asked.

"No, I don't want to see him again. I don't want an apology because I don't want him to know about..." she pressed her fingers against her flat abdomen. Then, looking up, she continued. "I'm going to keep it. It's a miracle. But I don't want him in my baby's life."

"Well, you are very brave to come on here and name your attacker. We wish you and your baby the best." The interview ended and the regular anchor for the morning took over.

"And there you have it, folks. Molly Haywood, a small-town girl from South Georgia, gaining nothing by telling her story."

"And what a sad story it is too, Bob," the co-anchor shook her head. "It's a tragedy when these women have to come out and share the most devastating event in their lives when local law enforcement failed them."

"Indeed, Sarah indeed, and I'll be honest, I followed Oisín O'Quinn's career for a long time, even interviewed him myself. It just goes to show, you can never really know someone."

"Mmm, very true."

"But in other news, doctors have discovered a rare strain of swine flu and why your dog may be susceptible to it. Stay with us after the break."

"What did you do?" Tony's voice rang in his ear, but Oisín's whole body tingled. His mouth was dry. His ears rang, his heart pumped blood so fast he felt lightheaded.

"I – I didn't do anything."

Byron walked over to him and sat next to him.

"I swear. I – I would never. Is she saying I ra-raped her?" His voice caught on the word. "She's... pregnant?"

"We have to get ahead of this. This is not good. I'll put together a statement. Get your ass to New York, now."

"Tony, I—"

"Save it. I don't care. I've got to work now. Get on your plane and get here ASAP." With that, Tony hung up.

Oisín turned to Byron. "You know I wouldn't. I couldn't."

"I know," Byron said. "I know but that doesn't help this situation."

"This is… my career is over."

"Not necessarily," Byron replied. "I don't remember her, and I don't think you do either."

"That doesn't matter, look at precedence. One story like this, true or not and I'm ruined."

"Let's get to New York. Let's see what Tony says. But text Naomi and tell her to call you. She deserves to hear it from you. I'll pack your bag but hurry."

Oisín nodded and sent Naomi a text as he headed down to get a cup of coffee, not that his shaking hands needed caffeine. He texted Callum, Willie, and Denis not expecting an answer so when his phone rang a text, he nearly dropped it.

Callum: You're full of shite, but one thing I do know, you'd never force yourself on a woman. Tell me what you need, my friend.

Oisín: Your support means so much to me. I'm heading to New York City. I'm transferring money to you because I'm taking the plane. Get your tickets and get home.

Callum: We don't need your money, Osh.

Oisín: Please. Take it.

Callum: Fine. Let me know what happens.

Oisín: I will. Thank you.

Byron walked down the back stairs to the kitchen, Oisín's and his duffel bags in both hands.

"Come on, I've already reached out to our pilot. He'll meet us there in an hour," Byron said.

Oisín nodded and glanced at his phone. There was no text or call from Naomi, but it wasn't even five o'clock yet and he hoped she was still asleep dreaming of him.

Naomi woke from a wonderful dream. She smiled as she stretched seeing the sunrise peeking over the horizon. Taking a deep breath, she reached for her phone about to text Oisín a good morning. Checking her phone, she saw the time was just before five-thirty and she had a text from him already.

Oisín (she changed his name in her contacts): Ni, please call me. Something happened and I don't honestly know what to do.

Naomi didn't hesitate. The text had been sent almost an hour ago. She sat up and dialed his number. It rang about four times before he picked up.

"Naomi?" His voice was loud, and she could hear an engine in the background.

"Oisín?" She questioned. His voice was stressed. "What's going on? Are you okay?"

"I—" his voice cracked. "I honestly don't know. There's... I didn't do it."

"Do what?"

He took a deep breath and let it out harshly. "On the news," he began. "A woman claimed that I – I..." he sounded on the verge of tears.

"Oisín, I believe you. Talk to me."

He breathed again. "She claimed I... forced myself on her. That I raped her and she's... she claims she's pregnant. I didn't do it, Naomi. I swear to you, I didn't do it. I never could. I swear, Naomi. I swear."

"Hey hey," she tried to soothe him, her heart aching for him. Was he a playboy? Yes. Was he one who looked at women as playthings? Yes. Would he violate a woman? Not in a million years and Naomi knew it beyond question. "I believe you."

A small sob echoed through the phone. "Thank you."

"It will be okay. What does your agent say?" She asked.

"Osh, we gotta go." She heard Byron on the other end call to him.

"Where are you going?" She asked.

"Tony wants me in New York to give a statement. We're flying out now."

"Oh," she answered. "Okay. Call me when you land?"

"You still want me?"

"Of course. This changes nothing for me. I believe you."

"But what if..." he paused. "What if—"

"What if you slept with her and don't remember?" She offered. At his affirmative noise, she continued. "Byron is at your hip at all times. Of anyone, he would know, right? Let's cross that bridge when or if it comes to it. All you need to do, is focus on getting to New York and doing whatever it is your agent tells you to do to get ahead of this."

He took another deep breath. "I wired the rest of the construction money to you and your dad. I hope it's enough. I don't know if I'll be back anytime soon. But please use it for whatever you need and let me know if you need any more."

"It'll be okay. I promise. I love you."

He whimpered slightly. "I love you, too. Thank you for believing me."

"Always. Have a safe flight. Call me when you land, please."

"I will, I gotta go."

"Okay."

With that, Naomi ended the call but immediately sent a text with *I love you* and the heart eyes emoji. Something to make him smile and flopped down in bed.

Knowing she would regret it, she opened her social media app and read the breaking news along with all the ugly and disgusting comments. Naomi knew there were bad people out there, both men and women, but to read some of the comments turned her stomach. They had crucified Oisín without question. They had taken the word of a woman and didn't care if it was true or not. Naomi prided herself on believing the stories of those poor women who had to deal with misogynistic bosses, coworkers, even on the street. She had been affected just over a month ago. She believed women when they claimed sexual harassment, abuse, or rape but were they *all* legit? Statistically, no. How many actors, singers, politicians, and nobodys, had false accusations hurled at them only to have their career torn down and when it came out that she had been paid by an opponent, or just lied because she wanted to tear someone's life down, the media printed a small paragraph with the retraction. All those stories, Naomi dismissed as rare and people should always believe the victim, but what if the victim was the man? All the faceless, nameless people that had happened to, blended into Oisín's face.

"Oh god," she breathed out as tears slipped out of her eyes and down her cheeks. People were saying horrible things about him, and Naomi could only hope he didn't read any of it.

There were so many times she wanted to reply on someone's comment where they said how horrible Oisín was. She wanted to tear them apart, rip them limb from limb for spreading lies but she couldn't and didn't. She had no personal social media account and wouldn't risk her father's company's reputation, but it made her so angry.

Yes, women should be believed, too few of them are. It was sad how often they weren't listened to or believed in a patriarchal society, but false claims are what perpetrated that type of society. Society would never grow so long as lies were allowed to go unpunished for either men or women.

Her heart hurt for him.

Chapter Thirty-One

Oisín and Byron sat outside his agent's office at eleven o'clock that morning. The pilot made good time, but they lost an hour due to the time change. Oisín wore his hat and sunglasses, but it wasn't enough. Paparazzi and news reporters crowded outside the front door to his agent's office Uptown and Byron had to push them back. They all shouted questions at him, but he ignored them and hurried inside the building, security holding them back.

They waited on the twentieth floor for Tony to finish his phone call. Finally, the secretary told them he was free, and they both walked in.

Tony looked ragged. His suit was rumpled, his dress shirt unbuttoned at the collar and his tie was loose around his neck. Tony glanced at the door and, with no preamble, spoke to Oisín.

"If you had anything to do with this, tell me now."

"Tony, I promise you I did not. Neither Byron nor I remember her at all. Have we checked her out? What's the full story?"

"We haven't had time. This hit us out of left field. We have two statements written. One that says you have nothing to do with it and will fight it. And one that apologizes and promises to get help for your sex addiction."

"I don't have a sex addiction. What the hell, Tony?" Oisín demanded.

"It's a viable excuse."

"No viable excuse. I'm innocent!" Oisín shouted. Tony said nothing and Oisín calmed. "What's the damage done?"

"Metric has pulled their offer but have told me they're open to discussion and wishes you well. Versace has issued a statement. For now, they're pulling all ads with your image. Your last shoot was set to launch in two weeks but that has been put on hold. Balenciaga has issued a public denouncement. GRP security firm has pulled their team. Byron's instructions are to finish here, drop you at your hotel, and report back to headquarters."

"They can't do that," Oisín gasped looking back at Byron.

"You don't pay him directly. He's on contract to us through GRP. They have ended the contract and are pulling your guards. I have spoken with the commissioner of the NYPD and he's offering four officers on rotation."

"I don't want NYPD. I want my bodyguard. The man I trust with my life."

"That's not an option."

"The hell with this! I'm innocent!" Oisín protested.

"That doesn't matter. She has public opinion on her side. In their eyes, you did it."

"So I have no recourse? I'll go down as a rapist?" Oisín demanded.

"No, of course we'll fight it. Counter it with a libel suit but for now, you need to read the statement and familiarize yourself with it. Then, we have a press conference in thirty minutes. You look like shit which is good. It'll sell the statement. Prep, I'm going to get more coffee."

Oisín sat in the chair with a huff. "How the hell did I end up here?" He asked Byron. Then, without waiting for a reply, continued. "Please don't leave me, By."

"I have to check in. But I promise I will make a case. I'll do my best," Byron said

Oisín nodded. "That's all I can ask. Thank you."

Byron nodded once and fell silent as Oisín read the statement.

Naomi watched Oisín take the podium on the TV in her living room. Her dad, the lads, and Naomi huddled together. Oisín's hands shook as he took a sip of the water they gave him. Then, he looked out at the crowd of reporters.

"Good afternoon," he spoke clearly even if there was a telltale vibrato to his voice. "I am standing before you today to proclaim my innocence of the charges brought against me by Miss

Haywood. I have no reason to doubt she was deeply hurt by someone but that someone isn't me. I profusely deny the allegations that I," his voice cracked. "That I raped her on June 2nd. I have two sisters, a mother, aunts, nieces, and many female cousins and friends and the idea I could... the idea I could do something so heinous is beyond reprehensible. It is disgusting. I am deeply sorry for her pain, but I can assure all that it has nothing to do with me. I welcome Miss Haywood to discuss this issue openly with me with an agent of her choosing, which I will gladly provide, to get to the bottom of this once and for all. I can only reiterate my innocence in this matter and hope to have this resolved fairly, impartially, and as quickly as possible. Thank you."

The reporters threw questions at him, but he was carted off the stage before answering.

Naomi stared unseeing at the TV.

"Well, let's hope the public hear the truth in his words," Callum stated.

"Aye, poor bugger," Willie replied.

"Who would do that?" She asked. "Who would lie about him like that?"

"A lot of people want their five minutes of fame, honey," her dad said. "She could have been paid."

"By whom?" She stressed. "Oisín has no enemies. No more than the usual person."

"Modeling is a tough business." Denis offered. "Maybe he crossed the wrong person."

"First someone shoots at him, now this? Something isn't right," Naomi said. "We need to find more info on the woman."

"Woah, who's this *we*?" Callum asked.

"I would have thought you'd want to help your friend fight this," Naomi stated.

"Well yeah, but I mean... we're nobody," Denis said.

"We're all he has."

They stared at her for a long moment, then nodded.

"We'll need reinforcements." Callum pulled out his phone and put it to his ear. "Killian, it's Callum, Oisín's in trouble."

Naomi sat on her bed, her back to the headboard, her laptop open on her bent legs. The day had passed in making plans to help Oisín. She had an idea. Finding Molly Haywood's social media through a friend of a friend, Naomi scoured through to see if she could find anything from June 2nd. When it wound up being a bust, she switched gears and looked for Oisín's. June 2nd he was at a party in New York City. After going through what felt like hundreds of pictures, not seeing Molly in any of them, Naomi searched for the party venue and found more. She did see Molly then, in two pictures. She was speaking to a man, but his face was obscured she saved the photos and printed them off. Then, she did a reverse image search, thanks to some fancy tech Callum had Killian install on her computer, on Molly's face. Wading through the dozens of articles of her claim about him, she found an archived news article from a few years back with her face, but her name was Molly Hester and she was married to a Dominic Jackson Hester. The name sounded familiar. She began her search for the elusive Mr. Hester when her phone rang.

"Hello?" She answered distractedly.

"Oh, sweetie, how are you? Are you okay? I can't believe it!"

"Olivia?"

"Who else? I can't believe it! I feel dirty being in his home! I feel dirty just speaking to him! And seeing you kiss him? Ugh! Honey, I'm so sorry! I should have stopped him. He's such a predator."

Naomi's whole body shook with anger at Olivia's words.

"You're more of a sexual predator than he is!" Naomi shouted. "How dare you judge him when you know nothing about him! You screwed ninety-nine percent of the guys in our high school and I'm willing to pay money that some of them didn't want you, but you coaxed and said how good you would make them feel. I remember your boasts. How dare you! Of anyone, Oisín is a good, kind, generous man who gives everything and anything he has to people in need. He is considerate, a gentleman, and he is worth one thousand times more than you. I'm sick of people like you, you are two faced, manipulative, and think just because daddy is rich you can have anything and everything you want. We're done, Olivia. I never want to speak to you again." Naomi hung up without giving her a chance to reply and threw her phone onto the mattress beside her.

"Honey?" She heard her dad's voice and looked up to see him standing in the doorway. A glass of wine and a plate with a sandwich in his hand. "What happened?"

"Olivia Harrison happened," she replied.

"What did she say?" Her dad came into her room and offered her the wine and sandwich.

"What everyone else is saying. Lies! All of it."

"You know I believe you and Oisín. I know he wouldn't do this."

"But?" Naomi prompted.

"But people aren't going to see it his way and even if some did... I hesitate to say, his career may be over."

"No, he loves what he does. I would hate for him to have to give that up."

"It's not up to you, honey. In the eyes of public opinion, he's done."

She shook her head at her dad's words. "I will do whatever I need to do to help him."

Bill stared at her for a long moment, then a soft smile appeared in his lips. "You do love him."

"God yes," she revealed on a sigh. "I love him so much."

"Then fight for him."

"How?"

"Go public. Tell the world who he truly is," her dad offered.

"He'd hate to have me involved. And how would it work? A small town contractor? Nobody would take me seriously."

"You love him, yes?"

"Yes."

"Then do anything for him."

Naomi stared at her dad for a long time then nodded. "Does Uncle Kei still have the contact at PCB News at 10?"

"Probably," Bill pulled out his phone and called his brother-in-law while Naomi took a bite of her sandwich. She woke her computer and continued her search on Dominic Hester.

Chapter Thirty-Two

It hadn't worked. Oisín sat in his penthouse apartment in New York watching yet another news segment about his statement and how behavioral and body language experts broke down his minute movements. They played the press conference he had after the shooting and one anchor kept saying that his erratic behavior could be caused by a number of different diseases. But one thing was always the same, they all sent their well wishes to Miss Haywood and hoped Oisín got what he deserved.

Oisín's head hurt, his heart ached, his whole body was worn out. Flopping back on the bed, he stared up at the ceiling. He hadn't slept well and though he tried to catch two hours after the press conference, he couldn't shut his brain off. Taking his phone in hand he opened his music streaming app and found the sound of waves crashing against the shore. Putting the sound on mid-level, he shut his eyes and tried to force his brain to stop thinking.

It lasted a few minutes until the waves were interrupted by his agent's ringtone. His stomach fell but he answered anyway.

"Hello?"

Tony just took a breath and let it out.

"Tell me, Tony."

"It's not good. Your sponsors have dropped you. The agency... They are wanting me to stop representing you."

"I didn't do this, Tony," Oisín's voice was pleading.

"I know. I know, Osh. I'm so sorry. I don't think we were ready for something this big. When you fired Nic—"

"Who's Nic?"

"Your PR Rep."

"The arse who didn't prep me right for the press conference?"

"Yeah, him."

"Of course I fired him. He didn't do his job," Oisín said.

"But, he would have had more experience with this," Tony said.

"What about the shooter? If we knew who was trying to kill me, maybe we can see if the two are related," Oisín offered.

"That's not going to happen."

"Why not?" Oisín demanded. "The shooting at La Playa Blanca should still be looked at. And the guy who attacked me on my run on the beach. Why haven't we found out anything yet?"

"Because."

"Because why, dammit?"

"The shooting at La Playa was a setup, okay? A PR stunt."

Oisín went silent for a moment.

"What are you talking about?" He finally asked.

"Nic thought your ratings needed a boost. He thought having something that looked like an attempt on your life would help drum up publicity. Of course, I'm sure he didn't realize the person would use live ammunition."

Oisín's ears rang. "You're saying that the shootings, where I was afraid for my life, were nothing but a PR stunt?"

"*Shooting* one not both. The second one, we still are trying to figure out. But PCBPD was notified so no further action was taken on their part."

Oisín closed his eyes.

"The important thing is, Osh, that you lay low. Let the statement do its job. This whole thing will blow over soon and they will be begging you to come back. You're the best model in the business," Tony said. "And I'm still your agent but maybe we could take a break until this is all over. Go home, take a load off."

"I'm in New York."

"I meant Ireland. They've frozen most of your assets but—"

"They've what?" Oisín demanded.

"Right, umm, the firm has frozen most of your assets. The company credit card, your line of credit, and the jet, but your bank account is still active."

"That's against my contract."

"This whole situation is against your contract, Oisín. Morals Clause."

"I'm innocent!"

"I know, but it doesn't stop them. Once you're cleared, everything reinstates."

"This is bullshit."

"I know. Listen. Go home. Take a week or two. Lay low. I'll call you."

Oisín closed his eyes again but nodded. He needed to go home. He needed his family.

"Fine. You need me, call me. I'll be home."

"Good. Trust me, Oisín, I'll keep digging. We'll get to the bottom of this."

Oisín hung up the phone. He needed to punch something, work off his anger. Slipping on his workout shorts and a t-shirt, he went to his private elevator and punched in the number for the fourth-floor gym.

He was blessedly alone and was able to run on the treadmill, punch the punching bag, and lift some weights in peace. Sitting on the weight bench, he pulled out his phone and searched flights to Shannon from New York. At least his bank account still had enough zeros that he didn't need the company's help. Finding a flight out in the morning, he purchased a ticket. Though he did splurge and took a First-Class seat.

Heading back up to his loft, it was weird not to have Byron by his side. He had been pulled from his post and replaced with four rotating NYPD officers which he refused after twenty-four hours. He didn't like strangers hanging around outside his loft and when he overheard one of them say they should be arresting him and not standing guard over him, he told them to go.

He hadn't spoken to Byron or Naomi in fourth-eight hours which was longer than he'd gone in years for Byron and over a month for Naomi.

He shot a text to Byron.

Oisín: I know it's not your job anymore, but I still look at you as my friend. I hope you do too. I'm on the 10:42 Delta flight tomorrow morning heading home to Shannon. I'm going to stay with my family for a while. I hope we can talk when I get back. I miss you, By.

Then another to Naomi.

Oisín: Ni, I'm sorry I haven't called, I've been holed up here in NYC. I miss you. I'm on an early-ish flight tomorrow. I'm heading home to Ireland. If you still want me to text you when I land, please tell me. I love you and I'm so sorry about all of this.

With that, he jumped into the shower, threw some clothes into a duffel bag, found his passport, set his alarm and crashed into bed. He didn't remember falling asleep but he woke to his alarm ten hours later. He called down to the concierge and asked for a taxi. Heading to the airport, he checked his phone. He had one text.

Naomi: Of course I want to know when you land! Don't be silly, this hasn't changed anything for me. I love you and I'm trying to figure out a way to help you. I have an idea, do you trust me?

Oisín: I trust you, love. Always.

Naomi: Good. Let me know when you land. Are you alone? Is Byron with you?

Oisín: Yes and no. Yes, I am alone, and no, By is not here. The security firm dropped me, just like everyone else.

Naomi: I swear I will destroy this woman if I ever meet her in person. She messed with the wrong man.

Oisín: What man is that?

Naomi: Mine.

Oisín couldn't admit how much that little word meant everything to him.

Oisín: I'm yours, truly. I'm at JFK. I'll call you when I'm through security.

Naomi: I'm going into a meeting in an hour, I'll text when it's over, if we can catch each other before you board, call me.

Oisín: Okay. Thank you for believing in me.

Naomi: I always believe in you.

Oisín smiled slightly and handed the taxi driver a fifty then grabbed his bag and backpack carry-on. He made his way to check-in and baggage check. He felt some eyes on him and he knew the sunglasses weren't enough to hide his identity. But some people didn't seem to care.

Once his bag was checked and he had his boarding pass pulled up on his phone, he made his way through security and toward his gate. The walk wasn't short, but he didn't mind, it gave him time to think. He hadn't told his family he was coming home and had dodged their calls. He didn't feel like repeating himself twenty times, so he waited. He would tell everyone together when he got home.

Finding his gate, he sat in a cluster of empty seats and pulled out his phone so as to appear non-sociable. But he still heard the whispers and even some pulled out their phones to, not so surreptitiously, take his picture.

The attendants came over the intercom to announce that their flight was on time and was being thoroughly cleaned. They would begin boarding soon. And they would board First-Class first. Oisín ducked down even further in his seat when he heard someone whisper his name. The girl was trying to be quiet but either her voice carried, or she wasn't as quiet as she thought she was.

It didn't matter because as he leaned forward, keeping his eyes on the ground, a pair of black Sketchers appeared before him.

"Well," a very familiar voice said. "This is different."

He snapped his eyes up to see Byron standing before him. "By?"

He grinned. "You didn't honestly think I'd let you leave the country alone, did you?"

"But I was pulled from GRP security."

Byron shrugged again "What is it I've heard you say? Sod 'em?"

Oisín couldn't help it, he burst out laughing, stood, and threw his arms around Byron. Pulling back, Oisín stared at him.

"I can't pay you what you were making, but I still have my bank account."

"That would make me your bodyguard. And a bodyguard would have to carry your luggage. Good thing I'm here as your *friend*."

Oisín chuckled again, the first rays of sunshine piercing his haze and he felt like weeping for joy.

"Besides, I miss your momma's cooking."

"Now boarding First-Class on Delta flight 1269 to Heathrow with connection to Shannon. At this time we will ask all First-Class customers to approach."

"Are you First-Class?" Oisín asked.

"You think I'd ride coach overseas? Been there, done that in the Marines, no thanks."

Oisín pulled his backpack over his shoulders, and they approached the ticket counter. The attendant greeted them with polite smiles, and they found their seats. Byron was across the aisle and down one from him and since there was no one beside Byron, Oisín asked the flight attendant if he could switch seats. Once he was next to Byron, Oisín felt like he could breathe again.

Naomi waited in the wings of the studio. Her uncle approached her with a soft smile.

"Are you sure you wanna do this, kiddo?" Uncle Kei asked softly.

"One hundred percent," Naomi answered.

Uncle Kei chuckled. "That's what your mother said just before I walked her down the aisle to marry your father." Naomi looked over at her uncle. "She would be so proud of you, Ni."

"One thing we Kekoa women will always do, is defend our men and do whatever we can for them."

"I know that," Uncle Kei smiled.

Another man approached wearing a headset and carrying a clipboard.

"All right, Miss Moon, you're next. Remember, look at the camera with the green light if you want to address the audience."

"Green light, got it."

"You're on in two."

It was the longest two minutes of her life.

Chapter Thirty-Three

"And welcome back. Well, everyone has at least heard of the explosive allegations against fashion model Oisín O'Quinn. Allegations, we should say, he has denied absolutely. But there's another story and we're happy to be able to bring it to you. We are joined by Naomi Moon, a good friend of Mr. O'Quinn who has heard the allegations and say... they're false. Miss Moon, good to see you."

"Good to see you, Jim," Naomi said.

"So you say you met Oisín O'Quinn a month or two ago and that these charges are untrue."

"Without a doubt."

"Tell us more."

"Well, my father and I own a general contracting business and we were contacted by Mr. O'Quinn who had recently purchased two properties here in Panama City Beach. He was generous and kind. He knew what he wanted but worked with us to ensure it was something we could do on a light crew."

"Why light crew?"

"My ex-husband is stealing our contractors. Luring them away with more money but cheaper product. So we were down nearly ten workers. There were times on Oisín's project that I wasn't sure we'd finish on time or on budget but when I went to Oisín he was gracious and out of his own pocket, hired friends to come out and help because he didn't want my dad to have another heart attack."

"How sweet."

"He is. We got close."

"Are you two dating?"

"I am not comfortable answering that," Naomi stated.

"But you are seeing each other?"

"Yes."

"What's your take on the recent issues he's facing."

"Well, I know beyond a shadow of a doubt he's innocent of this. He is a good, kind, caring, honest man. And not just that. I have evidence that prove this was nothing more than a plot to bring down a good man. It has come to my attention that his accuser was once married and may still be to a Dominic Hester. Mr. Hester, I have discovered, was Oisín's PR rep and he was fired six weeks ago for not prepping Oisín properly for a press conference causing rumors to run rampant. It's interesting to me how he was Oisín's PR Rep and as soon as he was fired this *story* broke. I believe Oisín would be very happy to submit to a paternity test for that unborn child she claims to be carrying."

"That's quite an accusation."

"And I have evidence, which I have turned over the PCBPD. And they have authorized me to reveal it here today."

"He's had a lot of people saying some very nasty things about him. What's your response to them?"

"Everyone who blindly believed without any evidence or giving Oisín a chance, my hope is that they learn. All women should be believed but with caution. Not every woman who comes forward is telling the truth. The great thing about our nation is that we are innocent until proven guilty. And Oisín O'Quinn is innocent. His designers have dropped him, and the media have said lie after lie about him. He's innocent."

"I'm sure he would be very grateful to you for clearing his name. If you could say anything to him right now, what would it be?"

She looked into the camera with the green light. "Oisín, I'm here for you. I love you. I'll see you soon."

"Well, there you have it, ladies and gentlemen. Naomi Moon clearing the name of Oisín O'Quinn with some hard evidence. I wouldn't want to get on her bad side."

"No indeed, Jim," his co-host said. "Thank you, Naomi for joining us today."

"Thank you."

The light on the camera trained on her turned red and the host continued. The stage manager beckoned her off stage and she handed over her microphone. Her uncle waited for her nearby and she hurried over to him.

"I'm so proud of you, honey," he said. "Now hurry." He pressed her passport, purse, and phone into her hand. "Boarding pass under your name. Go get your man. I like him. And I like the smile he puts on your face."

"Thank you, Uncle Kei."

"I love you, honey. Go."

She smiled at him, kissed his cheek, and hurried out the door.

It was good to be home, Oisín thought as he walked with Byron through Shannon airport. If anyone recognized him, they said nothing. This was home. Everyone knew him as Oisín O'Quinn, the youngest son of the former town vet, not the fashion model.

They got their bags, and he shot a text to Naomi that he had landed. Then, they headed out into the late August sun. As soon as they passed the automatic sliding doors to the parking lot, he took a deep breath.

"Welcome back to Ireland," he said to Byron who stood beside him.

"There's something... magical about this place."

"There is. It's nice to be home."

"So, how do we... *get* home? Do you have a car?"

Oisín opened his mouth to speak then closed it. He paused for a moment.

"I'm not used to having to figure that out. I guess I could call my brother or one of my cousins."

"Don't let me stop you," Byron grinned.

Oisín pulled out his phone but just as he was about to dial, a voice stopped him.

"Oisín? That you, lad?"

He turned to see his parent's old neighbor; Mr. O'Reilly and a young woman wearing a Harvard t-shirt standing near them.

"Yes, Mr. O'Reilly. Good to see you again, sir."

"Such manners! Not like the times I caught you with your pants down in my vegetable garden," the old man wheezed a laugh.

Oisín smiled nervously but the college student, clearly Mr. O'Reilly's granddaughter or great granddaughter looked at Oisín like he hung the moon.

"Yes, sir, I'm sorry about that."

The man waved him off. "You young'uns get up to all sorts of funny business." He laughed again. "But what are you doing back here, lad? I thought ye were in New York or Hollywood."

"I missed my family, sir."

"Ah, tell your da' I appreciate him coming to check on my cow the other day while your brother is out of town."

"I will, sir."

The young girl whispered something to her grandfather.

"Eh? What? Speak up, girl."

She blushed and glanced at Oisín. "Could we give them a ride?"

"A ride?" He asked. "Oh! Aye. Do you lads have a ride to your ma and da's?"

"We were just trying to figure that out, sir. It was a spur of the moment decision and a surprise, like."

"Well, I brought the Gator but there's room for the both of you lads, if you don't mind riding in the back. Come on."

Byron looked over at Oisín and mouthed *Gator?* Oisín shrugged.

They followed Mr. O'Reilly to the car park and sure enough there was the Gator. Oisín offered a hand to the granddaughter who blushed profusely and said a quiet *thank you* as he helped her up to the second seat in the Gator while Byron stowed their luggage in the back flatbed. Once they were seated on the drop-down hatch, Mr. O'Reilly started the engine.

"All set back there, lads?"

"Aye, all good. Cheers, Mr. O'Reilly," Oisín called back.

"Hold on then."

The Gator lurched into gear and Byron clutched the side of the hatch bed as a wide grin spread across his face.

"Just like when granddaddy was driving," he teased.

"It's not far."

"I love it," Byron replied.

As they rode in the back, Oisín pulled his phone out to check on a text from Naomi. There wasn't one. But there was one from Tony.

Tony: We're back, baby. Pop some bubbly and give that girl of yours a kiss. She's incredible.

Oisín's brow furrowed.

Oisín: What are you talking about?

Tony: Didn't you see?

Oisín: See what? I just landed.

Tony didn't reply, only sent him a link to a website with a video and an article.

The headline read:

Oisín O'Quinn Vindicated.

Molly and Dominic Hester, a Modern Day Bonnie & Clyde?

Oisín read on. Apparently, the love of his life had been up to a lot since he left. His former PR Rep had planned the whole thing with his wife.

He read the transcript of Naomi's interview and tears gathered in his eyes when he read her words.

I'm here for you. I love you. I'll see you soon.

Was that the meeting she had when she asked if he trusted her? Oh, he trusted her. He loved her. And he couldn't wait to see her again.

"Everything okay?" Byron asked.

He looked over and laughed through his tears. Offering his phone to his friend, Oisín watched as Byron read. The corner of Byron's lip tipped up. "I told you that woman is a keeper."

Oisín couldn't help the joyful laugh that burst out of his mouth or the tears that tracked his face. Now the world knew he was the victim of lies and the person who made that possible was the woman he loved more than anything in the world.

"I wonder where she is," Byron said.

Oisín clicked over to his text chain with her but there still was no answer, then he paused.

I'll see you soon.

She was coming to Ireland. She'd be there soon.

Oisín pulled up her dad's number and dialed.

"Bill Moon," he answered.

"Bill, it's Oisín," he called over the roar of the engine. "Sorry, can you hear me?"

"I can hear you, son," he said. "You landed in Ireland all right?"

"Yes, sir, just. Making my way to my parent's place. I was trying to get ahold of Naomi, is she home?"

"She's not, no," he answered but Oisín heard a little mischief in his voice.

"Do you know where she is?"

"Well, at this moment, probably somewhere over the Atlantic if her flight is on schedule which..." he paused for a moment. "It is."

Oisín's heart hammered in his chest. She was on her way to him.

"Thank you, sir."

"You're welcome, oh and, son?"

"Yes sir?" Oisín loved how subtly Bill started calling him *son*.

"You hurt my daughter and I'll enlist Byron's help, you understand?"

"Yes sir. I love your daughter, sir. I would never want to hurt her."

"Good, then you and I will never exchange blows."

"It would never be an exchange, sir. I hurt her, I stand still for you."

"Good to know. I'll send you her flight details but don't meet her at the airport, she wants to surprise you."

"It'll be tough. But I won't."

"Good. Tell Byron I said hello. The guys are with her too. Callum, Willie, and Denis."

"Good," Oisín breathed a sigh of relief, she wasn't going to be alone in a strange new country where they brought Gators to the airport. "Thank you."

"Welcome," Bill hung up and Oisín looked over at Byron.

"I think you have a little military crush there. He says hello."

Byron chuckled. "Ah, the Squids." He teased about Bill's branch of military.

"Were here, lads," Mr. O'Reilly called over his shoulder.

"Thank you, Mr. O'Reilly. Just here is perfect."

Oisín looked around and saw the gothic church and cemetery where generations of his family were buried. The row of houses in the Town Center made him smile and when the Gator came to a stop, Oisín jumped out as if the weight he was under had lifted. He let Byron grab the bags so he could thank Mr. O'Reilly.

"Just stay out of my vegetables, laddie," he wheezed a laugh as Oisín chuckled.

"I promise, sir. Good to meet you," he looked at the granddaughter who blushed and smiled. "And thank you," he said to her. She preened.

"I never believed her for a minute," she said.

"That means a lot."

With that, Byron came around to thank him for the ride and they stepped back as Mr. O'Reilly put the Gator in gear and drove off.

Oisín grabbed his duffel and headed to one of the cottages on the row. Byron walked next to him.

Before the garden gate even shut behind him, the door opened, and his mother came running out. It wasn't until he saw her, that his knees give out and he fell to the ground.

"Mama," he realized he was crying.

"Oh my darling," she wrapped her arms around him and held him to her tightly. "You're home. You're safe."

"Mama," he wept.

"Shh, shh. It's all right now, love. We've tried to call you, but we do understand. You needed to work through it."

"You don't hate me, do you?" He questioned, his throat tight with unshed tears.

His mother pulled back and cupped his face. "Now wait just a minute, Oisín O'Quinn. I carried you for nine months. Twenty. Six. Hours. Of labor to bring you into this world. Do you honestly think for one second that I would or could hate you? My darling, you don't know me at all if you think that. You're my son. My baby. If anything I wanted to tear them limb from limb for hurting you."

Her thumbs wiped his tears.

"I didn't do it, Mama. I swear I never touched her."

"Hush now, I know that. And you've been vindicated. I want to hear all about this woman who helped you." She helped Oisín stand. Byron giving an arm for him too. "Hello, Byron, dear, how are you?"

"Better now our Oisín is better, Mrs. O'Quinn. Thank you."

"I've told you before, dear, Mrs. O'Quinn was my dear mother-in-law. It's Rachael."

"Sure doesn't seem polite enough, ma'am."

"You southern gentleman will always have my heart. Now come inside."

"I thought I had your heart, love," Oisín heard his father say from the doorway.

"Among many other things Cabhan O'Quinn."

Oisín groaned as his mother winked at his father. "This is why I moved out," Oisín said to Byron.

"Oh hush, come on now, everyone's here."

"Everyone?" Oisín asked.

"Well, not everyone but a lot of us." She walked into the house and Oisín followed, Byron behind him.

Looking around the room, he saw his uncles Emmet, Innis, and Sean, along with his aunts Mara, Trish, and Ness and their brood and grandchildren. It would be easier to say who wasn't there as the O'Quinn clan was far too many to count.

"Everyone" Rachael got their attention. "Oisín's home."

Chapter Thirty-Four

Naomi turned her phone off airplane mode as soon as they landed and were taxing to the gate. Sitting in Business-Class, as she couldn't justify the expense of First-Class, she sat between Callum and Denis with Willie on the seat across the aisle.

"Welcome to Ireland, lass," Callum said.

The sun was setting as she looked out the window, but she smiled at Callum and sent a text to her dad to let him know she landed safely. Then checked the unread text from Oisín that just came in.

Oisín: Landed safely, love. I miss you. Call me tonight?

She wanted to reply especially when she got her dad's text back.

Dad: I'm glad you made it safely, darling. Oisín called. He knows what happened. He is looking for you. I dodged it as best I could.

Naomi: How did he sound?

Dad: He loves you.

Naomi smiled softly but followed the guys to the baggage claim to find their suitcases. Callum pulled out a set of keys and they all walked to his car in the parking lot. Once buckled in, Callum looked at her.

"B&B or Oisín's first?"

She glanced at the guys in the backseat then debated. They were all probably tired and wanted to head home.

Willie leaned forward. "For the love of god, man, just take her to our baby deer already."

For some reason, Naomi found that absolutely hilarious and burst out laughing.

"Oisín's it is then," Callum put the car into gear and began to drive.

The sun slowly set as they drove the relatively short distance to Oisín's parent's cottage. They were all quiet and Denis fell asleep in the backseat only to wake when Willie shook him as they arrived.

The village was exactly what Naomi expected. Rows of cottages, an old gothic church, and rows of shops, a pub, because of course there was one, and beautiful gardens lining the front of the cottages to the single lane road. Callum put the car in park and turned off the engine.

"You ready, Ni?" He asked.

"Oh yes," she answered. Though she knew as soon as she opened the door, her life would change, she grasped the door handle with confidence and swung it open. Her life would change, because Oisín would be there and that was something she would never hesitate to enjoy.

The doorbell rang and Oisín froze mid-sentence of telling his sisters about Naomi. Everyone was so excited he had met someone, though his mother wasn't happy that he planned on making his home in Florida, just as soon as possible.

He was explaining how amazing her renovation was on his home when the bell resounded throughout the cottage. His hands instantly grew sweaty, and his heart rate accelerated. His dad went to the door and opened it.

"Callum, Willie, Denis, good to see you, lads. Long time," Cabhan said and Oisín stood, suddenly nervous. His eyes turned to Byron who smirked.

"Mr. O'Quinn," he heard Callum say. "Wondered if Oisín could... come out and play?"

Cabhan's full bellied laugh echoed in the room. "And you hardly need any introduction, my dear. We saw you on the tele. But you're even prettier in person."

"Thank you."

She's here. She's here. Oisín wanted to shout it from the rooftops but instead, he felt every eye turn from him to the door as Cabhan reappeared leading four people into the house. Oisín's eyes landed on her and wouldn't budge. She scanned the room but as soon as she found him, she beamed, and he felt lightning strike his chest. He finally understood his grandfather, father, uncles, cousins, and brother. He knew what they meant now. And it was exhilarating and scary as hell.

"Hey there," she said.

"God, I love you," he breathed and raced to her. She met him halfway and he lifted her up in an embrace. Once he had her in his arms, his lips sought hers and she caught them. They kissed for what felt like hours, her in his arms, right where she belonged. Their hearts beating as one, everything about her screamed she was his and he would do everything in his power to prove to her he was worthy.

"Well, I'm offended," Callum's voice broke the haze of his mind. "I helped her find out who the bad guy was to. She gets the lip lock. What makes her so special?"

"Pucker up and kiss me, Call," Willie's teasing voice came next.

"I worry about you lads sometimes," that was Denis.

Oisín broke away from Naomi's kiss and slowly set her on her feet. She tucked under his arm keeping her arm around his waist and the other hand placed over his heart.

"Am I remiss in my attentions, lads?" He teased.

"Well, we did help her, flew over here with her, and drove her to you," Callum winked. "A little gratitude would be nice."

"You have my unending gratitude, Callum." Oisín squeeze Naomi shoulder and then stepped over to Callum, Willie, and Denis. "Thank you, all of you," he said, suddenly serious. "I can't say what your friendship means to me after so long. But truly, thank you."

"Ah, it was nothing," Callum grinned and pulled him into a backslapping hug. The other two followed and Oisín reveled in their friendships.

But then, someone cleared their throat and Oisín turned to see his family waiting for him to introduce them. He reached out for Naomi's hand and the feel of her slipping her hand into his unreservedly, made him smile.

"Everyone, this is Naomi Moon as you saw on the tele. And I'm in love with her. Ni, this is... nearly everyone."

"It's wonderful to meet you. Oisín has told me stories of his family and how amazing you all are. It's nice to meet the people who helped mold the man I love." Naomi said.

"Oh, come 'ere and give us a hug, lass. I'm Rachael, Oisín's ma."

Naomi stepped into his mother's embrace and sighed. His heart hurt for her. She hadn't had a mother's embrace in years. His ma pulled back and cupped Naomi's face, kissing her forehead.

"You are such a beautiful woman, dear. Inside and out. Thank you for loving my baby," she said.

"It's my honor to have the love of such a wonderful man," Naomi replied.

His mom sniffled as tears filled her eyes. "Oh honey, thank you."

Oisín's father stepped forward. "I'm Cabhan, Osh's da'. Welcome to the ever-growing O'Quinn family."

"Thank you. This is nice. It's just my dad, uncle, and me back home so it's nice to have a large family."

"Growing every day," Cabhan winked.

The door opened bumping into a snoozing-while-standing Denis.

"Oops, sorry," Oisín's cousin Aoife walked in. "Am I late?"

"Where have you been, girl?" Her father, Oisín's Uncle Emmet questioned. "We expected you an hour ago."

"Sorry, da'," she said. "Sorry Denis didn't mean to hit you."

"Ss— all righ'," Denis replied sleepily.

"Got caught in traffic getting out of the city," she smiled and embraced her mother, father, and Oisín.

"Aoife's my cousin," Oisín whispered to Naomi as they watched her make her rounds to the rest of the family. "Has a fancy financial job at a law firm in Dublin. She's the baby so Uncle Emmet and Aunt Mara worry."

"I think a father's worry is the same tone in every accent," Naomi winked.

Oisín chuckled and kissed the side of her head as he slipped his arm around her.

"Where's your brother?" Emmet asked his daughter.

"Which one?" She teased.

"Killian, smart arse," Emmet winked.

"Am I suddenly his keeper?" She questioned but there was more animosity in her tone than Oisín expected.

"Just curious, honey," Mara replied.

"You know more about him than I do these days."

"Oh honey," her ma said.

Oisín saw Naomi's quick confused glance at Callum and his answering slight shake of his head.

"Ni?" Oisín asked.

She looked over at him and smiled. "Later."

He nodded, knowing she would tell him everything later.

Once more introductions were made, Callum, Willie, and Denis said goodnight and drove home. Oisín and Naomi stayed on the sofa in the living room as one by one everyone went home. Rachael and Cabhan were saying goodnight to his aunt and uncle Ness and Sean as they headed out, when Oisín pulled Naomi close and held her tightly.

"I'm so glad you're here, love," he said.

"I had to come," she answered. "When I found out what that snake did to you, I had to help. I knew you were innocent. You never would hurt someone like that."

"Your trust in me is humbling. I haven't always deserved it, but I will do everything in my power to keep it," he replied.

"I know you will," she kissed him softly.

His parents returned and sat with them on the opposite couch.

"I'm sorry Lach and Corrie weren't here to meet you, Naomi, but I bet they will join us soon," his mother said.

"Any word from your agent, Oisín?" His dad asked.

"Just a text saying *we're back.* Nothing else." Oisín looked over at Byron who, for the first time, *lounged* in an armchair. "You heard anything, By?"

Byron shook his head. "I wouldn't be surprised if he doesn't call you tomorrow though."

"Well, you must all be exhausted and here we are keeping you up," his mother said grabbing the plates in front of them with a few uneaten crisps and crumbs of her apple crumb cake left.

"Can I help?" Naomi offered.

"I wouldn't dream of it, dear. No, you get some shut eye. There's a guest room next to Oisín's but I'm sure Byron will use that one. We have the girls' old room down the hall.

"Rae," Cabhan stopped his wife with a wink at his son. "I'm sure that's not necessary."

Rachael looked from Cabhan to Oisín and Naomi, then back to her husband.

"Oh," she realized. "Of course. You're both adults. Sometimes I forget."

"I appreciate the offer," Naomi replied.

"It's not like we can do anything other than *sleep* in my parent's house or my old bed," Oisín said.

"Of course, of course. Well, you have a good night and a good rest, dears. We will see you in the morning for breakfast."

"Goodnight ma, da."

"Goodnight," both Naomi and Byron said as they all headed down to their rooms.

Byron waited in the doorway of the guest room next door. "I doubt you'll need me, but just in case, I'm here."

"Thanks, By," Oisín said.

With that, Byron went into his room and shut the door. Oisín wrapped his arm around her waist.

"Do you want to stay with me? Or would you rather stay in my sisters' old room?" He asked.

She turned and slid her arms around his neck, stroking the hair on the back of his head.

"The fact you are asking and not simply expecting me to sleep with you, shows how much you've grown, Oisín."

"That, but also," he shrugged. "I respect you more than any other woman I've been with. I love you. And as much as I want to fall asleep and wake up feeling you beside me, I never want to take advantage of the situation or you."

A soft smile lifted her lips. "Then, Oisín O'Quinn, come and feel me beside you."

He let out a deep breath and kissed her.

Chapter Thirty-Five

"Oisín," he heard his father knocking on his door. "Oisín!"

The body beside him moaned and tucked tighter against him. He slowly opened his eyes as his nose was tickled with brown hair. He smiled softly and brought his arm around Naomi, who's head was resting on his shoulder.

"Oisín."

He looked to the door, sleep still clouding his mind. "Hmm? Da'?"

The door opened slightly. "All clear to open the door?"

Oisín rolled his eyes but caught Naomi's.

"No, Naomi and I are in the middle of wild and untamed sex. Shut the door and take ma out for breakfast if you know what's good for you."

Cabhan and Naomi laughed.

"If that's wild and untamed, I need to teach you a few things, lad," his da' said then opened the door fully.

"What's up, Da'?"

"Come to the living room quickly, there's something you need to see on the tele." He said then hurried back out the door.

Oisín flopped back down and clutched Naomi to him, burying his face in her hair, he moaned. "I like waking up with you."

She sighed and tossed one leg over his, cradling his jaw with her hand.

"Me too."

"Oisín!" His father called.

Naomi looked toward the door. "Maybe we should go see what he wants?" She offered.

"Or we could stay like this. Blame the jet lag."

"It's like noon, I think."

"And that's what seven in Panama City?" Oisín questioned. "Let's stay like this."

"We could, but not with Byron staring down at us," she said.

Oisín cracked an eye open, only to jump slightly in surprise. Byron stood at the foot of the bed, arms crossed, staring at them.

"Go away, you're not my bodyguard right now," Oisín grumbled.

"Actually, if you would get your butt out to the living room, you'd see that that isn't entirely true," Byron said.

"What?" Oisín questioned.

Byron turned and waved two fingers at him telling him to follow.

"Now I gotta see this," Naomi said, kissing him quickly but sliding out of the bed.

"No fair, you were warm."

"Come on," she said slipping on a sweatshirt over her sleep camisole and hurrying out the door following Byron.

Oisín sighed but chuckled. Waking up with Naomi was a dream come true. Having started as an endeavor to get her in bed for a few hours of fun, to thinking about forever with her, was a sobering feeling.

Tearing off the sheets, he padded to the living room, not bothering to put on a shirt. His parents, Byron, and Naomi were all gathered around the tele, cups of coffee in their hands. He wrapped his arms around Naomi from behind as his father pressed play and the screen came to life.

"Reporting live from Panama City Beach, we're bringing you breaking news in a developing story. Molly and Dominic Hester, fraudulent accuser and former PR Rep for Oisín O'Quinn have been arrested outside their home yesterday in New York City. The NYPD responded to a domestic violence dispute at eleven o'clock last night and found the couple outside their apartment complex arguing and Molly, it is said, was carrying a knife which she repeatedly tried to use on her husband and police.

"The twenty-six-year-old shot to fame when she came forward accusing Oisín O'Quinn, well-known fashion model, of sexually assaulting her resulting in a pregnancy. It has been confirmed that story is false, and she had been coached by her husband, O'Quinn's former public relations representative, to falsely accuse the fashion model as a sort of personal vendetta. It was also discovered that he was the perpetrator behind the increasingly aggressive social media attacks on Mr. O'Quinn and even went so far as to chase him down during his morning run on the beach and draw a gun on him."

Oisín's parents gasped and glanced at him but he was riveted by the sight of Dominic (Nic) being walked into the police headquarters in handcuffs.

"It should also be mentioned that the model's latest fashion campaign with Versace, has been reinstated and should hit stores in a few weeks. A statement from the model's agent came but a few moments ago."

Tony filled the screen speaking to a group of press. "No one is happier than I am to see Oisín's name cleared. I am happy to announce he is doing much better now that his innocence, which he strongly and adamantly proclaimed since the beginning of this ordeal, has been proven. I look forward to continuing to work with him and move on from there."

"Mr. Belladucci, do you have any comment on his fashion campaign?"

"I cannot speak in too much detail, but I can say I have received several personal calls showing support and I'm excited for the future."

"Mr. Belladucci," another reporter called out. "Mr. O'Quinn has a bit of a reputation, can you tell me if this experience has changed his view on certain matters?"

"I can say, Oisín is well aware of his reputation, but he has personally spoken to me and offered what help he can to Ms. Hester. She is a troubled young woman, and he is very moved by the situation. I know he has pledged money to the women's shelter in the Bronx to further their mission in helping battered women get the help they need."

"Did you do that?" Naomi asked.

"No, but it's a good idea," Oisín said.

"It's all PR," Byron replied.

"Mr. Belladucci, can you perhaps elaborate on his relationship with Miss Moon who came to his aid the other day by breaking this story?"

"That is his private life, but I am permitted to say he is indebted to her and is very happy to share their love with the world—"

"Are there wedding plans?" the same reporter asked.

"Woah," Oisín chuckled.

"That was fast," Naomi grinned. "Oisín, you didn't tell me. Did you know you're going to marry me?"

"Not yet, but it's something I've been thinking about," he kissed the shell of her ear. She shivered but grinned and didn't answer.

"That's up to them. Now, if you'll excuse me, I'm needed upstairs."

Tony headed up the steps of the agency's building and the camera panned back to the news anchor. Cabhan muted the television and looked at his son.

"It's over, lad."

Oisín took a breath but smiled then looked down at Naomi in his arms.

"Actually... I think it's just beginning."

Epilogue

Naomi woke to the feel of the warm Floridian sun shining down on her through the door to the balcony in the master bedroom. The door was open and the soft sound of the waves crashing against the shore lulled her sleepy brain.

Taking a deep breath of the warm salty air, she sighed and smiled.

"Should I be jealous that something other than me gave you such an... euphoric smile?" She heard from the doorway.

Sitting up, the sheets pooled around her waist. She grinned as her husband's gaze dropped down to her chest.

"Hey asshole, my eyes are up here," she breathed.

Oisín smirked and took his time lifting his eyes. "And beautiful eyes they are too."

"Flattery will get you everywhere, O'Quinn."

"Well... O'Quinn," he teased. "I certainly hope so."

He carried a tray with fresh fruit and two mimosas over to their bed. Setting it down between them, he sat on the mattress, his back against the headboard. Naomi took her glass of freshly squeezed orange juice and chilled champagne and clinked her glass to his. He never dropped her eyes as they drank and Naomi felt the caress of his eyes as if they were his fingers.

He leaned over to kiss her. The taste of orange prominent on his lips and tongue. "Happy anniversary, love," he whispered.

"Mmm, two months, that's quite an achievement that warrants mimosas," she teased pulling back and drinking again.

"Every morning I wake up with you next to me, warrants mimosas," he replied.

Naomi popped a piece of pineapple into her mouth and groaned.

"So good," she muttered.

"You know what day it is?" He asked.

She thought a moment. "Honestly, after the flight back from Hawaii the days have been muddled together."

He smiled softly but agreed. "It's the twenty-seventh," he said.

"Okay," she prompted taking another sip of her drink.

"A year ago today you... *bumped* into me in the Publix parking lot."

"Is it? Wow," she smiled. "Crazy you think I would have forgotten that." She beamed and leaned over the bed to the nightstand. Pulling open the drawer, she grabbed a gift wrapped box the size of a sticky note stack.

"What's this?" He questioned with a twinkle in his eye.

"Happy one year meeting anniversary, love of my life," she said and handed him the gift.

He took it gingerly, but his face lit with joy. Setting it on his knee, he reached over to his nightstand and pulled open the drawer, grabbing a small gift bag with pale green tissue.

"Happy one year meeting anniversary, and two-month wedding anniversary, wife," Oisín said and handed her the small bag.

She watched as he unwrapped and open the box. Laying inside was a braided leather bracelet he had been eyeing in Hawaii on their honeymoon, but she had it engraved with the date and the words, *Always Watch the Sunrise with Me.* He pulled it out with a surprised breath.

"Baby," he whispered. "This is amazing."

"So will you? Always watch the sunrise with me?" She asked.

"Always," he answered, slipping the bracelet over his hand and tightening the ties which were tied to small shells, to keep it on his wrist. "This is so cool."

Naomi smiled but turned to the bag he had given her. Pulling out the tissue paper, she pulled out a box and lifted the lid. A necklace lay inside. A circular shadowbox with a small shell next to a small pint of Guinness. Inside the shadowbox were scripted words that took her breath away.

Always Share 119 Seconds with Me. There was a silhouette of a couple kissing in the light of the moon.

"Oisín," she breathed. "It's beautiful."

He beamed like a little boy and offered to help her with the clasp. She lifted her hair and he placed it around her neck.

"Beautiful." Leaning forward, he kissed her. Their kiss stayed sweet and when they pulled back, he winked. "Want to take breakfast out to the balcony?"

"Absolutely," she beamed and got up, slipping on a pair of sleep shorts and camisole as Oisín took the tray out to their balcony.

Naomi stood in the doorway watching her husband as he leaned against the railing looking out at the water crashing against the sand. Their own slice of paradise. His broad back rose and fell on a sigh, but then something caught his eye on the deck below to his right. He stared for a long moment then threw his head back and laughed.

Naomi walked to him and looked over the railing only to see Byron and a woman glance up at him.

Oisín raised his hand in greeting. "I'll see you in a couple of hours for hair and makeup, Sheila," Oisín called down to them. Byron's eyes grew wide and Naomi bet, though she couldn't see from there, he blushed.

"Oisín, stop teasing them. He's entitled to a personal life."

"Yeah, but I've been trying to hook them up for over a year."

Chuckling, Naomi stroked his back and kissed his cheek. "You should have asked me. Sheila told me three months ago that she liked him. I got them to dance at our wedding. Pretty sure she went up to his room afterwards."

Oisín laughed again and wrapped his arm around her waist. "Leave it to my wife."

"When are you ever going to learn?" She asked.

"Probably before I'm ninety?"

"More than likely," she teased. "Oh, I had to tell you. I heard from Martin last night."

"Not exactly who I like hearing you talk about, love."

"Oh stop," she grinned. "You know we're just friends. But I heard from him via text yesterday while you were on the phone with Tony. Emilio is bankrupt. His car has been repossessed and the business has closed its doors as of Friday. Apparently, he had to deal with two class action lawsuits. One from his workers who claimed he didn't pay them what he promised and another from the clients who he cheated with his shoddy work."

"Wow." The corner of Oisín's lip tipped up. "Can't say I'm sorry for that. He should have read his Yelp reviews."

"I can't say I'm sorry for that either. I mean I am because I don't want anyone to go through that—"

"You're such a softie."

"I'm nice. There's a difference," she pouted teasingly. Her husband grinned and twisted a piece of her hair gently around his finger.

"And that's one of the things I love about you."

"Whatever, O'Quinn. Just remember I'm not always nice," she winked.

"Oh I know," he rubbed his cheek. "Still stings from a year ago."

Naomi giggled. "You kinda deserved that."

"I did," he agreed. "Now come here and let me help you forget that ex-husband of yours."

Oisín sat on the deck chair and pulled Naomi into his lap. She laughed as she wrapped her arms around his neck and kissed him.

"How long do we have?"

"Got to be on set in three hours."

"Plenty of time." She kissed him and slid her hand down his bare chest and to the waistband of his sweats.

"I like where your head is, love," he pulled her to him and kissed her deeper.

Oisín leaned over the female model as they lay on the shelly beach of Shell Island off Panama City Beach. The model was pretty with a pouty mouth, full lips, and sky-blue eyes. But as he looked down at her, he had to think of Naomi just to look interested.

His wife stood next to his agent, watching. He peeked over, seeing the sun catch the eight carat diamond Lotus flower engagement ring he had picked out in New York eight months ago and he smirked.

"That's great, Oisín, hold that," the photographer said. "Now look at me." His eyes tore from his wife to the camera clicking away. "Great. Oh yes, that's it. Perfect."

"Looking good, Osh!" Tony called.

Naomi's lip tipped up as she raised an eyebrow. He insisted on having his girlfriend, fiancée, and now wife at all of his photo shoots so nothing like what had happened, could ever happen again. Naomi was a star and had always been by his side. She took the paparazzi in stride and made good friends with both Sheila and Tony.

They had returned to America after three weeks in Ireland with his family and only at Tony's insistence as Metric had called again to reissue the offer. The hashtags on social media were blowing up and politicians on both sides of the aisle argued over policy reform. Oisín rolled his eyes at the old men's antics trying to never let a good crisis go to waste, but since he wasn't a citizen... yet, he said nothing.

Though he accepted the generous offer from Metric, he also had Tony look into creating his own fragrance line, *Vindication*. And that was what he was shooting that day as his wife of two months looked on. His best friend and bodyguard, who had quit his job at GRP security to create his own firm, stood beside her. The sun was on his back, the sand at his hands, and the Gulf of Mexico at his feet.

As they took a break from the pictures, Oisín walked over to Naomi and gave her a kiss. He would never change a thing. Going to Panama City Beach, Florida, was the best thing to ever happen to him.

an deireadh

Acknowledgements

Thank you for reading! I had such fun writing Oisín's and Naomi's story! And the little trip to Panama City Beach, Florida was just the icing on the cake. I met so many wonderful people who make an appearance in this story!

Lance and Sandra Boekenoogen, the owners of Panama City Beach's Spice and Tea Exchange! Thank you so much for your welcome and information about the city that was needed for Naomi, things off the usual beaten path for the tourists. I can't thank you enough for your hospitality and I am enjoying the spices and tea! Can't wait to go back!

Daniella, our wonderful server at the cabanas in at the condo pool! You were amazing and I just had to add your name as a cameo to this book!

Jesse Fedora, the amazing musician! Thank you for the incredible island music! I wrote a lot of this listening to you on the Steel Drums!

And to all the people who welcomed us and listened to my endless questions about the city! Thank you!!

Not all places named in this book are real locations, some have been renamed or changed altogether. But Pier Park is one place that is absolutely real and is an amazing experience. If you get a chance, be sure to check it out. The shopping and dining are incredible!

I would love it if you would consider leaving a review! Reviews are how authors get their name and novels out to the world!

On a more serious note, I want to stress my heartfelt love and support to anyone who has experienced sexual assault, harassment, abuse, or rape. We live in a culture that perpetuates that but it in no way justifies what happened to you. You are heard. You are believed.

If you or someone you know has experienced sexual assault, please contact the sexual assault hotline: 1-800-656-4673.

www.ingramcontent.com/pod-product-compliance
Lightning Source LLC
Chambersburg PA
CBHW072123020726
47501CB00003B/954